SPECIAL MESSAGE TO READERS

This book is published under the auspices of

THE ULVERSCROFT FOUNDATION
(registered charity No. 264873 UK)

Established in 1972 to provide funds for research, diagnosis and treatment of eye diseases. Examples of contributions made are: —

A Children's Assessment Unit at
Moorfield's Hospital, London.

•

Twin operating theatres at the
Western Ophthalmic Hospital, London.

•

A Chair of Ophthalmology at the
Royal Australian College of Ophthalmologists.

•

The Ulverscroft Children's Eye Unit at the
Great Ormond Street Hospital For Sick Children,
London.

You can help further the work of the Foundation by making a donation or leaving a legacy. Every contribution, no matter how small, is received with gratitude. Please write for details to:

THE ULVERSCROFT FOUNDATION,
The Green, Bradgate Road, Anstey,
Leicester LE7 7FU, England.
Telephone: (0116) 236 4325

In Australia write to:
THE ULVERSCROFT FOUNDATION,
c/o The Royal Australian and New Zealand
College of Ophthalmologists,
94-98 Chalmers Street, Surry Hills,
N.S.W. 2010, Australia

Emily Hendrickson lives in Reno, Nevada, with her husband. In addition to her Regency romances she has also written a Regency reference book.

HIDDEN INHERITANCE

Beautiful Vanessa Tarleton accepts a position repairing tapestries for the Earl of Stone, knowing full well his reputation as a handsome rake. She had heard gossip about him during her London season, but when her father gambles everything away, she knows the offer is too good to reject. Nicholas, Lord Stone, faces his own dilemma. He must wed an heiress to restore his nearly bankrupt property and to keep a promise made to his grandfather — but is the beautiful and wealthy Mrs Hewit the right choice? Although forewarned about the dangerously attractive earl, is Vanessa forearmed to resist his charm?

Books by Emily Hendrickson
Published by The House of Ulverscroft:

A PERILOUS ENGAGEMENT

EMILY HENDRICKSON

HIDDEN INHERITANCE

Complete and Unabridged

ULVERSCROFT
Leicester

First published in Great Britain in 2006 by
Robert Hale Limited
London

First Large Print Edition
published 2007
by arrangement with
Robert Hale Limited
London

The moral right of the author has been asserted

Copyright © 1989 by Doris Emily Hendrickson
All rights reserved

British Library CIP Data

Hendrickson, Emily
   Hidden inheritance.—Large print ed.—
   Ulverscroft large print series: historical romance
   1. Great Britain—History—George III, *1760 – 1820*
   —Fiction 2. Love stories 3. Large type books
   I. Title
   813.5′4 [F]

   ISBN 978–1–84617–858–0

LINCOLNSHIRE
COUNTY COUNCIL

Published by
F. A. Thorpe (Publishing)
Anstey, Leicestershire

Set by Words & Graphics Ltd.
Anstey, Leicestershire
Printed and bound in Great Britain by
T. J. International Ltd., Padstow, Cornwall

This book is printed on acid-free paper

For Coral, Julie, and Phylis — the best of friends and accomplices

Prologue

'Do you think she will do it? She is a Lady of Quality, after all.' Lord Stone slowly paced the oak floor of his library, about the only room in the ancestral pile of stones that was not in some stage of renovation. 'You're certain she is the right one, the woman I want?'

Robert Millbank, the Earl of Stone's steward and longtime friend, murmured his assurance. It was rare for Millbank to see his lordship's face set in such a deep frown. He was usually a man of decisive action, not one given to weighing a conclusion once reached. He sighed. Still, one did not usually offer the position Lord Stone could at last afford to fill to a young Lady of Quality.

At Millbank's sigh, Nicholas Leighton turned to give him an appraising look, then nodded in understanding. 'It has been a hard road, hasn't it? I confess there have been times when I thought the demands of the cent-per-centers would defeat us.' He ran a tanned masculine hand through the tumbled brown curls that graced his well-shaped head, putting them into further disorder. He had

1

never been a vain man, nor drawn to the airs of the town dandy or the magnificence of the Corinthian. Oh, he had done well enough on his own in London. But that was before he'd unexpectedly inherited, and was forced to take control of, a nearly bankrupt estate in the far reaches of Yorkshire. Now he had neither time, nor inclination, nor funds. A man of immense common sense, he had a priority list, and the woman was next.

'What is her name again? I will not have just anyone, you know. After all, she will be living here. I must consider her influence on Juliana.'

Millbank attempted to keep a stone face at that remark, and failed, cracking a hint of a smile. 'She is noted to be the very model of propriety. From what my cousin writes, she could have been the inspiration for the word 'proper.' '

Lord Stone's midnight-blue eyes flashed in unusual asperity. Gads, the chit wasn't here and she was already sounding like someone he wouldn't want around. Still, her credentials were impeccable. 'Your cousin believes it is but a matter of time?'

'Her father, Lord Tarlton, a baron, is a shocking wastrel. Finances, estate, both are in sad condition. Were it not for the attempts by this lady, everything would have gone long since. I imagine her aunt may offer to help, but my cousin writes that the woman is the worst sort of dragon. Your offer ought to be most providential for the young woman.'

'Yes, well, I expect you had better write and tell your cousin to make the offer on my behalf. You know the sum we discussed . . . all the details. I want her as soon as she can come. Her name, Millbank. What is her name again?'

'The Honorable Vanessa Tarleton.'

As Millbank began to write the letter he would send express to his cousin far away in Wiltshire, Lord Stone walked to the window. He stared at the low scudding clouds that tumbled across the sky. Things were coming together at last. It was like reaching the end of a long dark night. Still, he could not rest easy until he had fulfilled his promise to his grandfather with regard to his 'jewels on the wall.' With the coming of Vanessa Tarleton, that promise would be well on its way to fruition. And Nicholas Leighton, the Earl of Stone, always kept his promises.

1

'Really, Vanessa, I don't know why you must neglect me on such a horrid, rainy day. You know I must have the fire just so — I am certain I can smell smoke. My tea must be all of ten minutes late and my shawl has slipped from where you placed it. Really, my dear.'

The querulous voice of her delicate mother stirred Vanessa from her concerned inspection of the rain-soaked grounds beyond the house. Indeed, it seemed the rain had never fallen quite so hard, nor for so long a time.

The slender blond with a worried expression in her blue eyes released the pale pink silk damask draperies, a luxury her mother had insisted upon a few years past. Turning, she walked sedately from the tall bay window of the south salon to the fireplace, her faded muslin skirts flowing gently about her neatly proportioned figure. Though a dutiful daughter, she felt frustrated at the demands of her mother and aunt. Her father's arrival wouldn't help. He created more problems than he solved.

As she approached, she could see everything was just as it should be, the wood

5

burning brightly, not smoking in the least. She leaned one slim hand against the great carved oak chimneypiece. Making a pretense of studying the fire, she cast an oblique look at her mother. Vanessa took pains to conceal her concern over the weather from her mother and Aunt Agatha, lest her worries upset them further.

Sighing, she moved to placate her mother for the lack of attention in the past half-hour. 'The fire looks well enough to me, Mama, but I will have the footman place another log on for you.' Her soft voice betrayed no hint of the impatience or annoyance that beset her more and more. Were it not for the promise of release in the shape of her marriage to a nearby baron Lord Chudleigh, she would despair. She adjusted the Norwich shawl over her mother's thin shoulders. A sound at the door caught her attention.

Danvers entered precisely on time, bearing the silver tea tray. As was customary, he placed it upon the low walnut table near the sofa her mother favored, flicking a sympathetic glance at Vanessa before he left the room. Vanessa followed him to the threshold to softly request the footman bring more wood.

A derisive sniff heralded her Aunt Agatha's pronouncement from the opposite sofa,

...er skirts were spread in regal *display.*
...o not know why you complain, Elinor.
...at else can one expect from a daughter whose standards are not of the highest order? How you can tolerate her taking over your proper position is more than I can comprehend. In *my* day, young women knew their place.'

'If Vanessa visits the tenants on the estate, it is only to save me the effort, sister dear. You know my health will not permit anything so strenuous. In addition, I am persuaded her work with herbs under Mrs Danvers' direction in the stillroom has been most beneficial. When Vanessa marries Lord Chudleigh come August, she will be well-trained to manage his household. Though I don't know how I am to do without her, I must say.' The high, thin, plaintive voice ceased as tea and biscuits were consumed with an unladylike show of hunger.

In her words lay more than a hint of disappointment. Lady Tarleton was not best pleased that Vanessa had managed to snare no greater prize than a mere baron during her London Season.

Vanessa closed her ears to the flow of complaints she had heard all too often and for far too long. As her mother frequently bemoaned, if only Colin had lived, how different things might have been. With all to consider, it was possible her father might have paid more attention to the estate. As it was, from the day they received news of Colin's death in the Battle of Talavera, her father seemed to lose all heart, and matters began to fail. Her father, rarely joining his family in the best of times, now saw them even less. Vanessa heard the gossip, the tales of his gambling, his mistresses, the riotous living. While she attempted, with the help of William Hunt, their steward, to keep Blackwood Hall from tumbling into disaster, her father did his best to accomplish the opposite. And now it seemed he had succeeded.

Lady Tarleton waved a fragile blue-veined hand in the air with a dismissing gesture. 'I cannot place the least credence on this missive from town. It is mere spite, I am certain. Who would be so cruel as to tell us that Tarleton has gambled away the estate while at cards? I refuse to believe it.' Lady Tarleton sipped her tea, bit into her fourth biscuit. Her woeful sigh was heartfelt.

Compressing her lips a moment to still the words she longed to say, Vanessa bowed her head over the tea tray and poured a second cup of the finest bokea tea into her aunt's cup. The tea was by far the most expensive to

8

be found. Her aunt insisted it was the only thing drinkable, mused Vanessa, as she rose to return the cup to the lady with quiet grace. Gently she offered, 'Mr Hunt said the letter is from Papa's solicitors. I fear we must accept our fate unless Papa has found the means to redeem the property.' She did not add that it was highly unlikely such an event would occur. Her mother would have to face that truth soon enough.

Her eyes narrowed to a speculative slit, Agatha Cathcart mulled over the situation. 'Vanessa could always take you in with her when she marries,' she said to her sister, ignoring her niece even as she took the cup from her slender fingers. First caressing the triple strand of jet beads at her neck, she then smoothed the rich black watered silk of her gown. Though her husband had died but months after their wedding, Agatha had so enjoyed her status as a widow in deep mourning that she never left it.

She continued, assured of her audience, 'It seems a pity Tarleton neglects you so, dear sister. I know the war forced prices to rise — quite shockingly, in fact, and something really ought to be done about the matter — but with proper management, things could have been better for you. Of course, you will always be welcome to live with me if worse comes to worst. Never let it be said I turned my own sister away from my door when she needed me. I shan't take in that wastrel husband of yours, however, so do not expect *that* of me. *His* morals are past redeeming.' Since joining the Society for the Reformation of Morals, Agatha considered herself an arbiter of what ought to be done in the world. Her lips moved spasmodically in what for her passed for a smile as she looked at Vanessa. Were her niece to come under her roof, that miss would play a different melody if Agatha Cathcart had her way. And she always did; she saw to that.

'There is always the chance Lord Chudleigh will cry off when he learns the news. It may be my dowry is gone as well.' Vanessa's calm voice betrayed nothing of the tumult of inner emotions. She had learned never to betray an emotion nor to voice an opinion in her aunt's hearing. It was deemed unseemly for an unmarried woman. Yet the words against her father, however justly deserved, made her burn with anger. What gave Aunt Agatha the right to be so critical? Vanessa sat, a rigid, carefully controlled figure in worn pale blue muslin, her soft blond curls severely confined at the nape of her neck. It was all she could manage to deal with her two relatives in a pleasant manner.

Her sea-blue eyes were troubled as she

glanced once more out the tall windows to where the rain continued to fall in a heavy sheet. Her father was to travel this day from London. The roads would not be in best condition with all this rain. Perhaps he might stop until the weather improved, unless there was an element of time involved. She had heard of dispossessed owners having to vacate their homes with scarcely any notice. Mr Hunt said the settlement papers would be with her father; they would soon learn what was to happen. Naturally a gambler's debt of honor must be settled at once — never mind that it put a family out of their ancestral home. Her face masking her bitter thoughts, she feared for the future as she poured the tea and passed the biscuits.

Would Lord Chudleigh be willing to take her parents into his home after the marriage ceremony? She barely knew the man. It was a marriage arranged in proper fashion. She had met the baron at a ball . . . they saw each other a number of times at various social gatherings . . . he called on her with exquisite politeness. He had made the offer to her father, who accepted on her behalf, informing Vanessa of it later, after all had been arranged and negotiated. She hadn't been given the pleasure of accepting in person. That, her father had declared, was so much twaddle.

11

Women, he was fond of pointing out, had no head for business. Her secret amusement at her coping, with Mr Hunt's aid, with the affairs of the estate while her father gambled it away was a gentle irony not lost on her.

It was difficult to sit quietly attending the ladies when she would far rather be in the stillroom copying more herbal remedies or asking questions about household operations. If she must leave here soon, she might not have much time for such pursuits anymore. A sensation of helplessness assailed her, and she railed inwardly at the situation of women. She had done well to manage the matters her father ignored. Mr Hunt could handle things only up to a certain point. The final decisions came from Vanessa. It was she who came up with the solutions to the problems that daily rose to face the household. It was like being on a sled headed downhill toward a bottomless pond.

It had been difficult having Aunt Agatha with them these past months. For all the money the old lady supposedly had at her disposal, Vanessa saw no evidence of it as far as helping out with the added expense her stay entailed. Agatha was fully aware of their straitened circumstances, yet she insisted on the best of everything for herself. Vanessa had decided only that morning that, like it or no,

Aunt Agatha must either pay for what Vanessa considered extravagances or do without them. The finest bokea tea and sandal-wood soap were only two of a long list of luxuries Agatha demanded.

A soft rap at the door brought all three heads around. Vanessa bade the footman enter, noting his pale face, his nervousness. Not that Aunt Agatha wasn't enough to make the servants quake in their shoes, but his reactions did seem excessive. 'Yes?' He had undoubtedly come to attend to the fire, though no wood was in evidence. She motioned him closer, smiling kindly to reassure the poor young man.

Agatha's sniff was ignored as the distressed footman came toward Vanessa. 'Please, Miss Vanessa. Danvers says could you come with me downstairs straightaway?'

Aware of both her aunt's disapproval and her mother's total uninterest in any problems that didn't directly affect her, Vanessa nodded. Rising gracefully from the sofa, she spoke in low tones to the ladies. 'I will tend to whatever it is. 'Tis undoubtedly a minor crisis of some sort, like Cook is *again* threatening to leave.'

Even if it was to tend to a crisis, she felt a respite in hurrying from the room. Its overheated, stuffy air gave her the headache.

Or her aunt did. Either way, she'd barely sipped her tea before she'd longed to flee the room.

The marvelous plasterwork ceiling and the exquisite tapestries she had carefully preserved caught her eye as she walked swiftly through the upper anteroom to the central hall. Those tapestries would now belong to someone else, she thought with a pang of sorrow. She hoped whoever got the house would appreciate all the beauty there. Trailing her hand along the oak balustrade, she flicked a finger at one of the carved figures atop a newel post as she rounded a turn on her way to the ground floor. Across from her, the other half of the double flight of stairs rose in stately splendor to the upper stories, where her father's print room and her own turret bedroom were located in the west corner of the house. The house was as well-cared-for as she could manage on her minuscule housekeeping budget. But matters were coming to a head. The servants' pay was in arrears. The cook might very well leave for a better — and paying — position.

The double doors to the outer courtyard were open, and damp gusts of wind swirled in to cool the room. Vanessa shivered from the chill after being in the over-heated south salon. Danvers stood with his back to her,

14

looking out the doorway. Nearby, an eighteenth-century long-case clock chimed the hour. It was later than she thought. Tea tended to be a protracted event.

'Danvers, you sent for me?'

He turned, appearing worried and distracted. 'Yes, miss. Mr Hunt has gone with the men, but we felt you should be prepared first.' He seemed to struggle for his words, a sight such as Vanessa had never seen before.

'What has happened?' The chill draft struck her as premonitory. She looked to the open door, noticing the heavy rain falling, splattering on the cobbled courtyard with vehemence unmatched in her memory.

At her apprehensive words, Danvers straightened, then said with awful finality, 'His lordship's carriage has met with an accident on the road. I'm sorry to tell you he is dead, Miss Vanessa.'

She stared a moment at the neat row of twenty-four fire buckets along the wall, then sank onto the oak settle close at hand. Her mind was in a whirl. Papa? Dead? This couldn't be true! But even as she formed the thought, a carriage was entering the courtyard with Mr Hunt riding at its side. Though she seldom saw it, she recognized the carriage. Now it was splattered with mud, the damage evident. It stopped. Ignoring the water streaming down his face, a groom opened the door. Dazed with shock, she rose, slowly walked to stand by the massive oak doorway as the body of her father was removed and brought into the house. He had been covered with a blanket, which she did not seek to remove. She backed away from the men as they passed, unwilling to reach out to touch the body, a near-stranger for all he was her father.

Vanessa felt numb. She ought to feel grief, not this sense of reprieve. Yet he had been her father and was due a daughter's respect. She shut her eyes a moment. How different this was from when word of Colin's death had reached her. How she had mourned her dearest brother. Unlike her father, Colin had been very close to her and she had loved him best of all her family. Since then, she had often felt as though she merely endured.

William Hunt followed, tossing a packet on the mahogany side table. He turned to the lovely girl who watched in utter silence, placing an arm about her, drawing her away from the door as the body was taken away into the small anteroom off the hall. He removed his hat, handing it to the distraught butler. Hunt's graying hair was flecked with rain, his brown eyes soft with pity. His shoulders drooped as he considered the days ahead. It was a sad state of affairs.

'He died instantly. There was no pain.' Hunt urged Vanessa along to the brown drawing room, where a fitful fire burned low in the grate. He crossed to pour a small glass of brandy, then offered it to Vanessa, who stood staring out the window at the ever-falling rain. This was no time to faint, or have vapors, or do any other thing a woman of proper sensibility would do at such a happening. Vanessa knew she must contain her emotions yet again.

'Thank you, Mr Hunt. I believe you have more need of restoring liquid than I do. I shall be quite all right. I only wonder how to tell my mother. She is so fragile, you know.' Shoulders squared, chin up, she turned to face him, her eyes revealing nothing of her pain or her fears.

William Hunt searched the calm, beautiful face for signs of sarcasm. He found none. The kind, noble girl never spoke a word against that selfish mother of hers.

Vanessa continued, 'She is upstairs now, having tea with my Aunt Agatha. There will be a funeral to arrange. Will you send for the vicar? I am persuaded he will deal with mother better than I could.' Her eyes met his in a moment of shared understanding.

'One of the men has ridden off for him

already, miss. Mrs Danvers has supervised layings-out before — she will handle that. Do you want me to tell your mother?' He wasn't usually a coward, but facing Lady Tarleton at any time was not a thing to be relished.

'No, but come with me, please. I will tell her, and you can give me support if I need it.' She left the window, crossing to the door, then stopped. 'That packet? Have you had a chance to look at it? What news does it bring?'

'The new owner allows you some time to pack your personal belongings before you must leave. You may also take along things of a sentimental nature — within reason, of course.' His anger that this innocent girl must now cope with the entire problem of the estate firmed his resolve to do what he could to ease her burden.

'So the letter was not false, as Mother claimed. I thought not. I wonder what she will do?' She climbed the stairs with dragging steps, crossed the upper hall to the anteroom, then went through to where the two ladies still sat, their teacups empty, the fire burning with cheerful heat.

Her mother glanced at Vanessa's stiff figure as she entered the room. Vanessa's hands were clenched before her in an unnatural position, her face unusually pale. Lady

Tarleton broke off conversation with her sister. Her voice was sharp as she rapped out her question. 'What is it, Vanessa? I should think you could spare your poor mother the tribulations of the household. You know how overset I become at the least thing. My nerves simply are not up to what you could handle for me if you but chose.'

Vanessa was undeterred. 'This is not a small matter, Mama. It is your husband — '

Agatha's loud voice interrupted Vanessa. 'And what of him? Found an excuse not to come down and face us, I'll wager.' She rose from the sofa, an imposing figure in her black watered silk. Moving to stand near her sister, she wore an accusing expression on her face.

Vanessa walked slowly toward the two, her obvious reluctance to speak a puzzling thing. 'There has been an accident, Mama. I fear Papa was killed while traveling down from London.'

Lady Tarleton gasped. 'That cannot be. He would not serve me such a turn! You are too cruel to torment me in this manner, Vanessa. Was ever a mother so poorly treated by her own?'

'What Miss Vanessa says is true, my lady,' interjected William Hunt. 'I have just now returned to the house from where the accident occurred, bringing his body with me.' The steward concealed his distaste for the haughty lady next to her old dragon of a sister, Agatha Cathcart.

Lady Tarleton stared at Hunt with hostile, disbelieving eyes. His cool regard did not waver. Finally accepting what she'd heard, her ladyship swooned into an ugainly heap.

Vanessa turned to Hunt. 'Best ring for her abigail.'

While Hunt crossed to pull the bell cord, Vanessa knelt by her prostrate mother.

Agatha railed out, 'I knew he would come to a bad end. Did I not say so earlier? Gaming brings no joy; London is full of evil ways. Elinor ought never have married that man. I told Father he would be no good.'

Vanessa was scarcely able to hold her tongue. How she wished that for once she might speak her mind to this insensitive woman.

With the help of her abigail, Lady Tarleton was removed to her bed, with Agatha trailing behind, offering doleful comments, but no help at all.

★ ★ ★

The following days passed in a haze of fatigue for Vanessa. Aunt Agatha, for all her formidable pose, turned out to be useless in a crisis. Lady Tarleton was even worse. She swooned several times a day, leaving Vanessa to cope with everything that must be done. The funeral was held, possessions were sorted and packed up. Aunt Agatha made good her offer to her sister and invited Elinor to live with her. She also made it plain Vanessa was welcome as well, though she would be expected to help manage the household. Vanessa correctly interpreted this to mean her aunt intended to install her as an unpaid housekeeper.

A note from Vanessa's betrothed, Chudleigh, had arrived shortly after Lord Tarleton's coach. Apparently as soon as word seeped out of the disastrous gaming loss, Lord Chudleigh had taken pen in hand to declare the wedding off — in excruciatingly polite terms, of course.

One gray day not long after the funeral, Mr Hunt came upon Vanessa in the library, the one room she felt safe in occupying, as the sisters never read anything other than Agatha's tracts. It was not a pretentious room, for the past residents of Blackwood Hall had not been bookish men, nor inclined to spend their blunt on something they didn't use. Rather it contained a modest number of volumes, haphazardly stacked on their sides on two tall sets of plain shelves. The attraction of the room lay in the quiet to be found within its oak-paneled walls. That was something neither of the two older ladies enjoyed, but which appealed immensely to Vanessa.

'What troubles you, Miss Vanessa?' asked Hunt. When alone, they resorted to a familiar standing, rather like that of father and daughter.

She gave him a faintly ironic smile. 'It seems I have one worry less, at least. I shan't have to bother with postponing the wedding. The baron decided we shall not suit. No doubt the loss of my dowry had more than a bit to do with his decision. Odd, I did not think he was so short of funds. Perhaps he finds a bride so completely without home and hearth beyond the pale. Then again, it may be the scandalous manner in which I was deprived of this home.' Her wish to spare Hunt the sad details no longer mattered. She flicked a dismissing finger at the stiff sheet of paper bearing the baron's signature. She had kept the paper to remind herself of Chudleigh's unworthiness, a salutary lesson, and a reminder — should she need one — of her new station. Her face wore a bemused expression, certainly not that of a woman torn from her love.

'Do you intend to live with your aunt?' Hunt watched her face intently as he asked his question. The letter from Yorkshire had arrived. It was burning a hole in his pocket while he waited for a suitable moment to speak.

Vanessa couldn't control a shudder at the mention of her aunt. 'I know I ought to be grateful for her willingness to shelter us when we so desperately need help . . . but, oh, how I wish I had somewhere else to go.' She turned to pace the floor. 'As soon as she heard the news of Chudleigh, Aunt assured me she would be glad of my company. She then informed me that I would not be allowed to squander my time in 'frivolous pursuits.' What does she think I have done here, pray tell? I suppose she counts my harp playing as needless. No more embroidery, Hunt. I will be plying my needle on more useful items, turning sheets and the like.'

The steward thought her slender loveliness seemed most unsuited to a life of drudgery. Surprised at her outspoken words, but pleased at the opportunity speak, he cleared his throat. 'I may have a solution for you. I hope you do not mind, but I took it upon myself to make inquiries. My cousin works for Nicholas Leighton, the Earl of Stone, up in Yorkshire. The earl has been slowly restoring his castle and is now in need of a skilled needlewoman. He does not want just any person, as the castle is remote; whoever works there must needs live there as well. My cousin estimates the work will take some months. You are highly proficient at needle-work, especially in the mending of tapestries. No one could have done a better job on those hanging in the upper anteroom. Why not consider the position?' He wouldn't press. He wouldn't need to. All he had to do was allow her to be around her aunt a bit longer, Hunt decided shrewdly. He was confident Vanessa would grasp any chance to be away from the old harridan.

'How good of you to concern yourself with my future. I shall miss you, dear friend. It pleases me that the new owner has seen fit to retain you to manage the estate. I will feel somewhat better, knowing this is all in your capable hands.' She took another turn about the room, her face for once revealing her inner thoughts. 'I must confess that the offer from the earl brings an opportunity I had not expected. I promise to consider it with care. Can you tell me a little of him?'

'I've not met him myself. My cousin writes that he has an agreeable disposition. He is a fair man to work for; the servants are devoted to him. You could do far worse. As much as I dislike seeing you take a position, it will surely be better than living with your aunt.'

A soft scratching at the door brought a footman with a summons from the south drawing room: Vanessa's aunt wished to speak with her at once. Vanessa glanced back at Hunt as she made a reluctant move to the stairway. 'We will speak more about this later.'

William Hunt nodded as he saw the black skirts whisk around the door and up the elaborate staircase. Poor girl. Her grace and beauty deserved a better future. He hoped so sweet and kind a young woman would accept a way out of her aunt's clutches.

* * *

Vanessa sobered as she entered the drawing room, determined to remain calm despite her aunt's selfish demands. Ignoring the exceedingly warm and stuffy air, she dipped a proper curtsy, inquiring, 'You wished to speak with me, Aunt Agatha?'

'Your mother and I have decided you may as well dye all your dresses black. It is a waste of good money to bother with a dressmaker for new ones. Just get together with that Mrs Danvers and fix up a pot of black dye. I daresay that by the time you finish a year of mourning there won't be a man found who wants a woman as near on the shelf or ridden with scandal as you, not to mention your total

25

lack of any dowry. We three will deal together quite well. With a bit of tutoring, you will make a fine housekeeper, my dear.'

Vanessa couldn't bring herself to meet those eyes. Either she would give away her own anger or she would wince at what she saw revealed in her aunt's gaze. 'Dyeing fabric is not always successful. I will make an attempt. I cannot promise the results will be pleasing.'

Dismissed from her aunt's august presence, Vanessa fumed her way to the west turret room that for the moment was hers. She went to her wardrobe, pulled out her most hated dress, then marched down to find Mrs Danvers. It was her first act of rebellion.

Later, at the dining table, she meekly faced the ladies with the tale of dyeing fabric. 'I fear it did not go well at all. It is possible we were sold inferior dye, but the dress fell completely apart, the fabric in tatters. I would hate to think of the rest of my clothes meeting the same fate. I shall simply wear the dresses we had made when Colin died.'

Agatha exchanged a glance with her sister. 'I fear that will not do. We have already decided that your mother will have those dresses. They are far more elegant than you will need, my dear. Perhaps my housekeeper has a dress that would be suitable for your new position in life. You are nearly of a size, I believe. The dress can be altered to fit. As I mentioned to you before, Mrs Gates is due to retire. You are fortunate to have such a capable woman to train you.'

Not trusting herself to speak, Vanessa finished her meal in silence. Every morsel was forced down a tight throat. She refused to permit Aunt Agatha to starve her as well as turn her into a servant.

She excused herself as quickly as she could, pleading the headache, which for once was no fabrication. Hurrying up the stairs, she slipped into her room to undress and climb into bed unassisted. Agatha had assigned her maid to other duties.

Her sleep was troubled. Sometime during the night, she sat up in bed, her mind clear on what must be her path. She would go to Yorkshire. Surely her duty did not lie with her mother. That lady would be cosseted as much as she could wish by her sister. As for Aunt Agatha, Vanessa felt precious little obligation to move to her home and succumb to a life of drudgery and insults.

Vanessa's sleep was deeper, less troubled once she had made the decision to head north. She had had these middle-of-the-night revelations in the past, and always found them to be sound. The greatest loss she faced was her harp. Perhaps Hunt would allow her to store it here until she could send for it. It was the only thing she possessed that she desired to keep. The house and its contents had nothing but sad memories. No, she would set the past behind her. Perhaps while in Yorkshire she might find some means of creating a future that would not include Aunt Agatha. The prospect seemed most enticing.

2

Aunt Agatha was not best pleased. 'I cannot think what the world is coming to, young gels haring off to the wilds of Yorkshire without so much as a by-your-leave to their betters. Mark my words, young woman, you will be sorry if you leave the protection I offer you for God only knows what.' Aunt Agatha shook a plump finger at Vanessa, the black ruffle on her morning cap echoing her movement. 'And what do you know of this man, eh? All I have *heard* of him was of his exploits in London a few years back. The man is a rake, my dear! The hearts he broke, the life he lived!'

Agatha's dramatic sigh gave Vanessa the chance to insert a word or two. 'Mr Hunt has nothing but praise for Lord Stone, Aunt Agatha. However the earl may have behaved in the past has all changed. His servants revere him, others commend him for the effort he has made to restore the property nearly lost by his father and brother. It would seem he is a man to respect, not vilify.'

It pleased Vanessa to repeat what Mr Hunt had told her on the occasion of their second

29

conversation, when she had told him of her intention to accept the offer and travel to Yorkshire. She went on now, 'Is it possible, Aunt Agatha, that it could be the brother you heard talk of in London? His name was Damian, I understand.' Then, considering her aunt's age, she added, 'Or his father, perhaps?'

The rider earned her a glare from her aunt, whose chins quivered as she shot indignant words at Vanessa. 'Never! I do not get my facts muddled. Stupid girl! I cannot think how we could possibly be related. You are selfish beyond permission, to leave your poor mother at a time like this.'

Vanessa refused to quail. 'Had I married the baron as planned, I would have been leaving at any rate.' She suspected her aunt's only regret was the loss of an unpaid housekeeper she could bully to her heart's content. Vanessa didn't know what her prospects were in Yorkshire, but they must surely be better than whatever she might have had under Aunt Agatha's imperious thumb!

'Insolent chit! What has that to say to anything? Mark my words, girl, you will regret this. Your blue-eyed, blonde beauty will not help you in the least. You will be on the shelf and I will not lift one finger on your behalf. Nay, you can come crawling back before I will open my door to you.' With a vehement nod, ruffles all aflutter, Aunt Agatha shot Vanessa a look of loathing, then set off to the south drawing room, where she could malign her niece to her sister with impunity.

Vanessa placed a trembling hand over her rapidly beating heart. The prolonged exchange of words, more like a battle actually, had taxed her patience. More than anything, Vanessa disliked an argument. Yet how satisfying for once to hold her own with her aunt. Given time, she suspected, Aunt Agatha would eventually erode her newfound strength with continual carping. Nor did Vanessa have any illusions about her own ability to continue her slight defiance of her aunt's implacable will to control. Had she elected to accept her aunt's offer to join her household, she'd not dare oppose the old woman again. Nevertheless, it was comforting to know she could assert herself when necessary.

In a second bit of rebellion, Vanessa had countermanded her aunt's direct order and had Betsy returned to her personal service. It was but another step in gaining independence. She walked quickly up the stairs to join Betsy in the west turret bedroom.

Entering her bedroom with a thoughtful expression on her face, she found Betsy awaiting her arrival with a woeful countenance.

31

'You need worry no longer,' she said, waving a letter in the air, one she had carefully concealed from her aunt. 'I have had an answer from my friend in Kent. I recalled her mentioning that her sisters needed a maid. I told her how capable you are and she writes they will welcome you.' Vanessa placed the letter on the small bedside table, then crossed to where the trunks stood open awaiting her belongings. 'You will ride with me as far as London. From there you will take the mail to Kent, while I travel on to Yorkshire.'

'I don't know as how I can thank you enough, Miss Vanessa. That one would make my life a terror, she would.'

Vanessa said nothing. Rather she picked up her shawls to place them in the bottom of the first trunk. 'Yorkshire undoubtedly will be chilly after the mild climate of Wiltshire,' she commented. She studied the delicate white muslins, cambrics, and more elaborate dresses she had worn to social doings while in London not so very long ago. 'Do you think you could manage to sell the white muslin and these other dresses for me when we get to London? I hardly think I shall have any need for ball gowns or other elegant clothes in my new position, do you?' She held up a particularly favorite gown and added, 'And besides, white hardly seems the proper thing for a needlewoman, does it?'

The elegant black mourning gowns Vanessa had worn after Colin's death already lay packed in her mother's trunks. With no other blacks, Vanessa resigned herself to wearing somber-hued clothes instead of proper mourning for her father. Fortunately she possessed a brown tucked-silk crepe that would do well enough on those few occasions she needed to meet people, such as church on Sunday morning. She expected that, as in most households, the servants attended services, and Vanessa guessed that a needlewoman would fit into that category. Undoubtedly she would be something like a governess, or upper servant, certainly. She would know her place.

It would make no difference what she wore while she worked on the tapestries. Besides, no one at such a distant spot would know anything about her past. Lord Stone would not care one whit about her personal life. It was an appealing notion, now that she thought of it. Like starting afresh, in a way.

'Laws, miss,' cooed Betsy, 'you look elegant in anything you put on. I'd be pleased to help you however I can, though. A word or two will lead me to a place to sell your things.' Betty's confidence in getting about in a place like London amused Vanessa. Yet the maid was always one to manage. Betsy reverently smoothed a hand over a soft white muslin tucked and embroidered by Vanessa's own hand, destined for the sale pile.

Noting the look and touch, Vanessa smiled. 'I would appreciate it if you would take that dress for yourself, Betsy. I cannot bear to think of it on just anyone. As a favor to me?'

Betsy nodded, setting the admired dress aside. 'Thank you ever so, miss. Won't anyone else have as nice, I'm thinkin'.' The maid's eyes reflected her delight. 'Though I knows better than to wear it when I arrive. Many a maid's been turned away when the house-keeper got a look at her in a white dress. 'Twon't do for me to look above my place. I'll wear it iffen I find a young man to impress.' She set to work with her adored mistress, sorting the clothes. Those to be sold went in a pile on the bed: the garments making the trip to Yorkshire were wrapped carefully in tissue and placed in the trunks. Vanessa found her eyes straying to the view out her window rather than observing what was stowed in her trunk.

Vanessa paused as she gathered her dainty underthings, soft silk and finest linen. Every woman had a weak spot. Hers was exquisitely made underclothes and nightgowns. Her pale blue dressing gown was made of a delicate watered silk trimmed with lace and ribbon. It had a matching nightgown, fit for a trousseau, made for her wedding trip with Lord Chudleigh. A luxury, the ensemble might have fetched a fair price had she been willing to part with it. Which she wasn't. She thrust the delicate garments at Betsy, who folded them neatly, placing them at the top of the first trunk so they would be easily found when Vanessa reached Yorkshire.

Her departure from her girlhood home was accomplished with fewer complications than she would have believed possible. Desiring to catch the earliest stage she could, she bade her mother and Aunt Agatha goodbye the evening before her departure, her regret upon receiving such a cold farewell concealed beneath a mien of demure politeness.

At first light, Betsy helped her mistress into her clothes with the air of one aiding in an illicit rendezvous. The two consumed a hasty meal, then gathered up the baskets prepared by Mrs Danvers containing food to sustain them during the journey. It was still very early when they left for Devizes in the estate carriage, saying a fond farewell to the Danverses and Hunt before departing. Vanessa watched as Betsy looked back at the house.

'Ain't you sad to be leaving, miss? It's a powerful lovely place.' Betsy took one last look before settling back against the squabs, obviously puzzled at the lack of feeling in her mistress regarding the place where she'd spent her girlhood.

'No point in thinking about it, Betsy. That is all in the past. My future lies elsewhere.' Vanessa would not admit even to herself how desolate she felt to be going away from all she held dear, to an unknown tomorrow. Perhaps if her mother had been more sympathetic or her aunt more welcoming in her hospitality, Vanessa could have looked on her trip to Yorkshire as an interlude prior to joining the two women. The prospect before her was not comforting — a paid needlewoman in a nobleman's house. There had been no mention of his wife, but she hoped the lady would not be too difficult to deal with while Vanessa resided beneath her roof. That Lord Stone might not be married never crossed her mind.

At Devizes they bade farewell to the family carriage and booked two seats on the first public coach bound for London. The crowded conveyance headed north, then east on the old Roman road through Marlborough.

Vanessa's arrival in London was totally different from her previous trip. This time she came in a common stage and was let down at an ordinary-looking, though large inn. Its yard was full of travelers coming and going, dust swirling around, dogs nosing about, smells of food and people, leather and manure pervading the air. Fortunately, Mr Hunt had arranged accommodations for the two women. Vanessa signaled a hackney and set off for their modest hotel.

Once in her room, Vanessa surveyed it with a critical eye. 'It is small, but neat and quiet. I shall ask for a cot to be set up for you in the corner. I confess I am glad for your company. Let us eat our dinner, then enjoy an early night, shall we?' Betsy agreed. Vanessa would have liked a walk, but she had taken one look at the area around the hotel and decided it was safer to remain discreetly inside.

After a night's rest, Betsy set off with Vanessa's clothes neatly bundled up, while Vanessa hailed a hackney, directing it toward Savile House at Leicester Square.

Deposited on the cobbled street before the museum that housed Miss Susan Linwood's Gallery of Needlework, Vanessa took a deep breath, then hurried up the steps before she lost her nerve at approaching so important a person. Entering the principal room, she held her breath in anticipation. Then she expelled it gently as she viewed the first of the exquisite copies in needlework of the finest pictures of the English and foreign schools. She was glad she had handed over an additional sixpence for the catalog above the two shillings demanded for admission to this truly remarkable exhibit. According to the catalog, there were seventy-five works hanging here. From what she could observe, the coloring, light, and shade of the originals were indeed, as the catalog claimed, reproduced to perfection.

Scarlet broadcloth elegantly trimmed with gold bullion tassels and Greek borders draped the walls of the gallery. The guard standing to the far side of the room watched her as she moved along from one picture to another, intent, Vanessa supposed, on preserving the beauty of the needlework from hands that wished to touch. As if Vanessa would harm one thread of such magnificence!

Turning to the left, she went down a long and obscure passage toward a view of the cell of a prison. There she could see depicted the image of the beautiful Lady Jane Grey, visited by the abbot and keeper of the Tower the night before her execution. Vanessa studied the incredibly fine work before going on to the next exhibit, a view of a cottage, the casement of which stood open, the hatch of the door closed. On looking in, she perceived a fine and exquisitely finished copy of Gainsborough's *Cottage Children* standing by the fire, with chimneypiece and cottage furniture complete. Near to it was Gainsborough's Woodman, exhibited in a similar manner.

She felt almost overwhelmed at the wealth of beauty, all done with a humble needle and colored thread. Checking the small watch pinned to her dress, she noted that it was nearly time for her interview with the creator of all this remarkable needlework.

Let into a very plain room at the rear of the building, she took a moment to study the woman responsible for the exhibit. A dainty lace cap sat upon her head, a soft wave of brown-gray hair curving from a center parting beneath the cap's ruffle. The window directly behind her denied Vanessa a clear view of her countenance. Since Miss Linwood appeared to be in her middle fifties, perhaps she felt shadows kinder to a woman of her years.

Her voice, when she spoke, was soft, sweet, yet quite distinct, in spite of the distance between the two women. 'You desired my advice, Miss Tarleton?' Miss Linwood asked.

Vanessa nodded, grateful that Miss Linwood had plunged to the heart of the manner without any roundaboutation. 'I have been hired to repair some tapestries of great value. I brought my workbox with me, hoping you might advise me as to what materials I should take along with me to Yorkshire. I have a fair selection of yarns, from the repair on our own tapestries I have done over the past years. I will need more, I expect. I fear I will not find a plenitude of supplies up there.'

With that, Vanessa opened the rectangular workbox decorated with touches of ivory. A loose lift-out tray divided into compartments held a large variety of silk barrels, together with pinboxes, thimbles, thread waxer, needle holders, and emery.

The next half-hour was agreeably spent in listening and jotting down Miss Linwood's recommendations in an ivory-covered note-book. A reel box to hold the many reels of thread was suggested, along with a list of the most likely colors to be used, considering the age of the tapestries. Mr Hunt had been able to tell her that much about the work.

'I feel ecru is a most useful color, and you had best get a sizable quantity, both silk and linen. If the tapestries are as fine as you say, there may be a hundred or more shades. You will need a fair selection of wool yarns, for you do not know how severe the damage is, do you? Purchase the other colors in small quantity, I think. I believe you can order any additional amount you might need. Tell them I suggested you might do such a thing. Though I have all my yarns dyed for me, this shop is quite good.' Miss Linwood handed Vanessa a small card imprinted with the name of the shop she felt it best to patronize. When it came time to leave, Vanessa felt she was far better prepared to face whatever she might find in Yorkshire.

Leaving Miss Linwood, Vanessa went to the front of the exhibit to enjoy the needlework one last time before returning to the hotel and the journey before her. As she studied the self-portrait of Miss Linwood, she noted that others had entered the museum. Three gentlemen were standing across the principal room from her, with two ladies just entering. She was close enough to overhear the gossipy conversation among the gentlemen as they gazed at the depiction of a *Litter of Foxes at Play*. A review of the doings of nearly anyone who was anyone in the *ton* issued forth nonstop.

'Amazing works, ain't they?' said the eldest of the gentlemen, his quizzing glass raised to inspect the piece of needlework as he paused in his dissection of society.

'Indeed, they are. Wish my sister could do a quarter as well. By the by, Pryse, did I

41

mention I had a letter from Stone the other day?' This remark came from a younger man dressed in deep blue and pale gray, a Corinthian of high note, she was certain. His words caught her full attention.

'You don't say? How's he coming along these days?'

'In prime twig. Seems he's got things well in hand at long last. Pity that father and brother of his had such a run of bad luck. Went through prodigious sums, I heard. Known at every gaming hell in town, I daresay. Stone has reversed the damage. No doubt it won't be long before he comes to inspect the next crop of gels to make their come-out. Once he has the estate in shape, he'll need a wife, don't you know?'

The third gentleman, also dressed in the latest stare of fashion, added, 'I miss the old boy. He was the best of company, he was. Can't be much fun up there in Yorkshire. Dashed uncivilized place, I should think.'

'Have you seen the Leventhorpe chit? I believe she comes from up that way. Quite a jewel of the first water, gentlemen. If that is what Yorkshire has to offer, Stone may not come hunting down here after all. You know he never had any trouble collecting the ladies!' There was a nudge in the ribs to accompany this jocular remark. The three

42

moved on to inspect another picture, switching the conversation to another hapless soul.

Vanessa felt her cheeks warming. She had been frozen in her steps when she heard the name of Lord Stone, her soon-to-be employer. Usually so circumspect, she had actually listened to a conversation not intended for her ears! But she was glad she had paused. She was fairly certain they spoke of the earl. There couldn't be *two* Stones from Yorkshire of that description. Her new employer was not only unmarried, he might be looking for a wife! What implications that might have for her, she couldn't imagine, except that she would be alone, unprotected, in a house far away from anyone she knew. Her thoughts carried her out the door and into the hackney.

The clip-clop of the horse's feet on the cobbles was the only sound on the way to the hotel. There was much to consider. Mr Hunt had painted Lord Stone as a saint. Her aunt had made him sound like a devil. The truth must lie somewhere in between — but at what point?

Once in her room, she found Betsy returned. The maid fussed about her, bragging about the goodly sum of money obtained from the sale of the dresses. Vanessa was abstracted, pacing about the small room, pausing to stare out the window, which had naught but a brick wall as a view. At her maid's look of concern, she patted Betsy's arm.

'I heard something about my new employer today that upset me. Nothing bad, mind you. Just that I thought him to be married and he is a single gentleman.'

Betsy was as romantic as they come, and she cooed, 'La, miss, mayhap you'll marry the gentleman and settle down in Yorkshire. Then you won't have to worry none about the future or your Aunt Agatha.'

Vanessa laughed, shaken from her mood by the silliness of Betsy's words. 'Highly unlikely, Betsy, my girl. Lord Stone can have his pick. And that would never be a woman like me, with no dowry and only passable looks.' Vanessa accepted the fact that she possessed a pleasing countenance and nice manners. If she was aware of the lingering looks that came her way, she didn't reveal it in any way.

After a late luncheon in her room, Vanessa left the hotel, accompanied by Betsy. A visit to the shop Miss Linwood recommended found all the supplies Vanessa considered she might possibly need. Their cost depleted her sum of money by a worrying amount. Two years before, she would not have given a thought to spending so much. Today, every penny added up far too quickly. She could only hope her employer would reimburse her for the expenditure.

'My dear Miss Tarleton! It is you, is it not?'

Vanessa turned from paying for her purchases to meet the curious eyes of a lady who had known her parents well.

'Lady Randolph.' She smiled politely. 'How nice to see you.'

The older woman noted Vanessa's dress, the brown tucked-silk instead of the deeper black that was most proper. 'I was sorry to learn of the death of your father. Your dear mother?' Her look sharpened with interest for a tidbit or two to share with her friends.

Willing her face not to blush with the shame of her father's gaming losses, Vanessa replied somewhat stiffly, 'She has gone to reside with her sister, my lady. I am going to visit friends in Yorkshire before joining her.' Vanessa could only be thankful the coffee-brown silk she wore was acceptable, though not as often seen as black for mourning. She carefully refrained from announcing her employment as a needlewoman. The deliberate omission was a vanity she hadn't expected to discover in herself. Perhaps it was a disappointing facet of her character, yet Vanessa despised the thought she might become the latest *on-dit* for gossiping tongues.

'You will not be returning from the wilds of Yorkshire to Blackwood Hall?'

Lady Randolph knew very well the estate had been lost. Everyone must know by now. Vanessa glanced to where her ladyship's ivory-faced daughter selected silks for a piece of embroidery. 'No. From Yorkshire I will travel to my aunt's home, I expect.' Unless a way could be found to avoid it, she added mentally.

Lady Randolph vividly recalled Agatha Cathcart from the one and only time she had met her. A look of sympathy flashed across her face. 'Best find a position as a governess, my dear.' Lady Randolph turned away to answer a question raised by her daughter. Vanessa felt an unaccustomed twinge of envy. It was not so long ago that she too had selected anything she pleased, with no regard to cost. Now she took advantage of the distraction to murmur something appropriate, then left with all possible haste.

Jolting along in the hackney with Betsy sitting patiently across from her, Vanessa studied the parcels in her lap. It would be a humbling experience to have to request being repaid. At least she would no longer have to worry about having an excess of pride. It would be as Lady Randolph predicted. The

46

day Vanessa finished the tapestries, she would have to seek a position of some sort. How often was a needlewoman in demand? Perhaps if she did well, she could obtain a similar position elsewhere. It was a pity that the main English manufactories of tapestries had failed, or she might seek a reference from one of them for preservation work. Her smile at that thought removed the anxious frown from Betsy's face. Noting her maid's concern, Vanessa attempted to make the rest of the day as pleasant as she could. The two ate dinner in their room, settling to bed early. Both spent a restless night.

Betsy left first on the Dover Mail. Vanessa firmly quenched a feeling of abandonment. She lifted her chin, picked up her sober skirts, and climbed into the Yorkshire coach. She was thankful it was a morning in June, which, while chilly, did not have the rawness of half-past five on a January morning.

Four gleaming chestnuts seemed ready to set off. The coach stood prepared for her trip. Ostlers were thrusting baggage into the boot; it swallowed up everything thrown at it, it seemed. Vanessa had seen her own trunks stowed near the bottom before she settled onto her seat next to the right window, facing forward. It would have been cheaper to sit atop the coach, but she intended to travel straight through to York, thus saving the price of rooms. It would be folly to be out in any weather, risking a fall when tired. There was a limit to her thrift.

The sound of the horn, with its cheery, 'Oh, dear, what can the matter be?' seemed melancholy to Vanessa as the coach lurched forward and rumbled out of the yard and through the cobbled streets of early morning London.

At the George at Huntingdon, Vanessa was hesitant to venture into the inn without a maid to lend her countenance. Still, a hot meal appealed. A young abigail or governess had sat opposite Vanessa; a parson and his wife and a chinless clerk also bound for York were the other riders on the journey. The sixty miles they had traveled seemed like an age, yet she knew there were far more to cover, nearly two hundred in all, according to Mr Hunt.

At an understanding look from the governess, Vanessa joined the travelers for a hot meal, sitting quietly with the governess.

The horses were changed, the passengers climbed back in, and they set off again. The parson and his wife left at the next stage point. The others prepared to endure the night of jostling over the north-bound road. Vanessa closed her eyes and tried to sleep, seeking to discourage conversation.

It was not, perhaps, the best solution. With nothing else to occupy her mind, her thoughts moved naturally to the one thing remaining at the back of her head all the time — Nicholas Leighton, the Earl of Stone. Would he be a cold, hard man? Surely he could not be so very bad if Mr Hunt's cousin vouched for him. That gentleman was held in the highest esteem by a man she had known most her life, dear Mr Hunt.

So, given Mr Millbank's approbation, surely she must consider Lord Stone to be a man of . . . consequence? But what was he really like? she mused. Would he be a remote tall blond with piercing blue eyes, or possibly a dark romantic with Byronic leanings? Soon she would know.

First impressions were important, she believed. She hoped she could set herself to rights at the inn where they stopped in York before continuing on to Stone's Court.

Her longing for a feather bed grew as the hours passed. Vanessa felt every bone and muscle in her body protesting vehemently. With every hour that passed, she wondered if she was doing the right thing in coming such a great distance.

When at last she stumbled from the coach at the inn at York, she first sought information about her transportation to Stone's Court. A man would have to be sent out, it was explained. She then sought a room where she could restore herself and take a nap. She was so tired, not even the thought of a hot meal enticed her. Her final thought before drifting to sleep on a blessedly comfortable feather bed was of the earl. Was he a devil or a saint?

3

Vanessa peered eagerly from the window of the carriage. On either side of the road lay a deer park of some magnitude. They had entered the gates of the property some time before, and it seemed they had ridden for ever so long. She could see a few fallow deer wandering beneath the trees of the fine woods. It was a tranquil scene of exquisite beauty, like a hand-tinted etching in a picture book.

Relaxing against the squabs, she reviewed the morning's events. Vanessa had intended to rest only a short while before continuing on to the Leighton estate. When shown by the landlady to a tiny room where she might refresh herself, she had slumped on the bed and fallen into an exhausted sleep within seconds.

Hours later, the sympathetic landlady shook her awake with the information that the groom from Stone's Court was below. The sleep had been vastly restoring, however, even if it left her feeling somewhat fuzzy in the head. Vanessa paid her bill with gratitude. She could envision herself arriving half-asleep and making a terrible impression on her new employer. If she saw him. Of course, it might be that she would deal directly with the steward, Mr Millbank. She hoped she might request a meal. Her store of food was depleted, and her stomach had been protesting since she left York. She ought to have taken time for lunch at the inn.

Her attention was caught by the double row of lime trees they now passed between, and she leaned forward once more to look out the window. A mist had descended over the area, blotting out the distant view. The damp seeped in around the carriage door and penetrated her cloak. She shivered — more with apprehension than with cold, however. She was so close.

There was a rattling of gravel beneath the wheels as the coach turned. All at once she could make out a ghostly shape. It was a building, appearing like one solid rock of stone, rising in austere splendor before her. She drew in an awed breath. Narrow windows looked down on the forecourt. The structure bore a definite resemblance to a fortress of old.

The carriage drew to a halt, the door was opened, and Vanessa was helped down. The groom hesitated, then swung up and sat by the coachman as he drove the carriage away around the curve of the drive. Alone, feeling abandoned in the misty gloom, Vanessa looked about her.

She stood on the lower level of the broad steps leading to the double doors, one of which stood partially open to the mist. Cautiously, wary as a doe, she moved toward those doors. She could hear muffled sounds echoing through the damp air with eerie foreboding. Truly, this residence lived up to her employer's name.

There was no butler in evidence, yet they must have been expecting her. Then she realized she ought to have sought the servants' entry. Yet the carriage had stopped here. Puzzled, she poked her head around one of the tall doors, then gasped.

Within was a lofty central hall, the likes of which she had heard described by a friend after a visit to Blenheim Palace. There were two large and two smaller arches, quite elaborate in design. The walls above were frescoed, with musicians, muses, and an array of gods and goddesses silently serenading.

The fantastic sight was set aside as she renewed her determination to seek the servants' entry. Just as she turned to leave, she caught sight of a man crossing beneath one of the archways, his footsteps echoing on the white-and-black marble floor. He neared the central portion of the hall, directly under the filtered light from the dome, before she realized he must be the steward, Mr Millbank.

His height was above average and his shoulders were impressive, though he wore a plain white cambric shirt, open at the neck. Surely the earl would have an exquisitely tied cravat above a waistcoat of elegant design? Nankeen breeches were tucked into well-worn boots, not the sort she expected to be worn by the owner of this romantic pile of stone. However, those legs were well-formed and nicely muscular, revealing an athletic inclination. He was handsome in a careless way, in spite of tousled dark-brown hair and a smudge of ink on his cheek.

The sight of the ink smudge confirmed her first impression. Taking a steadying breath, she stepped forward to speak to him. His down-to-earth look appealed to her, most reassuring amid the grandeur of the house.

'Hello?' She cleared her throat, then took another step to place herself in his path. He lifted his eyes from a sheaf of papers held in one very well-shaped hand to give her a puzzled look, as though wondering what on earth she was doing there.

'I am Miss Tarleton, sir. The coachman put me down at this entrance, though I daresay I should have sought the servants' entry. Perhaps you could contact my employer, Lord Stone, to tell him I am come?' She gave a look about her, unaware of the amusement and appreciation for this fresh beauty that crept into the midnight-blue eyes of the man she faced.

'Welcome, Miss Tarleton. If you are not too fatigued, perhaps you might like a tour of your new home for the coming months. I assume it will take you some time to effect the repairs to the tapestries?'

Nothing was said about contacting his employer, and Vanessa was too delighted in his company to risk repeating her request. He tucked the papers under one arm, then extended the other to her. Vanessa, gratified to find the steward was such a personable man, smiled brilliantly up at him, nodding her pleasure at the thought of a tour of the house — if you could call so grand a place by such a humble word.

'I am well enough, sir. Though the road north from York is not smooth, the carriage made the trip tolerable.' She beamed a second smile at him, her eyes assuming a sweetly grave expression. 'If the tapestries are anything as described, and neglected for so very long, it could well take some months. I must confess to a bit of apprehension.

Though I have handled the preservation of the tapestries at Blackwood Hall for many years, they are not quite the age of these. Those date merely from the seventeenth century. I understand the tapestries here are much older, and I fear they may be difficult to work on.'

'I was told you are highly skilled. How does it come that a young woman who should be doing nothing more than concentrating on a Season in London should spend so much time at tapestry repair?' His eyes met hers with a shock of warmth in them that shot to her toes.

A hand fluttered to her throat as she responded in soft, breathless tones, 'I enjoy needlework, sir. Our tapestries needed tending and I did it.' She hated to reveal there had been no money to hire a weaver to make repairs.

They entered a large saloon that she thought must be lovely on a sunny day. Facing south, with many windows, it possessed a cheerful aspect even in this misty light. The furniture, what still remained in the room, sat concealed by holland covers. She could hear echoes of lumber being dropped on a floor, the sound of voices, the rasp of a saw. The pungent odor of fresh paint drifted about them.

'We thought you might find this an acceptable place to work. It has good light, and a large table could be set up here to accommodate the tapestries. I assume you will want to lay them out to work on them?'

The idea of working in this grand room was a bit overwhelming. Then she remembered she was the daughter of the late Lord Tarleton, and not some mere weaver. Giving him a suddenly confident smile, she replied with serene charm, 'It sounds admirable to me, though it seems a large room for the task. Will it not be inconvenient to you to have it thus occupied for so long?'

His voice was warm and confiding. 'The entire place is in the midst of refurbishing. Not all the furniture will be returned. A good many new things will have to be ordered, I suppose. What is the latest vogue in London?' He held on to her slender hand by simply bringing his arm close to his body. Common sense told him she was merely a tool toward his goal. But his other senses were clamoring to be heard, and they gave distinctly different reactions. The needlewoman had turned out to be exceedingly lovely.

'There is an Egyptian influence, according to Mr Ackermann's Respository. I quite enjoy the simple curving, rather classical lines, though I wonder at some of the lions' heads and paws and caryatids depicted. I do feel that a crocodile couch and a sphinx sofa are perhaps going a bit far. I have nightmares of entering a salon simply swarming with beasts.' She gave a light chuckle that the listener found enchanting. 'The Prince Regent is much taken with the Chinese style in furniture and decoration. When I attended the celebration of his appointment as Regent, I observed numerous examples in his apartments.'

Vanessa abruptly ceased her chatter. She did not intend to impress anyone with a past now gone. She moved with him as he guided her through the subsequent rooms, listening intently to all he explained. His voice was pleasing, husky and deep. The warmth of his body through the fine cambric of his shirt was strangely comforting. She ought to have objected to the intimate manner in which he tucked her arm so tightly to him. Instead she found she quite liked it, and said nothing. His body was firm, well-muscled, unlike Lord Chudleigh's.

'This is the music room. Somewhere underneath all that holland cloth is a pianoforte. Do you play?'

'Not the pianoforte. I play the harp, but mine is stored at Blackwood until such time as I have a place for it.' Desiring to change the subject, she asked, 'This is a rather drafty old place, is it not? I hope I do not regret leaving the warmer climes of Wiltshire for this desolate spot.'

A faint smile touched his lips. The most irresistible urge to tease the possessor of those delightful blue eyes came over him. Why not? It wasn't often he was able to be someone else. 'I feel certain *you* will not find it so harsh. You found London pleasant?'

A suddenly wayward tongue permitted her curiosity, fed by long hours in the coach, to escape. 'The gossip in London is that Lord Stone is fond of high living. Or at least the ladies. I should think this would be quite boring for a man of his apparent interests.' She paused, then plunged on, heedless of indiscretion. 'Is he such a shocking rake as I have heard?'

The man at her side gave a little cough. 'You heard much gossip while in London?'

Vanessa nodded, confiding, 'I vow, between those wicked tales and the stories of his many sins from my Aunt Agatha, I was almost ready to overlook my dire need for this position.'

He glanced down at her worried countenance. 'And are you in dire need?'

She gave her head a doleful shake. 'If you but knew my Aunt Agatha, you would have no need to ask.'

'Dragon, is she?' He was all sympathy, recalling the remark made by Millbank.

'Indeed. I suppose it is that very trait that makes me hope the earl is closer to my steward's praise than my aunt's awful predictions. I have no desire to join her household.' In her delight at the beauty of the house, she failed to note he did not answer her question.

The man at her side frowned, then directed his remarks to the room they were entering. What would this charming creature say when she discovered who he really was?

She emitted an unconscious sigh as they continued to the end of the house, where the sight of the long gallery brought her to a halt. It was in the process of extensive alterations. Here the paint smell was strong. Odd pieces of lumber were scattered in tumbled piles, and carpenters bustled about, intent on their tasks. They cast darting glances at the two who entered, but said nothing.

Vanessa was embarrassed at the faint rumbling of her empty stomach. She gave her companion an apologetic look, then sighed. 'I do hope I can get some sort of meal before too long.' She politely omitted mentioning her missing meals. She turned from his concerned gaze to look about.

A light and airy feeling pervaded the room,

in spite of the fact it was narrow and long. What must have been three rooms originally now opened up on one another, separated only by arches to form one great gallery. The carpenters were occupied in decorating the elaborate window surrounds. At the far end, a painter could be seen wielding his brush. As she passed under the first arch, the central part was revealed to be an octagon with a domed ceiling. It seemed a room to be found in a palace, not some ordinary manor house. Though Blackwood Hall had been a fine example of the latter, this was far grander, almost palatial.

The man at her side placed his hand over hers, a most pleasurable feeling. 'We must see to your needs. The remainder of the tour can wait, I am certain.' He paused as a man with a long roll of what appeared to be architectural plans bustled up. Vanessa missed his look of irritation.

The man inquired, 'Milord, if I could have but a moment of your time. I have drawn in the changes you requested in the octagon and would have you inspect them.'

Vanessa drew back as though stung. This was obviously not Mr Millbank, as she had first thought. The man she felt so comfortable with, had shared amused looks and chuckles with, was her employer, the Earl of Stone!

She had so hoped to make a favorable impression on the man, and now he must think her a veritable featherhead. And the things she had said! How humiliating!

Drawing in a vexed breath, she pulled away from his side, ignoring the flash of annoyance that crossed his face as she stepped toward the door. 'Thank you, milord. I will seek the housekeeper. I am certain she will assist me.'

'Miss Tarleton . . . ' His expression was thunderous.

Vanessa paused at the far entry to the long gallery and nodded graciously at Lord Stone. 'Perhaps I shall see you later, milord? Thank you for your kind attention.' She dipped a very proper curtsy, then fled past a startled painter.

The corridor with its marble busts and statues of great antiquity normally would have fascinated her at any other time. Now as she hurried along the white marble tiles, she was torn between hunger and an embarrassed desire to seek refuge in her assigned room, wherever it might be found. He had known who she was and deliberately refrained from telling her his identity. What a fool he had made of her! His amused glances now assumed a totally different aspect. She gritted her teeth and clenched her fists in anger as she thought of what she would like to say to that dissembler. Oh, he had not actually lied to her, but he had allowed her to believe he was Millbank. He must be well aware she would not have spoken with such an easy manner had she known he was the earl. Furious, she stamped around the corner even as she berated herself for allowing her tongue to run away from her. What an odious man, and to think she must face him again. Aunt Agatha must have the right of it: he must be a devil and a rake.

When she arrived once more at the arch that led into the entrance hall, she saw a very tall, thin, almost cadaverous-looking man dressed in an impeccable black dress coat with crisp white tie checking the view from the open door. His melancholy mien draped about him like a shroud. The absent butler?

'Ahem.' She caught his attention at once. 'I am Miss Tarleton, newly arrived from London. I just spoke with Lord Stone. Perhaps I could be shown to my room?' She tried to curb her ire, and gave him a hopeful look, not expecting too much from what must be an aged family retainer.

Jet-black eyes studied the Lady of Quality who stood politely before him. His brisk voice startled her. 'I am Peverly, Miss Tarleton. I regret I was unable to meet you when you arrived. The house is in a bit of disarray at the moment, as you can see. I'll ring Mrs Murdoch. She will show you to your room in the west wing.' He spoke the words with a sense of importance, as though she should feel honor in such a location. He marched over to tug a long rope on the wall.

The entry of a short, rather plump woman dressed in rusty black was most welcome. She looked as though she might be a cozy soul, a woman Vanessa might find to be an agreeable co-worker.

'Mrs Murdoch, show Miss Tarleton to her room in the west wing.' The woman faced him as though in silent argument. 'As his lordship specified,' he added. There was an unyielding command in his voice. Vanessa was aware of a feeling of conflict between these two.

With seeming reluctance, Mrs Murdoch turned and motioned Vanessa to follow her up the stairs. Around one end of a broad arch Vanessa discovered a staircase with several landings, each displaying a collection of some sort. She ignored these, concentrating on the housekeeper. She could almost feel the animosity with every jangle of the keys on the chatelaine which dangled from Mrs Murdoch's ample waist. Her body fair bristled with indignation. Vanessa could only wonder what had upset the woman so.

The hall was carpeted in faded red wool of some age. With a sinking heart, Vanessa trailed down it behind Mrs Murdoch. It was not an auspicious beginning to what might well be an uncomfortable few months. They paused mid-point in the hallway. The housekeeper opened a heavy oak door and gestured. Vanessa sidled past the rotund lady with a sense of unease.

''Tis the blue room,' Mrs Murdoch announced unnecessarily. The pale blue walls echoed the deeper blue of the hangings on the painted four-poster, the satin-striped chair covers, and the lovely chaise at the foot of the bed. 'His lordship said to put you in here. I can't spare a maid for you. You'll have to do fer yourself.' She pointed out the desk, washstand, wardrobe, and elegant dressing table with a curt wave of her hand.

Vanessa wasn't certain what she had expected, but it wasn't such a fine room. From the expression and manner of Mrs Murdoch, it wasn't what the housekeeper felt proper.

In a manner unconsciously like the one used when dealing with servants at Black-wood Hall, Vanessa graciously dismissed the housekeeper, every drop of her genteel blood evident. 'Thank you, Mrs Murdoch. I'm sure this will be most satisfactory.'

Vanessa wondered at Mrs Murdoch's attitude. There existed more than a hint of hostility in her manner that had nothing at all to do with the butler.

'I would like a light meal in my room, if you please. My journey has been long and tiring.' Then, deciding to end an argument before one could begin, she added, 'Lord Stone gave instructions, I believe?' She faced the woman in black with a cool, unswerving stare.

Once free of the uneasy presence, Vanessa walked to the window. It looked down on the forecourt, dimly perceived through the heavy mist. Turning around, she surveyed the room. Creamy paper was tucked untidily into a box on the writing table, a pen lay in readiness. On the dressing table, a silver-backed mirror, slightly tarnished, was placed next to a brush and other implements necessary to beauty, showing an equal lack of attention.

The room wasn't obviously unkempt, but there was a feeling of a deficiency to be found within, as though the work was done infrequently and with half a heart. The wood on the lovely wardrobe was dull and the beautiful Turkish carpet looked as though it had been a good many months since it had had a brushing.

A soft rap on the door brought a comely

maid, who announced, in a breathless voice, 'I'm Katie, miss. Her highness said I was to see to you. Mr Peverly done told her I was, that is.' Katie grinned with evident glee at this. She placed the tray of food on the dressing table, pushing aside the silver mirror and other things with an utter disregard for possible scratching. 'Your trunks are here. I'll see to your things while you have your tea.' She motioned the footmen who carried the trunks, directed the placement, then banished the men with an impudent grin.

While Vanessa ate her plain but filling tea, Katie hummed to herself as she hung away the gowns.

'I'm that glad to see you here, miss. His lordship will be happy to have those tapestries repaired, he will. We know he made a promise to his grandsire, and he always keeps his promises, he does.' She gave a critical inspection to each gown before hanging it away. 'I must say, miss, 'tis a blessing you brought some pretty dresses with you. I daresay they will put a nose out of place, looking all the crack. I fancy you'll stick a needle in Mrs Hewit's air-dreams, I do.' She gave a delighted giggle.

It seemed the good Betsy had taken advantage of Vanessa's abstraction to sneak several of her favorite evening dresses into the trunk. How vexing. The money would have been welcome. Still, she had meant well.

'It is nice to feel welcome by someone,' Vanessa replied before thinking, while wondering who this Mrs Hewit might be. Vanessa brushed down her very crumpled dress. She had best change into something else, which, while it might be wrinkled, would at least be clean. She removed a lilac sprigged muslin from Katie's hands and shook it well before changing into it from the practical dress she had worn for traveling.

Katie gave her a shrewd glance. 'Don't be lettin' her highness put you off none. She's an old dragon, that one is. Sweet young thing as you be has to learn to hold her own. Still, I 'spect you'll manage. Got round Mr Peverly without half-trying, you did. Our Mr Millbank will find you a rare sight.' She chuckled with evident glee at the thought, then walked to the door. 'I'd best get back, or the old dear will have my head. If Murdoch permitted, I'd press out a gown or two fer you. She's a sorry old scold. Just be kind to our poor Lady Juliana, we all do love her, we do.' With that last remark, she disappeared around the door with the now-depleted tea tray and was gone.

Vanessa wondered who Lady Juliana might be and why those belowstairs felt pity for her. Katie possessed a very forward manner, doubtless revealing what she ought not. Vanessa was well aware that little went on in any great house that the servants didn't know. In fact, she felt sometimes that they knew things before they happened.

With most of her clothes put away and her tea finished, she longed to see the tapestries. Her night things and lingerie could wait until later. She suspected Lord Stone would have taken her to the tapestry room had they not been interrupted by the architect. The very thought of the further indiscretions she might have uttered, not knowing who her audience was, made her cheeks burn.

The best way to find her way back to her room was to count doors as she went, which she did. The staircase was more impressive than she recalled, the landings revealing exquisite treasures collected long ago, though she could see a few places where something was obviously missing. If Lord Stone's father had been like her own, the items had been sold to pay gaming debts and not yet redeemed.

At the foot of the stairs she turned in the opposite direction from where she had traveled earlier with her host holding her arm in such a lovely manner. Peverly was absent from the hall again, but the great entry door was shut. It didn't make the hall any warmer.

Fires had been lighted in both of the fireplaces. What a roaring blaze it would take to heat *this* lofty area.

Several rooms away from the hall she found the tapestries. Even in the murky light of the ebbing day, the colors were vibrant, like fine gems hung on the wall to gleam softly down upon the viewer. Walking closer to then, she inspected the borders, noting signs of fraying, broken threads. Fortunately there were no large areas where moths had attacked or the weaving had disintegrated. But there were a great many places where reinforcement was needed. She could see that even at this distance.

The man at the door paused. No bonnet now hid her glorious wealth of golden hair that richly gleamed in the candlelight. Her gown, while rumpled, was becoming to her slenderness, and she was an appealing vision.

'What is your opinion? I have not waited too long for repair?' His words hit Vanessa with soft surprise.

Glancing back to see Lord Stone, she quelled a sudden nervousness with difficulty. What would he say regarding her foolish words? 'I think not, milord. While it is true they are in a sad state, they are not past redemption.' Her cool, perplexed gaze seemed to amuse him.

'Peverly reported you went this way. I knew where to find you.'

'I did not see him anywhere.' She thought back to the hall, quite sure no one had been about. Her eyes flashed with remembered ire at this man's deceit.

'He has a snug retreat behind a screen near one of the fireplaces, his only problem being a tendency to nod off now and again.'

'He ought to be suitably pensioned off at his age.' Her voice was reproving. 'Surely he has given many years of good service to your family.' She stopped, appalled at her impropriety in speaking out. Hadn't she said enough before?

The responding chuckle caught at her heart. 'I doubt if anyone could persuade him to leave. I have the distinct feeling Peverly is convinced the house will not continue without his overseeing the job.'

Momentarily overcoming her anger, Vanessa gave him a wistful smile. 'Like our Danvers, I suspect.' It was not her place to wonder at the friction between Peverly and Mrs Murdoch, marking it down to the jealousy between a retainer of long standing and someone who was more newly come to the position. 'Mrs Murdoch has been here many years?'

Lord Stone walked to inspect the frayed

edge of the largest tapestry, shaking his head that the beautiful weavings done in the fifteenth century should be in such a sad condition. How his father could have ignored such a priceless treasure was beyond him. 'Actually she has been with us but two years. Mrs Hewit was kind enough to direct her to me when our previous housekeeper retired.' His regard was again humorous. 'You see, some of our older servants *do* retire.'

Here was another reference to the absent Mrs Hewit. Vanessa would not succumb to the desire to ask who this lady was. It was none of her affair. 'It is good to have helpful neighbors when in need,' she replied.

He ignored her remark. 'I am looking forward to seeing the tapestries worked upon. They were dear to my grandfather's heart. He often referred to them as his jewels on the wall. Sad to see them like this.' He gently shook the tapestry, releasing a faint cloud of dust. Clearing his throat, he continued. 'Will you feel quite able to begin tomorrow? We, Millbank and I, did not expect to see you so soon. I recollect your remarks on your journey. It would have been better had you rested a night on your way here. I fear you will be too tired.' He turned from his examination of the tapestry to study her.

Vanessa was quite certain her cheeks were

as pink as the gillyflower in the tapestry at her side. 'Not so, milord. I will be able to commence my work first thing in the morning. Indeed, I find I am anxious to do so. These hunting scenes are truly beautiful. Ours depicted the seasons and were a very gay collection of scenes. One wonders if the ladies of the day really wore those fantastic garments to watch their huntsmen bring home the game. They look so tranquil, so removed from the world about them.' She pointed to an elegant lady in a fur-trimmed damask gown of vivid blue, belted in crimson. A fine gauze veil draped from a heart-shaped rolled headdress to cover her haughty face.

'I am glad styles have changed. It would be a shame to see that lovely hair hidden beneath a headdress.' His gaze lingered on the shining blond curls below the narrow braid of hair that coiled about her crown. The admiration in his eyes surprised her.

For a moment she melted in the warmth of that gaze. Then her hand flew to her head. 'Oh, dear, I have been remiss in forgetting my own cap. I am not so lost to propriety as to go about without something on my head, milord.' She wanted him to realize she was aware of her place, that she appreciated her respite from Aunt Agatha's dominion. Her eyes were turbulent with distress. 'I want you

73

to know I will do my utmost to repair these lovely tapestries with all due care. Perhaps I may consult with Mr Millbank come morning in regard to the worktable?'

Her look was anxious for many reasons. It would not be proper for her to be putting herself forward as an equal. All that had changed in a drastic way when her father played one too many games of cards. Turning, she walked toward the door. 'I will bid you good evening, milord.'

'What? Are you too tired to join us for dinner? Perhaps it might help if I promise not to tease you again. We dine at country hours here. Do say you will eat with us. Millbank and Juliana will be desolate if you don't.'

She halted at the door, cheeks aflame, head proudly up, not turning to face him. In a low voice she brought forth one of her fears. 'I had expected to eat in my room, like many a governess does.'

'Nonsense, it would only create more work for the maid. You will see enough of your room, I am certain. I will expect you at the table in an hour.'

Vanessa nodded, still not risking a look at his face. She didn't want to see the pity she was certain she would discover there.

4

A contemplation of her wardrobe contents brought a dissatisfied look to Vanessa's eyes. 'I would feel better if I could wear black gowns,' she softly announced to her lilac sprigged muslin. Her distress was deeply felt. It was too bad of Aunt Agatha to confiscate her black gowns. Though she was aware that black washed her face of color and made her look slightly ill, still it was what was fitting and proper. She felt a great urgency to prove to that pair of laughing deep blue eyes that she was a very proper lady, not to be trifled with in the least!

She hung away the muslin dress she had worn briefly to view the tapestries, while debating what to wear to dinner. The gowns Betsy had saved out for her were going to be most providential, it seemed. Vanessa hadn't expected to join the family for meals. It was a relief to know she wouldn't have to present herself before those knowing dark blue eyes in dowdy clothes. She reproved herself for her vanity even as she reached for an old favorite of hers.

She pulled out the deep sea-green sarcenet,

its neckline edged with a delicate lace ruff. The skirt had been all the crack before she left London, tiers of vandyking bordering the hem. While the color was not that of mourning, she doubted if any in this household would spare a thought for her status. The advantage of this dress was that it was exceedingly decorous in its line. There was nothing of the sheer, figure-clinging look to it. The sleeves fitted discreetly to her wrists, ending in a dainty fall of lace. She dug in her trunk to find a small lace evening cap for her head, smiling at her reflection in the mirror as she placed it neatly over her blond braids.

Tomorrow she would wear a proper day cap. She was certain she had tucked in several before closing the lid of the trunk. The cambric caps, edged with a frill and tied under her chin with a straight lappet, would be further evidence of her most prim demeanor. It would be the sort of proof of her propriety she needed after her indiscretion.

She was slipping her foot into a slipper slashed over the toe with the same sea green as her dress when the door slowly opened. A plump young woman of perhaps seventeen with a rather spotty complexion and anxious blue eyes peeked around, then smiled and bounced into the room.

While Vanessa stood silent, taking wary assessment, the other beamed a look of extreme good nature. 'Hullo! My brother, Nicholas, said you had arrived. How splendid this is! I am Lady Juliana, and I am excessively glad to see you, you know. This is a horridly dull place. How happy I am that you have such a friendly countenance. Now I will have some company. My brother spends all his time with accounts and Mr Millbank. I get quite tired of his seesaws, first ignoring, then scolding me.' She slowly absorbed the quiet elegance of Vanessa's costume, then looked down at her own dress. What she saw made her grimace. 'I suspected what Mrs Hewit chose for me was not quite the thing, but I fear it may be even worse than I had believed.'

This outspoken frankness was ignored until the addition of that name. Vanessa was unable to stand it another moment. She at long last succumbed to her curiosity. 'Just who is Mrs Hewit? And your dress is not so very bad.' She was afraid her reassurance was half-hearted. The dress was in appalling taste. The white muslin would have been unexceptional, except that it was overflounced, overberibboned, and made its wearer look nothing more than a plump, overdecorated pigeon.

Furthermore, it had a distinctly childish look to it.

'Mrs Hewit? Pamela Hewit is a neighbor lady who has an exceedingly great desire to be of help to my brother. She is in and out of this house until I could scream with vexation. She fobbed this dress on me with the most sickening smile. It makes me look like a stuffed goose. I think she did it to make herself look slim and charming by comparison. She offered to help *dear* Nicholas in dressing his baby sister.' Lady Juliana made a pained grimace, then fiddled with the ribbons on her dress as she continued, 'She lives at Primrose Hall, a manor house east of here. She so fancied the name of her home — her former husband's, actually — that she will wear nothing but yellow. Makes me fairly ill when I see her.'

'I see.' Vanessa stuck her foot into the other slipper, then walked to the chair at her dressing table. Fingering the hand mirror on the table, she turned to look at Juliana. If the poor child could lose some of that puppy fat and clear up that skin, she could be quite lovely. Her hair was lighter brown than her brother's, but very drab and dull. There might be golden highlights lurking; it was hard to tell. Vanessa longed to attempt a restoration on Juliana; however, that wasn't why she was here.

'I don't suppose . . . ' Lady Juliana began, then plumped herself down on the chaise, quite resembling a pigeon on the nest. 'You must be dressed in the latest fashion from London. I cannot wait to see Harry's face. I say, you are not in the market for a youngish husband, are you?'

Her fears were so transparent that Vanessa couldn't refrain from a smile and shook her head. 'Much as I might like the security offered by marriage, there are precious few men looking for a dowerless wife.' She gave the awful dress Lady Juliana now picked at, a considering look. 'You know, we might take a few of those ribbons off, and perhaps see if a flounce might disappear without damaging the dress fabric. If my Betsy were only here it would be a simple matter.'

'Could you?' Lady Juliana popped up from the chaise and slowly rotated so Vanessa could get the full effect of the tiers of flounces and excess of blue ribbon.

Taking pity on the beseeching eyes and remembering what it was like to feel so uncertain, so gauche, Vanessa nodded. 'I'll get my scissors.'

Lady Juliana stood quite still as Vanessa took her pair of silver-handled, steel-bladed scissors from her workbox and proceeded to snip some of the excessive number of ribbons from the dress. When the pile had grown to a satisfying size, she then knelt to examine the rows of flounces at the lower part of the skirt.

'I do believe two tiers can be removed. Shall I?' Vanessa glanced up at Lady Juliana, who nodded vigorously in return. As Vanessa carefully snipped away, she said, 'If you like, I could check your other dresses for you. I daresay Mrs Hewit hasn't been to London for some time, else she would know what is all the vogue.'

Juliana giggled. 'I would be greatly surprised if Pamela Hewit has been south of Yorkshire in her life. Mrs Hewit is fond of putting on airs, if you know what I mean.'

'Well, I expect I shall, if she is in and out of here as often as you say.' Vanessa took a deep breath, then asked the other question that had been lurking on her tongue for some time. 'Is there some manner of understanding between Mrs Hewit and your brother? I only ask because that might explain her interest in you.'

'Goodness me, I hope not.' Juliana's sigh was heartfelt. 'I shudder to think of sharing a roof with her. Considering my lack of looks, I doubt I'll attract an acceptable suitor, despite the generous dowry Nicholas promises to offer.'

This bit of frankness brought Vanessa up short. It was simply not *comme il faut* to be discussing the private life of her employer in this fashion. To change the subject, she remonstrated, 'My dear, whatever gives you such an idea? I am persuaded you could be a very lovely girl with a little assistance.'

'That is what I was going to ask you before,' bubbled the delighted Lady Juliana. She watched one flounce cast aside as Vanessa tackled the other, partially hidden beneath the uppermost flounce. 'You have such beautiful skin and your hair is like spun gold. You look like the fairy princess in a book Nicholas gave me for Christmas one year. I would be so grateful if you could help me. I know I must look a quiz. Harry doesn't even know I exist.' Her sigh was a mournful gust.

'Well . . . ' Vanessa's reply was cautious and considering. 'I do have my recipes for skin care with me. I had expected to be married this August, before my father died. My betrothed decided he needed a bride with more money,' she added dryly. Vanessa was surprised that it hardly stung to recall the baron's defection. 'In preparation, I copied down our housekeeper's herbal remedies for nearly everything useful. I daresay your housekeeper has a number of the ingredients in the stillroom.'

'Mrs Murdoch?' Lady Juliana asked with disbelief. 'If she has anything other than elderberry wine in there, I will be vastly surprised. The lady does not bestir herself to look for such things as herbs. Though she does have a way with desserts.' Lady Juliana sighed again and added, 'As you can see.'

Nodding thoughtfully, Vanessa perceived that this household badly needed a firm hand, a woman's hand. Obviously the young Lady Juliana was not the one to have a go at Mrs Murdoch. Undoubtedly it would take one such as Mrs Hewit. Then she recalled something Lord Stone had said earlier. 'I believe it was Mrs Hewit who recommended Mrs Murdoch for the position as housekeeper here.'

Lady Juliana gave an approving look at her deflounced and deribboned dress. 'That is true. After Papa and Damian died, our old housekeeper retired, and poor Nicholas had so much to do. Mrs Hewit's offer was very providential . . . for Mrs Hewit, I dare say. She has been here ever since.'

'You mean Mrs Murdoch?' Vanessa politely clarified.

Lady Juliana shook her head. 'I wish I did. I mean Mrs Hewit. I think she has set her cap for Nicholas, and I don't know what to do about it. So far, he has been too busy to take much notice of her, but she is always around. I fear she may get to be a habit, and Nicholas will ask her to wed him because she is so convenient.'

'I somehow doubt that of Lord Stone, but one never knows what a man might do.' She grimaced as she thought of his earlier behavior. Vanessa gathered up the excess of ribbons and flounces to place them on the desk, then turned, motioning Lady Juliana to the mirror on the far wall. 'It meets with your approval?' Vanessa picked up an armful of filmy nightgowns from her trunk to place in a drawer, then paused to watch the delighted young woman as she twirled about, admiring the new look of her gown.

'It does look better, does it not?'

The wistful gaze tugged at Vanessa's tender heart. 'As soon as I can, I'll check your dresses and find remedies for your skin and hair. We shall have *you* looking like a fairy princess before long, just you see!'

'Really, Miss Tarleton,' drawled a husky, very male voice as Lord Stone paused by the open door, which had never been closed after Lady Juliana's entry, and stood looking at Juliana. He jerked his head in the direction of the stairs while glaring at his sister.

Lady Juliana timidly stared back at him, bobbed a curtsy to Vanessa, saying, 'Thank you extremely for your help.' She then scuttled past him with the air of a fat mouse escaping a lean and hungry cat.

'We were about to go down for dinner, milord. Did you wish to speak with me?' Vanessa was not a young miss like Lady Juliana, ready to flee at a dark look from Lord Stone. She clung to her poise, facing him with, it was to be hoped, well-concealed racing heart. He had changed his clothes, and now she could see how badly she had misjudged him earlier. His corbeau jacket must have been tailored by Weston. It stretched across those shoulders she'd noticed before with a remarkable fit. The linen of his neck-cloth was arranged to a nicety above a waistcoat that impressed her with its utter simplicity and good taste. Raising her eyes to meet his, she absently noted his hair was now arranged à la Titus. How long would it be before he ran those impatient fingers through it, she wondered, returning those delightful curls to tumble in charming disarray? He must drive his valet into a tizzy.

'I could not help but hear what you said to my sister. I hesitate to issue a scold, but isn't it rather cruel to speak to her thus? She has always been plump, more so these past years. What can you accomplish that Mrs Hewit and Mrs Murdoch cannot? I cannot permit

84

you to raise false hopes. You were hired to mend tapestries, not meddle in family affairs . . . my family affairs.' He looked down that aristocratic nose, his eyes, now darkest blue, flashing in anger.

Vanessa clenched her teeth as she bit back the words she longed to fling at his pompous head. He spoke of propriety and yet he invaded her room?

She said in soft tones, 'I find your sister quite charming, milord. You must know that a girl of her age becomes aware of her appearance and desires to look her best.'

His face was unchanged. A cool, remote look veiled his eyes. He was behaving in a disgustingly pretentious, arrogant manner, one he had a perfect right to, mind you. And it made her absolutely seethe. No wonder his little sister turned to sweets for consolation. When Vanessa could speak with a reasonable degree of calm, she answered, 'Surely you can see for yourself how she is maturing? I have no desire to meddle or interfere, but she has my sympathy. I see little harm in lending a bit of assistance.'

Vanessa's hands tightened their hold on the filmy nightgowns she still held, crushing the delicate fabrics to her bosom. This was not the way to speak to your employer and remain employed! Yet he must see how he was neglecting his young sister, the harm it was doing her.

'I repeat, it is none of your affair.'

Vanessa was quite tempted to speak her mind. She gave Lord Stone a troubled look. 'I believe it far better for her to obtain help from one who is knowledgeable than try some outlandish scheme. It is only natural that she wishes to look nice, you know.' Vanessa could not remain silent. Perhaps it was because there had been no one to champion her when she badly needed help.

'Enough! You are most impertinent, Miss Tarleton. I was informed you were a very proper lady, one who might set an example for my sister.' He glanced away, then added, his voice cool with politeness, 'I am well aware it is the height of impropriety to eavesdrop on a private conversation, much less invade a lady's bedchamber. Normally I would not, but it does permit this speech without fear of being overheard by one of the servants. Contrary to your belief, Juliana's welfare is important to me. I will not have her hopes lifted to impossible heights, only to have them dashed.'

Vanessa wondered precisely what else he had overheard. The next time she got together with Lady Juliana, they would be sure to shut the door! With a shock, she realized she fully intended to disobey the earl and help his dear young sister to improve her looks and dress. What was in this Yorkshire air that turned her into such a rebellious woman? She was shocked at her outburst. Of course there had been his perfectly odious behavior earlier, when he teased her with his deception. That had been quite horrid of him. She also sensed she felt an increase of freedom from the restraints she had known all her life. To be sure, she must remember her position, but he needed her skills, and she was a lady, not one born to the role of servant. It was different from waiting upon her mother. This man brought out a latent rebellion in Vanessa that she hadn't known existed. There was something about the man that riled her. He disturbed her peace.

He took a deep breath, then nodded. 'Dinner will be served shortly. I don't like to keep Cook waiting. Shall we?' He took note of the armload of delicate silk and sheerest lawn in her arms, the azure wisp, a froth of white, the neck ribbons trailing in gay abandon. 'That is, after you stow that delightful armful of fabric. Nightwear, Miss Tarleton? I hadn't suspected that beneath such a proper exterior beat the heart of a courtesan.' His eyes gleamed a gentle taunt at her.

Cheeks burning with anger and embarrassment, Vanessa crossed to shove the pile of nightwear into a drawer, slam it shut, then exit the room past his sardonic gaze. This man was going to drive her to lengths she never before had contemplated. The resounding click of her door sounded to her like the cocking of a pistol — aimed at her head.

As Vanessa marched ahead of him, Nicholas watched the rhythm of her walk, the grace of her slender body as she floated regally down the stairs. A mental image of Vanessa, her blond hair unbraided and hanging down her back, clad in that azure confection, shimmered before his eyes. It was an alluring, intriguing vision, one he could quite happily dwell upon for any amount of time.

At the foot of the stairs, Vanessa turned, shattering the vision with her cool words. 'I shall endeavor to remain as proper as possible, milord.' She walked ahead while a wistful recollection of azure appeared before him, then faded.

He muttered something that sounded a bit like, 'That I will believe when I see it,' then joined her.

Vanessa gave him a sharp glance as she walked at his side toward what she presumed was the dining room, but he gave no further indication of his pleasure or displeasure. Apparently one did not exchange words within the hearing of the servants. Which was only proper, she reminded herself.

They passed the tapestry room to find a charming dining room where Lady Juliana awaited them with an apprehensive look in her eyes. The paint smell lingered here, but not to a point of objection. The furniture was graceful Hepplewhite and Sheraton, the wood more polished than in Vanessa's room. Hunting pictures graced the walls, freshly painted a buttercream color. A multitiered chandelier hung above the table, its brass gleaming in the candlelight. It looked quite new, and Vanessa suspected it had been an addition during the refurbishing of the room. Two mirrors were hung to reflect the light of the candles, bringing a cheerful atmosphere to a room now inhabited by wary people.

Lady Juliana cast a timid look at her much older brother. 'Is everything all right? You are not come to blows?'

Vanessa felt the warm clasp of his hand on her elbow as he guided her around the room. 'Not yet.' The richness of his voice was too close for her ease. His reply was terse, yet Vanessa felt hope, for it wasn't angry as before. Perhaps he might be made to see reason in regard to his sister and her desire to improve her looks.

A stir at the door brought another gentleman into the room. Lord Stone slanted a lazy smile in his direction. 'Ah, Millbank, at last. You must meet the newest addition to the household. Miss Tarleton, *this* is Mr Robert Millbank.'

Vanessa compressed her lips a second as she realized that Lord Stone was reminding her — an unkind thing of him to do — that she had mistaken him for his steward. It seemed Lord Stone hadn't appreciated the slight. Pity. It wasn't her fault if he was in an untidy, plainly dressed condition when she arrived at the door. There hadn't even been the butler to assist her.

Turning to face Mr Millbank, she gave him the benefit of her most heartfelt smile. 'I am indeed pleased to meet you at last, Mr Millbank. I have heard so many fine things about you from your cousin, Mr Hunt, I almost feel as though I know you already.' She extended her hand, liking the firm handshake from a man much younger than she had expected, given Mr Hunt's age.

It was clear to Lord Stone that Miss Tarleton made a conquest of Millbank with the first glimmer of her smile. By the time she finished her encomiums, he was well and truly done for. It irritated Nicholas that the lady in question should be so full of praise for his steward when she had been so coldly condemning to him only minutes earlier.

'Perhaps we could all be seated and continue the conversation while the food is served?' The gruffness of his voice startled everyone.

Vanessa slid onto her chair with a fluttering in her heart. She hadn't anticipated sitting next to her tormentor all through dinner. She had been so very hungry, and now she wondered if she would be able to eat a bite.

Juliana sent her a reassuring smile from her place at the other end of the table. She dipped a spoon into a hearty bowl of vermicelli soup and the meal began.

Mr Millbank spoke first, surprisingly. He seemed to be completely unaware of any tension between Vanessa and Lord Stone. 'And how was my cousin when you last saw him? I am glad he is to remain at Blackwood Hall. It would be difficult for an older man to find as good a position.'

Vanessa found it hard to reply, conscious of an aching in her heart that she would never see her beloved home again. 'He was quite well, I believe. He is a fine man, near as like a father to me these past years. Indeed, I do not know how I might have managed without his help and advice.'

Lord Stone looked down that nose of his and inserted, 'He was your father's steward, was he not?'

Vanessa knew he implied that it was Hunt's job to manage the estate, not hers. Lifting her chin slightly, she slid him a glance. 'My father showed no interest in the estate, milord. Even so fine a steward as Mr Hunt must needs consult with someone from time to time as regards decisions.' She brought her spoon to her mouth and slowly savored the soup, giving him another glance to see how her words sat with him. She caught a bemused expression on his face and wondered at it.

'Tomorrow we shall have neighbors to dine with us,' the earl said. 'Mrs Hewit and Harry Featherston will join us at table.' He shot a hard look at Juliana. 'I expect you to oversee the menu with Mrs Murdoch this time, Juliana. Last time we had guests to dine, Mrs Hewit was required to lend assistance. It is past time you took up your duties around here.'

Vanessa nearly gasped at his cruelty to poor Juliana. Having spoken with Mrs Murdoch but once was enough for her to know that Lady Juliana would find it difficult going. Vanessa sent an encouraging look at the pale young miss seated near her, longing to place a comforting hand over the one that trembled.

She gave an almost imperceptible shake of her head when Juliana made as though to answer her brother. The visible anger, once expressed, would only have made things worse, Vanessa was quite certain. Why Lord Stone treated Juliana in such fashion was a mystery, but if things proceeded at an equally spanking pace the remainder of her stay in this household, Vanessa didn't doubt she would know before too long. She felt as though she had been plunged into the heart of a maze and was having to feel her way to the exit.

The soup plates were deftly removed, to be replaced by dishes of stewed veal with rice, cold lamb, and dressed cucumber. It was not the type of meal to serve to company, but Vanessa felt flattered she was received as family. Juliana picked at her food, causing Vanessa to wonder how she had gotten so plump if this was an example of her eating habits.

When currant dumplings and a fine gooseberry tart were brought to the table, much was revealed. The footman served Juliana a goodly helping of each dessert before she as much as indicated a preference for either. Vanessa wondered at that. Surely it wasn't proper for the footman to take it upon himself to make such a decision. Unless someone had given him instructions before-hand. She searched Juliana's face for a clue, then applied her spoon to the dainty helping of gooseberry tart she had requested.

Lady Juliana led the way from the table as the men settled down for a conversation that appeared to deal with sheep.

Taking a deep breath, Vanessa spoke with care. 'Forgive me for being intrusive, Lady Juliana, but you did ask for my help. Was it you who ordered, in advance, servings of both desserts to be placed before you?'

Lady Juliana leaned against one of the few chairs in a small salon next to the tapestry room. This room, too, had been painted and was now being restored to usefulness with fine oils rehung on the wall, small tables replaced.

'No.' She shook her girlish curls vigorously. 'They always do it. I expect they all know how excessively fond I am of sweets.'

'Since it seems to be a problem, you might countermand the order, whoever gave it. For I am persuaded that no footman would serve you such unless so instructed by someone.'

Lady Juliana was much struck by this reasoning, and collapsed on the chair with a very thoughtful expression on her plump face. 'It must have been Mrs Murdoch. Only she has the authority to do a thing like that.

Certainly Peverly would never take it upon himself. But why?' She looked up at Vanessa with all her puzzlement clearly written on her face.

At the transparency of her expression, Vanessa wondered if Juliana's feelings for Harry Featherston were as obvious when she saw him. Poor dear girl. Vanessa firmed her resolve to assist Lady Juliana all that she could.

Juliana drifted over to fidget with the fringe of the newly hung draperies. 'You will like Harry. He is amazingly handsome and excessively well-bred. Nicholas finds him quite agreeable. Indeed, I scarcely get to see him at all. Nicholas drags him off to his library first chance. I wish . . . '

Flinging the drapery fringe aside, Juliana sighed with impatience. 'Would you like to join me in the music room? I must know if you play. Do you? It is one of the great pleasures I have, to be able to indulge myself at the pianoforte. Come.' She beckoned with an imperious gesture of her hand, then bounced from the room with a youthful exuberance.

Following more sedately — after all, she had no idea when Lord Stone might leave the dining room, and heaven forbid she be found comporting herself with a lack of refinement

— Vanessa trailed behind her. Juliana had tugged the covers away from the instrument by the time Vanessa entered the room, and soon was skillfully drawing forth exquisite sound from the pianoforte. Had Vanessa played, she would have been reluctant to attempt it after this performance.

Lady Juliana beamed at the round of applause from Vanessa following her rendition of Scarlatti's Cat's Fugue. Vanessa returned the smile.

'You play with a delicacy quite rare, Lady Juliana. It is unusual to see such grace and tasteful style in one so young. I quite admire your agile finger technique. I have no ability to speak of on the pianoforte. My direction lies with the harp.' Vanessa gave a sigh, wondering if she would ever be able to apply her fingers to the strings of her own beloved instrument once again.

Lady Juliana looked to the doorway behind Vanessa and demanded, 'Do you hear that, Nicholas? I have a kindred soul in Miss Tarleton. Is there not some way we might find a harp for her to play? I would dearly love to engage in duets with her. It would be vastly entertaining for us all, would it not?' Her plea was softened by an appealing smile.

Vanessa turned to discover Lord Stone standing far closer to her than she liked.

Giving him a cautious look, she tried to be casual in her walk to the pianoforte, where she felt a refuge in Lady Juliana's proximity.

'Your harp is stored at Blackwood Hall, as I recollect.' Nicholas looked, really looked, at his young sister, noting the improved appearance of her gown, the eager smile which bloomed on her face. Why hadn't he observed how much she had grown up, how badly she needed taking in hand? Pamela had assured him Juliana was content with her plumpness and her lonely hours at the pianoforte. Obviously she was not. It irritated him no end that this woman, this stranger, should enter his home and in minutes see what he had not perceived. 'I will see what I can do, Juliana.' He nodded at her, then turned his thoughtful gaze upon Vanessa. 'I have instructed Peverly to assist you in the morning as to the setting up of a worktable and anything else you may find necessary.' He bowed, quite correct and cool, then left the room with no further words.

A chill seemed to have fallen over the room after his departure. Even Lady Juliana felt it, mused Vanessa as she watched the young lady rub her hands over her arms.

'You can be certain Nicholas will do something about a harp, but what, I wonder?' Lady Juliana poked at the keys of her pianoforte with an idle finger as she turned a speculative gaze on Vanessa.

Joining Lady Juliana in her exit from the music room, Vanessa also wondered just what Lord Stone might do once he discovered that she had no intention of forgetting her resolve to help his darling young sister. Recalling the ferocity of his frown earlier, she decided perhaps it was as well she didn't know. It could very well cost her some much-needed sleep!

5

Peverly magically appeared before her eyes as Vanessa rounded the corner of the great hall to search for him the next morning. The screen behind which he discreetly retired from time to time was inconspicuous to a high degree.

'You startled me,' she exclaimed in a breathless gasp. Then she smiled at him and, like Mr Millbank, he was captivated by her charm. 'I must seek your help, Peverly. Did Lord Stone tell you about the worktable I shall need?' She wondered if the kindly old butler, his grim appearance so at odds with his gentle ways, would recall any command given more than ten minutes before.

'Indeed, miss. I have instructed the footmen to set up a large table in the saloon. Please follow me.'

Vanessa walked behind the stiffly erect old man into the spacious saloon. In the morning light, she saw that the walls were hung with pale yellow silk, with an abundance of gilding on the delicate designs of the ivory coffered ceiling. Elaborate surrounds, equally decorated with gilding, framed each of the

99

paintings, which had been cleaned and newly restored. By daylight she could see that the marble mantels of the fireplaces had caryatid supports, and she hoped the earl wasn't offended at her remarks of yesterday. These caryatids were in exceptional taste, however. She suspected his questions yesterday were simply to draw her out — or tease? — for the saloon gave all the appearance of being done by someone who knew very well what was all the crack in London.

The footmen had assembled a long table taken from some workroom in the house, and now were covering it with white holland linen over a thin padding of some sort. At her approving nod, Peverly straightened even more, if such a thing were possible, pointing out in less frosty accents than usual that this was also at his direction. 'The table was dusty and dark, miss. I made sure you would want not only a clean surface but also a white padded one. Mrs Peverly always fussed about such, you see.'

'I confess it is more than I hoped to find. Thank you for your care, Peverly. If the men could bring the central tapestry here first, I shall begin with it. I perceive it is the worst damaged.'

The elderly butler cast a scrutinizing look around the area before executing a stiff bow, his bones creaking audibly, departing with the footmen following smartly behind him. Soon she could hear things being moved, calls for another ladder.

A maid entered with a small tray upon which sat a fat brown teapot that Vanessa recognized as a fine example of the local Rockingham ceramics. In the shape of a peach, the amusing pot was filled from a hole in the bottom. Nodding to the girl to place the tray on a small satinwood table, Vanessa applied herself to a cup of tea and the tiny cakes with it.

Taking the cup and saucer with her to one of the tall windows, she sipped as she gazed off into the parkland flowing south from the house. Sitting on a rise, the house commanded a fine view of the greens, a remarkable fountain that she must be certain to see more closely, and the lush forest in the distance. It was quite an improvement from the gray mist which had blanketed the area upon her arrival. Judging from the manner in which the trees bent and swayed, a brisk wind was blowing. She could make out the figure of the Earl of Stone in the distance as he rode across a field with Mr Millbank at his side. There was no mistaking who was who this morning.

A warmth crept into her cheeks as she

considered her calamitous entry into her new position. What a way to begin! Not only had she mistaken the earl for his steward, and said perfectly awful things about him, but she had dared to argue with him about his treatment of his young sister! It seemed as though she had been possessed. But it also seemed the earl was a forgiving man. At least there had been no words exchanged when she entered the breakfast room just as he was about to leave with Mr Millbank. Of course she had not completely forgotten his horrid behavior upon her arrival.

Vanessa had been wary when she discovered he had not left the room as yet. She had awakened early and decided she ought to show her employer she really did know what was proper of one employed to repair tapestries. She was not here as a guest to take her leisure in bed of a morning.

His greeting had been equally proper. 'Good morning, Miss Tarleton. I trust you shall have a busy day. If there is anything you need, refer to Peverly . . . or Millbank.' A smile lurked in his eyes as he solemnly bid her goodbye. But, she sighed, he had been distant in his manner and she felt quite put in her place as a needlewoman. Not that it was a terrible position. From what Mrs Danvers had explained before Vanessa left home, they were considered skilled and important people. Indeed, Woburn Abbey employed two such ladies all the time. It might be possible to graduate from needlewoman to the loftier job of housekeeper if she applied herself. It couldn't take more than twenty years of diligent work! The very thought of spending all those years in hard servitude was depressing. A house-keeper literally ruled the house, except for the area covered by the house steward. It was up to her to keep the linens in order, do the regular sewing, the preserving and sweet-making, among a great many other tasks. The vision of Mrs Murdoch at work in the stillroom on the confectionery that seemed in far too great abundance brought Lady Juliana to mind.

Lady Juliana had yet to appear on the scene this morning. Apparently she remained in her room with her hot chocolate and rolls rather than face her brother this early in the day. Upon arising, Vanessa had dug into her things to find her recipes for the healing lotions and applications for skin, plus the tisanes to be drunk to promote improved digestion and a lessening of hunger. Later she would seek out Mrs Murdoch and find out precisely what herbs might be found in the stillroom. That lady was not to be seen at this hour. No doubt she was occupied in handing out supplies for the day or working at her accounts.

The bustle at the entry to the saloon brought Vanessa's attention to the doorway to discover the enormous tapestry being carefully carried to the work-table. Dust filtered into the air, making her long to give the tapestry a good shake out-of-doors. One didn't treat priceless, fragile things like that, however, and she decided she might try a tender brushing to remove some of the accumulated residue of many years.

Nodding with approval at the superior care the footmen gave the tapestry, she then dismissed them all, smiling with gratitude at the elderly butler as he moved to the doorway. 'Thank you, Peverly. I can see this household is in excellent hands.' Her kind words brought a faint smile to crack the stiff façade he usually bore.

Once left to her own devices, Vanessa began to unroll the tapestry to examine it with her lens. It was similar to the odious quizzing glasses she had so despised when she made her come-out in London. This, however, had a neat ivory handle to match other articles in her work-box, and was used for much better purposes than adding to the pretensions of a dandy.

She paused in her inspection. How odd to

discover the tapestry was lined. Perhaps it was due to the rather strange lumps, most likely an old form of trapunto, she observed beneath a number of the tapestry birds. Satisfied with this simple explanation, she continued her scrutiny.

She was humming to herself in a quiet manner when she sensed another presence in the room. Glancing up, she found that Mr Millbank had entered and approached her table with cautious steps.

'I thought I saw you riding out with Lord Stone a while ago.' Vanessa welcomed him with a gracious smile.

'Simply checking on one of the fields to be worked. How does the tapestry look? We are very grateful you were able to assist us in this restoration, Miss Tarleton.' A faint flush crept over his cheeks as he drew closer to where she worked at examining the weaving. He seemed a nice young man, neat, polite. 'I have heard fine things about you from my cousin over the years. He much admired the way you helped him at Blackwood Hall. I would appreciate the benefit of your good advice should you see anything here.' He frowned, considering something at small length, then spoke. 'At present we are involved with the restoration and a great many improvements. It is an exciting time for a man interested in new developments. Still, it prevents me from investigating as I would like.' He briefly thought again, then added proudly, 'Lord Stone is much taken with the latest improvements. I daresay you'll not find a fire engine or arrangement for bringing water to the house that is more advanced than what we have here.'

'A fire engine? How wonderful! I'll confess I have a great fear of fire.' Vanessa had noted with delight there was a water closet in her dressing room. Also, it appeared from the stubs of pipes concealed behind a screen that plans existed to bring water up to the room as well — a vast improvement over carrying water up in pails that could easily spill on the way. Though she had visited in a few great houses over the years, this was the first time she had found so convenient an arrangement in her dressing room. 'The, er, facilities in my dressing room are quite fine. I can see where the earl is a true progressive.'

'He is a good man to work for, indeed. Demanding, yet fair.' Mr Milbank edged closer to the table where she bent over the weaving to add, 'I wish to repeat how pleased I, er, we are you came. I know something of the circumstances that faced you at Blackwood Hall. I am glad you decided to come to us.'

Vanessa raised her head to stare out one of the windows, noting the tossing branches of a tall oak as she did. 'I suppose Lord Stone knows as well?' she inquired in a flat, low voice.

'Yes.' He made no attempt to soften his reply. Indeed, there was no reason why he should. Yet she felt it keenly, the knowledge that her circumstances were known and perhaps speculated over by others. Especially the earl. For some reason, that bothered her the most.

'His father died two years ago, his brother as well, I believe.' She felt compelled to know more about the man who employed her. Mr Hunt had been discreet in the extreme.

'Yes. Both were killed in a boating incident. A sudden storm blew up; their boat capsized. It was a great tragedy.'

'Mr Hunt mentioned that Lady Stone died many years ago. How did they manage with Lady Juliana? She is such an appealing, unaffected girl. Surely someone must have had the care of her?' Vanessa felt a stirring of sympathy for the young Nicholas, motherless, going his own way for so long, then assuming control of the nearly bankrupt estate and a young sister as well. Still, he ought to have paid more attention to Lady Juliana.

'Her governess remained for some time

until called home to tend her dying mother. Somehow, another governess was never found. What Lady Juliana needs at present is a companion. I hope you will not object if she seeks you out when you are not working on the tapestries. It gets very lonely for her here, and Lord Stone is much occupied with the improvements.'

'I shall welcome her whenever Lady Juliana seeks to spend time with me.' Vanessa considered taking Millbank into her confidence regarding the plans made to help Lady Juliana improve her looks, then decided perhaps it would test his loyalty to Lord Stone too far.

Shifting to something else that had occupied her on her journey north, she asked, 'While in London I spent quite a sum of money purchasing yarns with which to mend the tapestries. Shall I be reimbursed for that?' She loathed asking, almost begging, for the money, yet if he knew her circumstances, he also knew she had few shillings to spare.

'But of course. Tell me the amount, and it shall be repaid at once.' He was all brisk business, the trustworthy steward to the hilt.

She smiled at the indignant tone of his voice. Although she had dealt with anxious tradesmen when funds were low and Mr Hunt elsewhere, it was new for her to be seeking funds. She'd survive this and other indignities as well, she supposed. Aunt Agatha would say it was good for her soul. 'Thank you, Mr Millbank.' She flashed him an appreciative smile, dismissing the kindling gleam in his eyes as a mere trick of light.

She turned back to the tapestry, not intending to rebuff Mr Milbank, but feeling it imperative she keep at her job. 'There are several areas here that are quite damaged, I suspect. I believe I can effectively repair them. Tell his lordship I feel it is not too late, as he had feared.'

'Tell his lordship what?' The hearty voice from the entryway caused Mr Millbank to quickly draw back from the table where he leaned over to examine the area Vanessa pointed out.

Her mouth dropped open slightly as she beheld the apparition that stood grinning at her from the door. And this was the man so concerned with propriety? 'Milord?'

'Look the very devil, I expect. Had a bit of a run-in with a very determined animal.' His grin was infectious. Vanessa found herself looking at him with an answering twinkle in her eyes. A smile hovered over her lips but refused to allow itself to settle.

Vanessa expected him to mention a wild dog at the very least, when she noticed a bundle of white fur cradled in his arms. She rose, crossing over to where he stood, wary at the light in his midnight eyes, unable to decipher their depths. 'What is it?'

As she bent over the mass of dirty white fur, a paw equipped with sharp claws reached out to bat at the lappet of her mobcap. She hadn't bothered to tie it just to work quietly at the tapestry. Now, snagged in a set of claws, it slid off her head and a tangle of golden hair cascaded down and over her shoulder. Her hands flew up to rescue her hair, but it was too late. As she gave a narrow look at the animal, two eyes opened, one golden, one green.

Lord Stone's voice was amused. 'I suspect the cat is considered bad luck in the village, with those strange eyes. I found some lads beating it with sticks as I left to come home.'

Vanessa immediately forgave the disaster with her cap. 'Poor thing. Perhaps I may have it?' She held out her arms, a pleading expression in the now-turbulent sea-blue eyes.

The familiar stirring that had come over Nicholas last night hit him again as he beheld the very feminine woman before him, her eyes so soft, hair in magnificent disarray. She was more beautiful than she ought to be, given her penniless state. His glance slid over to where Millbank also stared as though turned to a statue at the sight of the spun gold that fell in such a tangle. So that was the way of it, was it? Nicholas pushed aside the annoyance that surged up within him.

Vanessa noted the annoyance that briefly flashed over Lord Stone's handsome face. Assuming it to be a reaction to her disheveled state, she attempted to smooth back her hair with one hand as she stroked the cat with her other. 'I must apologize, milord. I will contrive to manage my own hair in time, but my maid was always so capable. I do miss her help. In the meantime, I hide it beneath this cap, you see.' Her expression was a mixture of embarrassment and rueful apology.

He shook his head in dismay that this elegant lady should be reduced to doing for herself because of her father's wildly extravagant living. Nicholas handed her the cat, then impulsively gathered the mass of spun gold in his hands, as he had secretly longed to do from the moment he saw it, tucking it beneath and into the cap that had hung crazily from one shoulder all the while. 'There. That will do for the moment. I will instruct Mrs Murdoch to see you have a maid to assist you. It wouldn't do to have that hair falling over your eyes as you try to sew, would it?' He managed a neutral look, while his hand lingered a moment longer on a recalcitrant curl. It had shaken him to feel that living silken treasure in his hands. He stood so close to her he could detect the scent of bluebells, his mother's favorite flower, his too, for that matter. The delicate fragrance hovered in the air between them like a perpetual breath of spring. Her appeal was undermining his resolve to remain aloof. Determined to retrench, he moved away. 'You will do me a favor if you can tend to the animal. I never could abide to see the weak and helpless set upon.' His voice was brusque, his attitude cool, correct. He bowed slightly, then left the saloon to repair his tattered condition.

Why did she feel as though he had done something wickedly dangerous to her hair, when all he had done was to tuck it beneath the cambric-and-lace cap? There had been an affecting gentleness to his touch. Every stroke of his hand had brought a frightening reaction within her. Taking a deep breath, she stared down at the filthy, malnourished cat and gently patted his head. 'Hercules or Ajax? I wonder. Or perhaps Agamemnon might do?'

'I beg pardon?' Now that Lord Stone was gone, Millbank felt safe in drawing closer to Vanessa.

'The cat must have a name. I wonder what Greek hero would be most suitable as a namesake.' She walked toward the hall, studying the cat as she went. 'Hercules, I think. This poor animal has prodigious strength for a cat, to withstand those boys and the awful neglect of its past owner. I won't demand twelve labors of him as Hera did, however. This cat shall be quite fine and welcome if it will but keep the mice from my room.'

She accepted that Hercules would be hers to care for. It seemed every cat around home had found its way to her at one time or another. Odd, how this poor mistreated creature had settled down in her arms after fighting poor Lord Stone quite royally. Obviously this was a cat who appreciated the ladies. She gave Hercules an approving pat on the head. 'We shall brush you and feed you properly, and you will find you are feeling much more the thing quite soon.'

Hercules snuggled closer to the lady. The cat's expression seemed to show it knew it had fallen into a first-rate spot.

'What on earth do you have in your arms, Miss Tarleton? Never say the tapestry is falling to bits and shreds!' Lady Juliana flew down the last of the stairs and hurried to Vanessa's side. 'I do believe it's a cat! Just wait until Nicholas sees it in the house. He

113

believes cats belong in the barn and the kitchens.' She stretched out a tentative finger and Hercules took a swipe at it, his green eye assaying the value of this person who hovered near his protectress.

'Well, it was your brother who dumped the animal in my arms with instructions to see to it. And I will, most assuredly,' she added softly. Echoing the thought Nicholas expressed, she knew she could not bring harm to a weak and innocent creature. Wryly she appended that Hercules seemed capable of taking care of himself. It was only a gang of little boys with big sticks that were too much for his presently weakened condition. Once the cat had his strength back, Vanessa was confident Hercules could handle anything. She sailed out to the kitchen, a curious Lady Juliana trailing in her wake.

Cook, once being appraised of his lordship's desires in the matter, found a tempting array of meats for Hercules. The cat abandoned his attempt at being dignified, and hungrily gobbled the food before him. Vanessa watched while leaning against a scrubbed wooden table.

'You actually intend to keep him? I cannot believe it.' Lady Juliana giggled at the thought of Nicholas yielding to this bag of bones and fur.

'Hercules shall stay in my room, for the most part. Though if he is like the cats at home, he will be fiercely independent.'

'Then how can you say he will be yours?' Lady Juliana accepted a muffin from Cook, ignoring the frown from Vanessa at this nibbling.

Vanessa shrugged. 'With cats, you have to be willing to let them choose, give them freedom. If they know they have your affection, they may stray, but they will return to your side.'

Juliana finished off her muffin, then replied, 'That sounds like Mrs Hewit's description of how to retain a man's attentions.'

Vanessa raised expressive eyebrows. Across the room Cook choked on whatever it was she was tasting. 'As to that, I cannot say, not having deliberately tried to capture a man, nor having any experience in keeping one.'

Lady Juliana drew closer, her curiosity obviously stirred. 'You were betrothed, were you not?'

Vanessa made a rueful face at her inquisitor, knowing Lady Juliana was hungry for feminine talk of any kind. 'I fear my attraction for him was a plump dowry, not my person. And I . . . I felt it my duty to accept.'

She bent over to scoop Hercules up into her arms, keeping her face hidden from sharp eyes. What her father had arranged was only proper. Vanessa had had no call to wish it could be otherwise. She had never known any marriage that she could call a happy one, though she had heard that such a thing existed. In London, she had observed, there were couples who went contrary to accepted *ton* behavior and were much seen together, their mutual affection obvious for all to note. It would be lovely, if true.

'Now the cat has finished his meal, I shall give him a bath.' Vanessa smiled a look of encouragement at Hercules.

'Never say you would put a cat in water!' Lady Juliana put her hands before her face and laughed. Cook abandoned her work at the stove and joined in as well, her hands resting at an ample waist, arms akimbo.

'I refuse to have fleas in my bed!' Vanessa laughed back at them. Minutes later she stealthily carried Hercules toward a wooden bucket of warm water that had a bar of strong lye soap lurking, in its depths. The yowling didn't last long, for once Vanessa swiftly scrubbed the cat clean, she ducked his head beneath the water. At Lady Juliana's horrified gasp, Vanessa replied, still watching the sputtering cat with care, 'The fleas all go to his head, then I drown them.'

'Well, I never,' exclaimed the amazed cook

as Vanessa cuddled the sodden cat in a thick bundle of clean rags to dry him off. A shy scullery maid took the tub away.

'Now to do something for you, Lady Juliana.'

Lady Juliana sidled away from the animal being vigorously dried. 'No bath for me, if you please. I prefer my room.' Lady Juliana edged around the table as though she really believed Vanessa might pop her into a bucket.

'The sooner we commence on your program of improvement, the better. I want it made known to all that you are not to indulge in those muffins and cakes and such. Fruit, my old nurse insisted, is the best dessert. Or perhaps a wedge of cheese with biscuits. We shall want simple, nourishing foods, Cook. Chicken and veal, or any fowl, for that matter, fish as well. I shall see Mrs Murdoch about the herbs right now.'

She extended a totally changed Hercules to Lady Juliana. Gone was the filthy, matted hair. Hercules was now a somewhat fluffy cat with a marvelous tail that twitched uncertainly as he surveyed the room, the gold-and-green gaze searching for further indignity.

'That cat does not want me, only you, Miss Tarleton.' Lady Juliana backed away toward the door, then hastily left the kitchen.

117

Vanessa, resigned to the clinging cat, made her way to the stillroom. There was no sign of Mrs Murdoch. The cash book was open to the current entry page. Vanessa absently wondered if the entries in Mrs Murdoch's book were as precisely ordered as those in Mrs Danvers'.

Looking further around the room, she found a sad collection of herbals on a high shelf. A small bottle of oil of almond sat next to a tin of lupin powder. Upon inspection, the tin proved nearly empty. The flax seed seemed rancid and needed tossing out, Vanessa thought. She was checking the unpleasant remnants of dried strawberry leaves when the door opened. Without turning around, she announced, 'The herbals are in a sorry state, Mrs Murdoch. If you like, I shall endeavor to collect as much as possible, such as cowslips and elder flowers. I shall need some fresh watercress to make a soothing skin ointment for Lady Juliana. I cannot believe you do not have a fresh supply of rosewater or lavender in here. Perhaps there is a local source where you may purchase them?' The tone of her voice left no doubt as to her opinion of a housekeeper who would not have a goodly amount of fresh herbs for mixing into remedies.

She continued, 'You grow feverfew, do you

not? And I shall want some meal of oats. Cooked with vinegar, it will make a nice paste to remove freckles and spots. Poor dear, she has such a problem.' She shifted Hercules to snuggle into her shoulder as she reluctantly turned to face the housekeeper. The expression on that dour face was sure to be unpleasant.

'Good heavens!' she whispered.

Before her stood the superbly dressed figure of her employer, Lord Stone. He was all that was elegant and proper for visiting or company. With sinking heart she recalled that Mrs Hewit and Harry Featherston were due for dinner today. Just what she needed in her disheveled state. Oh, well, perhaps Vanessa would be expected to eat in her room with guests come.

'You might well seek divine intervention on your behalf. I thought I made it clear you are not to attempt any manner of restoring course on Lady Juliana. When I met her on the stairs a short time ago, she mentioned you had bathed the cat and now were checking Mrs Murdoch's stillroom for herbs to do something equally improving for her!' His voice was low and utterly scathing in his anger. It cut harshly into Vanessa's tender sensibilities.

'It is one thing to set about removing fleas

from a cat, quite another to embark on a program of improvement for my young sister. Juliana has always been plump, she looks fine just so.'

Something burst within Vanessa at his angry, smug pronouncement. 'Do you know your young sister has resigned herself to spinsterhood due to her appearance? Those spots on her face are from overindulgence in sweets and, I suspect, a lack of fresh air and exercise. From what I have heard, she does little around here but nibble treats prepared for her by Mrs Murdoch. I have become quite fond of Lady Juliana since I arrived. She seems a dear girl, and not one to be consigned to the shelf without an attempt made to rescue her. It would be well if you would take an interest in how her time is spent. I fear she has been very lonely here.' Aware she was trespassing further, but deciding to plunge deeper into the troubles facing Lady Juliana, Vanessa added, 'And when did she last get decent gowns from a *good* dressmaker?' Normally Vanessa would have bitten off her tongue rather than speak so to a gentleman. But this man fired her to an anger never before experienced. The cat was silently dropped to the floor as Vanessa prepared to do battle.

The earl stepped forward. She backed

against the wall of cupboards. His hands reached out as though to shake her. He gave a sigh of frustration, then dropped his hands to his sides. 'Leave Juliana alone. Stop meddling in what is none of your affair. I do not need advice from a rejected spinster on how to prepare my sister to accept a marriage to someone!' At the sudden distress in her eyes he was driven on. 'She will marry eventually, and well. I have set aside a handsome dowry for her. There will be no magical ointments or damaging drinks. I saw enough of the effects of such quackery while I was in London.'

His eyes burned with a wrath seeming greater than warranted. Vanessa longed to lash out at him, but found her tongue had deserted her just when she had need of it most.

'Now, go up to your room and take that cat with you. I expect to see you changed and down here later for dinner this evening with all this nonsense out of your head.'

Vanessa watched in silence as Lord Stone turned and marched from the stillroom. As she gathered her poise about her, Mrs Murdoch entered, the sly look on her face revealing she had heard all. Unable to tolerate an exchange of words, Vanessa nestled Hercules in her arms to slowly make her way upstairs. Regardless of what that insufferable man thought, she would not give up. The memory of Lady Juliana's eager face, so full of hope and appeal, refused to allow that. The battle lines had been drawn. He called her meddling? She would show him.

6

'Rejected spinster.' The words burned in her ears as she carefully shut the door, then placed Hercules on the end of her bed. Lord Stone couldn't possibly know how mortifying it was to be in her position, nor how difficult it was for her to keep up appearances, the calm façade, the proper mien. Even when he was a second son, he'd had money and a position in society. Men might run to debts, but they didn't suffer the rejection a woman did when out of funds, did they? It seemed to Vanessa they simply looked for a platter-faced spinster of sufficient wealth to wed.

Suddenly she caught sight of her reflection in the mirror by the wardrobe. Her hands flew to her head, then picked at the shoulders of her dress. It was too, too amusing for words. Tears stung her eyes as she laughed, a bit hysterically, at the miserable picture she presented.

Golden wisps of hair straggled from beneath an untidy cambric-and-lace cap. Her dress was spotted with dirt and water from the energetic bath given Hercules. A smear of dirt angled across one cheek. She looked like the lowliest scullery maid. It was no wonder Lord Stone had been so disgusted with her. Drat! Oh, double drat!

Well, the blue jaconet muslin was undoubtedly ruined. There was nothing Vanessa could do to restore it to its former glory. It had been a favorite, a neat, pleasing dress with a high neck and softly puffed mid-length sleeves. As she stripped the offending bodice from her arms, there was a gentle knock at the door, opened immediately by Katie.

The unabashed grin from the freckle-faced girl was most improper, but Katie didn't care about such, it seemed. 'Mrs Murdoch sent me to wait upon you, milady. Seems she got orders from Peverly, who got them from his lordship himself, to see you were taken care of in a fine way.' The pert maid bustled over to assist Vanessa with the skirt of the dress as she attempted to slip it off.

'Tsk, tsk, Miss Vanessa. What a terrible mess you have made of this dress. Never fear, Katie will fix it.'

Normally Vanessa confided in no one, least of all a maid. Now, however, her life had been turned upside down. 'My dress isn't the only thing I have made a mess of today. I had so hoped to help Lady Juliana with her skin and weight. Now *he* most likely will never let me near the dear girl. Look at me! I am a disgrace, my hair in a tangle, clothes a complete disaster.' She dashed away an errant tear that had the temerity to attempt a slide down one cheek.

'Don't give up yet, milady. All is not lost.' Katie deftly slipped a wrapper around Vanessa as she steered her forlorn mistress away from the mirror.

'You shouldn't call me 'milady'. I'm only an Honorable.' Vanessa sniffed. Her mouth was set in a brave line.

Katie said in reply to this bit of truth, 'That may be. For according to Peverly — who heard it from Mr Millbank — your father, God rest his soul, was a baron and your mother a lady to her fingertips.'

Vanessa turned to inspect the contents of her wardrobe. Was there nothing missed by the servants? She'd as soon Mr Millbank had remained silent. 'Lord Stone expects me to dine downstairs this evening. I did not expect to be invited to keep company of the family when they entertained. Thank heaven I have something suitable to wear.'

A knock on the door brought forth a line of footmen with steaming tubs of water. Katie directed them to the dressing room. As the last one shut the door behind him, she motioned to Vanessa. 'In you go. A nice bath and you'll feel more the thing. Come on now, milady.' At Vanessa's look, she added, 'Well, and I'm sure you will be, someday. I'm just practicing.'

Allowing herself to be led to the copper hip bath, Vanessa further permitted her hair to be washed and her back gently scrubbed until the depressing afternoon faded into manageable misfortune. Her favorite scent of bluebells wafted up from the water. 'Katie, I appreciate the scent today, but that bottle is all I have left. I must guard it, for I can't afford another on what I am paid as a needlewoman.'

The maid sniffed. 'That so? Well, leave it to Katie, milady. I suspect Mr Millbank will want you to be happy.'

Before Vanessa could caution Katie to refrain from asking for scent for a needle-woman — a scandalous request it was, too — Katie had left her wrapped in a huge sheet of a towel. Gathering up the brushes and combs, Katie motioned Vanessa to the other room. It took surprisingly little time to dry the delicate strands of golden hair before the fire with Katie brushing and brushing in soothing strokes.

With a certain amount of pride, Katie said, 'Just wait until you see the hand I have with hair. After which we will get you dressed to face that Mrs Hewit. I fancy you want your

126

best armor on for her!'

'I think I'll put on my stays and petticoat first, Katie.' Vanessa was determined to keep some semblance of control over her life.

Katie merely smiled, and hurried to assist Vanessa into the very fine stays of white buckram stiffened with whalebone, lacing up the back, with the steel busk giving a perfect line to the body. Vanessa had no need to have Katie pull at the lacings as many woman did. Her small waist needed little assistance, but fashion decreed the stays, and the gusseted inserts did support her full bust. The latest thing in dainty drawers of fine cotton went under the sheer linen petticoat edged in embroidery and lace.

'Ready, milady?' Katie motioned to the stool before the dressing table, then busied herself with the brush and comb.

When Vanessa looked in the mirror sometime later, she was amazed to see the vision reflected. Katie had done up her hair in short ringlets at the side and a coil of hair on her crown. The pale gray-blue dress of silver-shot sarcenet had a square neckline that set off her slender white neck and smooth shoulders quite nicely. All traces of the miserable day were erased, leaving her looking more than presentable.

Joining Lady Juliana in the hall moments

later, Vanessa squeezed the hand offered her in a comforting way. 'Do not fret, my dear. It really is not all that bad.'

'I had wanted to impress Harry, you know. If he even sees me, I will be amazed. Was Nicholas terribly severe?'

Vanessa thought of the tongue-lashing she had endured earlier. 'I have had worse, I daresay. Please do not give it another thought.'

Her face downcast, figure drooping slightly, Lady Juliana nodded. 'I promise. It was a lovely notion while it lasted. Nicholas is a plaguesome old wigsby.'

Vanessa thought that while the earl might be narrow-minded and possibly crotchety, he was hardly elderly. She wished she might break one of those hideous vases she had observed in the newly opened drawing room neatly over his thick skull. Handsome as he might be, he certainly didn't know anything at all about young girls in the throes of love. No matter if it might appear calf love to him, it was real to Lady Juliana.

Peverly proudly escorted his ladies to the drawing room, murmuring that Mrs Hewit was ahead of them.

Across the room Vanessa saw a slip of a woman whose head was crowned with glorious chestnut curls dressed in a fairly recent mode. She was wearing a thin sarcenet gown of daffodil yellow, a lovely complement to her dark hair. One dainty hand toyed with an artful curl that draped down toward a lamentably flat bosom. Vanessa thought with complacency of her own nicely endowed figure, then scolded herself for her vanity. Taking a deep breath, she advanced, Lady Juliana in tow, toward the woman who might very well take over the earl and the household as well.

Lady Juliana might not have had much training, but she did well in the introductions. The ladies dipped the faintest of curtsies, sizing each other up all the while.

'I understand you are to repair the tapestries. How excessively kind of dear Nicholas to include *you* in the family gathering.' Pamela's sweet smile didn't falter one speck at the slur Vanessa suspected was deliberate.

'Mr Millbank and I are deeply grateful of the honor done us, I'm sure. I was told you live near here. Not very far, I gather?' Vanessa gave a hesitant smile. The barely concealed animosity from Mrs Hewit was puzzling. Surely a beautiful woman with a blissfully fat purse and a sizable piece of land need have no fear of an impecunious needlewoman.

'Nicholas . . . that is, Lord Stone' — Mrs

Hewit blushed rosily at her supposed gaffe — 'is my nearest neighbor to the north of my property. He has been tremendously helpful in the past two years since my husband died. I am determined to help him all I can in return. Do you not like the vases I selected for him?' She caressed one of the hideous vases Vanessa had seen earlier.

It was extremely difficult to repress the shudder that threatened to sweep over her frame. Vanessa was saved by the entry of Lord Stone with Mr Millbank close behind him.

'Good evening, ladies. Pamela, you look more charming every day.' Lord Stone cast a dark look at Vanessa as though to say that she would never equal his definition of the word.

Mr Millbank ignored the chestnut-haired beauty, turning instead to Vanessa. 'How is Hercules coming along?'

A reluctant smile crept out as Vanessa met his eyes. 'That animal has gobbled up all that Cook sent up, thanks to your kind directive. When I left my room, he was boldly ensconced on my pillow, sound asleep.'

The comment had reached Lord Stone's ears and he walked closer. 'You won't have to share your bed with fleas? The bath you gave the cat did the job?'

The smile on Vanessa's face faded. Nodding, she made her reply curt. 'He is quite clean, thank you. Well-fed at the moment too.' Memories of the altercation that had followed that bath returned, with a distressed look flashing briefly to her eyes.

Walking up to stand as close to Lord Stone as propriety allowed, Mrs Hewit intruded, 'A cat? But I thought you never allowed cats in the house, Nicholas.'

Explanation of the circumstances of Hercules' introduction to the house was spared, thanks to the entry of Sir Harry Featherston. The butler even cracked a hint of a smile as he showed the young man into the drawing room.

By now, Vanessa felt Peverly to be a shrewd judge of character. If he liked Sir Harry, he must be all right. She fell back to let the others greet Sir Harry first, calmly waiting to meet him while observing the reactions of the others. Mrs Hewit dismissed Sir Harry immediately in the manner of one vastly above him. Mr Millbank treated him with a deference due to a man of good birth and fortune. Sir Harry was clapped on the shoulder with a show of close friendship by Lord Stone. And poor Lady Juliana looked as though she wished herself a million miles away.

Vanessa could have shaken the young man as he made a polite good-evening to each of the assembled. Even to her, his aplomb and polish were evident. Good breeding was obvious in all he did and spoke — except when it came to Lady Juliana. He flicked her a casual glance and patted her head gently.

'How go your days, Sprite? Keeping out of trouble?'

Lady Juliana blushed a deep rose, gave him a spaniel-eyed look, and murmured a vague reply. Her incoherence was sad, but the benign indifference bestowed by Sir Harry to a young girl head-over-heels in love was utterly crushing. Vanessa wondered if he had any conception how his words wounded. And whatever possessed him to call her Sprite? Anyone less of a sprite, she had yet to see. Once, perhaps, the young Lady Juliana might have been a delicate sprite. Now . . . well, there was the potential. Perhaps Lady Juliana might reveal the reason for the pet name, but Vanessa would never hurt the dear girl by probing. At least he *had* a pet name for her. That was a step in the right direction, Vanessa supposed.

His eyes were friendly as he greeted her. 'Nicholas said he was bringing a lady here to repair the tapestries. He is fortunate to acquire someone who not only has skill but charm and beauty as well.' His cheerful countenance denied anything more than politeness, but Vanessa could see Lady Juliana was not best pleased with the attention being given a needlewoman, even if she was an ally.

'You are too kind, sir. Lord Stone and Lady Juliana have been most gracious in welcoming me to their home.' Vanessa took a careful step away from Sir Harry and Lord Stone. She had no desire to annoy either of the ladies in their pursuit.

Beside Lord Stone, Mrs Hewit made an impatient gesture. She, too, thought the needlewoman had received more than her share of regard.

Vanessa silently blessed Peverly as he entered the drawing room to announce that dinner was served. Thinking of the gong Aunt Agatha had demanded be struck to announce the evening meal with an earth-shattering effect, Vanessa bit back a grin.

'You find the thought of dinner to be pleasing?' Mr Millbank bent to quietly enquire.

'I was just thinking.' Vanessa softly explained what she had recalled, and joined Mr Millbank in gentle laughter.

At the far end of the table where he stood after showing Mrs Hewit to her chair next to his, Nicholas frowned at the sight of his steward and the needlewoman sharing an intimate moment. He ought to feel grateful that Millbank seemed to have taken an interest in the needlewoman. Third son of a baronet, Robert Millbank deserved to find a good woman to wed. The two would be admirably suited to one another. Nicholas wouldn't be losing a steward, he would be gaining the permanent services of a needle-woman. Not cheered by the thought, for some odd reason, Nicholas set out to be charming to the guest at his side. Such an engaging woman did not deserve to be neglected. He was well aware she found him attractive. She was not an unpleasant armful, either. As well, she had her husband's lands, willed outright to her, and all his wealth to boot. Marriage to Pamela Hewit would solve all his problems for some time to come. Pity it did not seem more appealing.

The dinner was well-served under Peverly's eagle gaze. When it came time for dessert, Vanessa sought to meet Lady Juliana's eyes. They exchanged a knowing look. At Peverly's direction, the footman brought around a tray of rhubarb tarts, meringues, and lemon cream, offering to each person what he wished. Instead of handing Lady Juliana a plate with all three desserts, the footman placed a small portion of meringue before her in a most discreet manner. Vanessa noted that Lord

Stone had not observed this alteration of past practice.

However, Mrs Hewit had. 'What? Is someone being cruel to you, dear Juliana? You usually sample all the desserts on the table. Is there someone new who does not know your fondness for sweets? Peverly,' she demanded in a sharp tone, 'see that Lady Juliana gets her usual portion of dessert.'

The elderly butler darted a quick glance at Vanessa, then looked to Lord Stone at the head of the table. Surprisingly, it was Lady Juliana who spoke. 'I find I simply cannot eat another bite, dear Mrs Hewit. How kind of you to be concerned.' She lifted her chin, then continued, 'I am not a child anymore, to be stuffing myself with sweets.'

It was discouraging to note that Sir Harry paid little attention to what was going on at the moment. He applied himself to his lemon cream with polite pleasure.

Lady Juliana studied the delicate meringue on her plate, took one bite, then pushed it away with a look of unhappiness on her face.

It was fortunate that the time soon came for the ladies to depart from the dining room. Lady Juliana arose after a quick look to Peverly. His nod was most discreet. Only Vanessa, who was watching the little scene, caught the exchange.

In the hall, Lady Juliana smiled at Mrs Hewit with gracious charm. 'Let us go to the music room. Have you seen it since the painters have done with it? All it lacks is a harp to make it complete.' She said the latter to Vanessa, unaware of the lump it brought to Vanessa's throat.

As they entered the music room, Pamela Hewit examined the alterations in the decor with a proprietorial eye. 'I must say, it turned out better than I expected. I suggested it be hung with a deep red silk, but you know how stubborn men are. Nicholas said the pale greenish-gray would provide better light for the musicians. Bah! As if an extra branch of candles would not do the thing. Am I not right, Juliana?' She watched with narrowed eyes as Lady Juliana seated herself at the pianoforte, adjusted the branches of candles on either side of the music stand, then began a simple piece of music.

A feeling of unease settled over Vanessa as she watched Mrs Hewit study Lady Juliana while she played. Perhaps that lady was noticing that the simple white dress with the blue ribbons was the same as the many-flounced, many-ribboned dress she had ordered for the girl. She had.

'Is not that the sweet dress we found for you when we last made a trip to York? But what have you done to it? Or did that maid of yours damage it?'

Sending a warning glance to Vanessa, Lady Juliana spoke up in defense of the changes. 'I wanted a few alterations. I am no longer a child, as I keep trying to remind everyone. Only the infants wear so many flounces and ribbons, I suspect. At least, I find this style suits me better . . . now.' Her smile was as sweet as the lemon cream served at dinner. Vanessa could see no hint of malice in it, nor, she suspected, could Mrs Hewit.

Ignoring the answer, Mrs Hewit demanded, 'Help me with my shawl, dear girl, and perhaps you can locate my fan about somewhere. I seem to have misplaced it.' She fluttered a rather vague hand in the air while casting a sharp look to see that Juliana did her bidding promptly.

Juliana found both items on the sofa, handing them to Mrs Hewit with calm politeness before resuming her place at the pianoforte.

With a restless movement, Mrs Hewit rose from her chair and walked to stand by the lovely Brentwood pianoforte. She turned to smile at Vanessa. 'Did you know that Herr Beethoven owns a piano similar to this, by the same maker? Sometime you must persuade Juliana to play that sonata of his for you.'

137

'She means the Sonata Number 26 in E-flat, the 'Fare Thee Well' sonata. It sounds most romantic.' Lady Juliana grinned at Vanessa behind Mrs Hewit's back.

Shrugging her pale yellow sarcenet gown enough for the shoulders to slide a bit more, Mrs Hewit sniffed. She shot a look at the needlewoman that said she doubted Vanessa knew what good music was. 'For now, perhaps you will play and I will sing. Are you musical, Miss Tarleton?'

'I don't care to sing, madam. My talents lie elsewhere.' Vanessa's look was rueful.

A superior smile flitted to Mrs Hewits small, prim mouth. 'Of course, I forgot your needlework for the moment. Juliana, shall we?'

When the gentlemen joined the ladies in the music room, it was to the gentle strains of a pleasant tune that taxed neither Lady Juliana's nor Mrs Hewit's abilities.

'Millbank,' demanded Lady Juliana with a sparkle in her pretty eyes, 'you must join us.'

Smiling shyly in return, Mr Millbank went to the corner of the room and picked up a violoncello, then sat on a chair pulled over to the side of the piano by a thoughtful Sir Harry. Lady Juliana cast a longing look at Sir Harry before resolutely turning her attention to the music.

It was possible, Vanessa decided, that Lady Juliana completely forgot about her seemingly hopeless affection for Sir Harry while she played the delicate piece of music. It was a lovely minuet performed with superb clarity and feeling by both musicians. Lady Juliana was far and above the average talent found at the after-dinner musicale in the homes Vanessa had visited before her father's death.

With the conclusion of Mozart's Sonata in E minor, written, Mr Millbank explained, originally for the pianoforte and violin and adapted by himself, the group dissolved into quiet conversation. A footman entered with a tray holding tea as well as dainty cakes.

Aware that Lord Stone had moved too close to her side, Vanessa edged toward Mr Millbank as she exclaimed, 'Lady Juliana is quite the professional in quality of performance. I vow you could hear nothing better anywhere. You are very accomplished as well, Mr Millbank.'

He seemed pleased with her praise. 'I am sure you play well too, Miss Tarleton. My cousin has remarked upon your skill at the harp.' He nodded in approval of whatever he had heard from his cousin. Vanessa had no doubt it was rather biased.

A shadow crossed her lovely face before she gave a thin smile. It was difficult to listen to the lovely music and not join in as she dearly wished to do. 'That was most gracious of Mr Hunt. He has had to listen to my practicing over the years, I fear.'

'Clearly you repine for your harp. We shall have to see what we can do about that, Millbank.' Lord Stone's voice was polite, though a bit cool.

'You don't play an instrument, Lord Stone?' Vanessa inquired.

'Harry and I constitute a devoted pair of listeners. Right, Harry? Not everyone is gifted in that way, you know.' His voice was now completely uninterested.

Feeling oddly chastised, Vanessa withdrew slightly, finding she was able to sip her tea in relative peace while she watched the others. She enjoyed observing people from a distance. One could see the little byplays. For instance, Lady Juliana made such valiant attempts not to gaze at Sir Harry, while Mrs Hewit made no effort to conceal her attraction to Lord Stone. The reactions of the gentlemen were interesting as well. Lord Stone flirted with a remote charm, while Sir Harry ignored Lady Juliana as though she didn't exist. When he did speak to her, as earlier, he tended to treat her as though she was about two- and-ten.

While Lord Stone might have forbidden

Vanessa to attempt to help Lady Juliana, he hadn't stayed to receive an answer, Vanessa mused. There was such potential in Lady Juliana. The loss of those extra pounds would make all the difference. Her face glowed in the candlelight, and how pretty she would be with a less plump face, those spots and freckles gone. Vanessa determined anew she was not going to allow Lord Stone to deflect her from her original purpose in regard to Lady Juliana.

Turning to answer some small remark by Mr Milbank, she decided to get Katie to help with the plan. If, indeed, Katie could 'fix everything,' she would make an excellent co-conspirator!

Sir Harry drew close to where Vanessa and Mr Millbank stood. 'I knew a Colin Tarleton while I was in Spain. Could he have been a relative of yours?'

Vanessa paled, but calmly faced him. 'He was my brother, Sir Harry.'

'Oh, I say, I am sorry.' He looked as though he would have done anything to take back the words just spoken. He glanced at the floor as Vanessa sought to reassure him she was fairly recovered from the loss.

'It has been two years now. Much has happened since then. Did you know him well?' Earnest desire to know all warred with the knowledge that she ought to postpone this talk until a more proper time.

A serious expression slipped over Sir Harry's nice face. 'I should say I did. If it hadn't been for your brother, I and several other men might have died of our wounds at the Battle of Talavera. He was a fine man and was sorely missed after he was killed.'

'Please, tell me what you remember. We heard so little about his part in the battle, and the letter informing us of his death was so brief.' Vanessa moved closer to Sir Harry, forgetting all the others in the room. Of these, Mrs Hewit was the only one who seemed pleased that Sir Harry could tell Vanessa the details of her brother's life during the war in Spain.

Before Sir Harry could begin, Lord Stone stepped forward. 'Perhaps it would be better if Harry came over tomorrow to fill you in on the details?'

His voice was gentle, but Vanessa was once again reminded, however subtly, that she had gone beyond what was proper. Whatever must Lord Stone think of her now? Her desire to know about Colin had pushed her beyond the line. Colin and she had been quite close, and she missed him dreadfully. She gave Lord Stone a strained glance, then turned once again to Sir Harry.

'His lordship is correct, you know. I would not wish to bore these kind people with such stories as can only be of interest to myself. If you would be so good as to speak with me at a later time, I would deem it a great kindness.' Her eyes pleaded with him to understand without her having to say another word about it. Mrs Hewit looked entirely too pleased at the matter, and Lady Juliana appeared to glower silently at Vanessa from behind Sir Harry's back.

Recollecting himself, Sir Harry nodded, then murmured something polite about calling the very next day to apprise Vanessa of her brother's fine qualities as a young officer in the field of battle.

At that moment Peverly entered the room to speak with Lord Stone, his voice a barely distinct murmur, as the others drifted toward the pianoforte, where Lady Juliana now seated herself, her hands lightly skimming over the keys in a pretty country air.

Lord Stone nodded as Peverly concluded, then joined the group. 'I am indeed sorry to have to break in on the music, but it has begun to rain, and Peverly feels it may turn into a storm before long. You know too well what that does to the roads hereabouts. I took the liberty of calling for your carriage, Pamela, yours too, Harry. I am afraid this

143

puts an end to our friendly evening. The fortunate thing is that we can look forward to many more. Perhaps next time we can test our skill at a game of whist?'

He tucked his hand beneath Mrs Hewit's elbow as he guided her to the door, where a footman held her pelisse. Peverly materialized with a huge black umbrella to assist the lady to her carriage. Vanessa could see Mrs Hewit was not pleased to leave, but after extracting a promise from Lord Stone to assist her with a small problem on her estate, she left in a flurry of yellow cloth.

Sir Harry spoke softly to Vanessa to assure her he would most assuredly call upon her on the morrow — unless the storm became too severe. Vanessa, conscious of the unhappy Lady Juliana not far away, was warmly polite anyway. The young gentleman was to bring her information she had longed to hear. Lady Juliana must realize there was nothing romantic involved in the least.

'You cannot know how eagerly I will be awaiting your visit, sir.' She curtsied deeply in her gratitude, beaming a heartfelt smile that included everyone who still stood in the hall. Sir Harry allowed Peverly to hold the umbrella for him, not too proud to receive help. After all, a fellow did not have Weston up here to provide a new coat on the spur.

When Peverly returned, the door banged shut with a resounding echo. He departed for a warm fire and a bedtime glass of port. Lady Juliana paused on the stairs to peer down at the three who remained before giving a sniff, then marching up the remaining steps to the upper floor and her room. Suddenly recalling an urgent desire to go to bed, Millbank said his good-night, and that left Vanessa to face Lord Stone alone.

'I fear Lady Juliana is not best pleased with me tonight. I had better go up to explain.' Her words faded away as she found Lord Stone motioning her to the warmth of the drawing room nearby. A fire burned low in the grate, and candles were near to the guttering point in the wall sconces. 'Milord? I hope I did not displease you by requesting that Sir Harry tell me about my brother. I have missed him so much.' It was the only thing she could think of at the moment that might have annoyed him. Surely the earlier dispute was over and done with?

Lord Stone hemmed and hawed a bit before coming to the point. 'I observed Juliana this evening. I must concede that you have a point.' He held up his hand before Vanessa could think of anything to say in response. 'A point, I repeat. That does not mean I condone a regimen of quacking her with concoctions and whatnot. But my little sister has grown up more than I realized, and for that awareness, I thank you.'

'Handsomely said, milord. Perhaps in time she might have a new dress or two? Let her look over the fashion plates from London for a bit. You know it is always the anticipation that beguiles, often more than the realization.'

Nicholas stared at the needlewoman who had turned his placid, hardworking life upside down, one way or another. 'We shall see. I daresay you have the right of it in this regard. I shall talk to Juliana about it tomorrow.' He added in the mildest of tones, 'Do you think it kind to flirt with Sir Harry under my sister's very nose — if she indeed is fond of him?'

Vanessa had turned to leave the room, sure the conversation was at an end. She paused at his last words. 'I have no personal regard for Sir Harry. I much prefer her friendship to any nebulous interest that might spring from that direction.' She looked back to meet his eyes, now shadowed by the failing light, wondering what in the world was going on in that head. 'I am well aware that no gentleman as handsome and well-set as Sir Harry will consider marriage with anyone but a woman with a goodly dowry . . . such as Lady Juliana has, for example. I believe I know my place.

And,' she added as an afterthought, 'nothing other than marriage would do for me, you see.' She skirted a small table by the door to flee up the stairs to her room.

Nicholas walked to the fireplace, leaning against the cool marble with one hand as the other rubbed his forehead. Life had suddenly become exceedingly complicated.

7

Vanessa sleepily batted at whatever was tickling her nose a few times before realizing Hercules sat at her side, waiting impatiently for her to rise. An elegant tail curled around right beneath her nose. Beyond her window she could see white clouds in a race across the sky, playing tag in a game they could never win. She slipped from her bed and was attempting to do up a plain round gown of printed green cambric when the door opened and Katie entered, tiptoeing with great stealth before realizing Vanessa was already awake and up.

'Here, and let me help you, milady.' Katie skillfully hooked up the back of the dress, then nudged Vanessa to the dressing table, where Katie's prowess with the comb and brush was again demonstrated.

Deciding it was pointless to fuss over the undeserved title Katie persisted in giving her, Vanessa quietly left her room, walking softly down to the breakfast room for a bite to eat. There was no one in view when she entered; she relished the total peace in which to eat her substantial meal. She intended to begin the actual stitching this morning, but first she must hunt around for a few of the herbs for Lady Juliana. How thankful she was that Lord Stone was nowhere in sight.

The herb garden was deserted. Dew clung to the spider webs draped from arching branches of rosemary, and a wood warbler could be heard from the other side of the brick wall surrounding the garden. The air was fresh and sweet-smelling. As she searched the neat rows for familiar plants, a saucy bullfinch, its crimson breast a cheerful contrast to the tiny white blossoms of the blackthorn, nodded a good-morning to her. Other than feverfew, she found few of the plants she sought. It would mean facing Mrs Murdoch about the stillroom.

Deciding to try a paste of oatmeal and vinegar before she went further afield, Vanessa paused in the kitchen to consult with Cook a few moments. After finding Cook was in complete agreement with her, and quite willing to help where she could, Vanessa hurried to the saloon.

The hours passed quickly as she studied the tapestry, then neatly worked one repair after another, taking tiny, nearly invisible weaving stitches in the aging fabric. It was as well that a lining had been added at some point along the way. Surely it helped prevent more serious deterioration and damage to the tapestries. It was frustrating when she paused for a cup of tea to find that only one small corner of the tapestry was done.

Idly she smoothed the woven surface out, then again noted the odd lumps in the better-preserved area of the tapestry. She hadn't paid all that much attention to it before, as it clearly did not need restoring. The lumps seemed to be primarily located beneath the brilliantly colored exotic birds that flew here and perched there amid the elegant lords and ladies of the hunt. The reason for the lining became quite evident. Trapunto involved a stuffing with backing, and it could be a very old form of trapunto she hadn't come across before. Certainly she hadn't discovered such in the tapestries at Blackwood Hall. Perhaps she ought to investigate or report it.

Then she thought of Lord Stone. He might dismiss it as unworthy of merit; indeed, he might consider it nothing more than meddling in a matter that need not concern her. She was here solely for the purpose of mending the tapestries, not to explore the unusual stitching in them. Truth to tell, she had plenty to do without looking about for other tasks. His caustic remark about her meddling in the affairs that were none of her concern still stung. Vanessa had *never* been so accused in her life.

'Ah, there you are. Peverly said you were hard at it. May I join you?'

The attractive smile from Sir Harry revealed what Lady Juliana found so appealing. 'But of course.' She pointed to a chair not far from where she worked, then carefully inserted her needle into the weaving so as not to lose it, while he drew the chair close to the worktable.

'I happened to see Nicholas riding toward the north of his property so I thought I would take this chance to talk to you about your brother.' Sir Harry grinned at her with a nice twinkle in his eyes.

Flushing with a combination of annoyance at Lord Stone and eagerness to hear about her brother, Vanessa nodded quickly. 'It was thoughtless of me to enquire last evening. Naturally it is a subject best left to the two of us.' She sat poised in an attitude of expectancy, waiting.

Sir Harry studied his hands for a moment, as though reluctant to tell his story. Vanessa shifted slightly on her chair, and he looked up at her before clearing his throat. 'Yes, well, I expect you heard something of the battles leading up to Talavera. We were starving, you know, worse than dogs hunting for something to eat. The government had promised money for supplies and animals, but we never saw it.' He paused again in reflection, bitter, from what she could see. 'Late on the twenty-seventh of July there was a fierce battle. The Frenchman, Jourdan, lost, we later heard, one thousand and three hundred men in forty minutes. He had been too confident, never having faced Wellesley before. During that night we actually met the others who had survived the battle by the little river that flows there, men from both sides drinking to quench that awful thirst. It helped a bit, but oh, God, we were so hungry.'

He drew a ragged breath, as though the simple retelling of the battle brought a dryness to his throat. 'The next day was worse. Sherbrook with the Guards suffered heavily after going too far. Anson's brigade got caught in a narrow ravine. It was terrible. I was hit in the leg and was weak with hunger so couldn't go far. There was no medic within sight or sound. Then late that day a fire caught in the dry grass of the Cerro de Medellin. If it hadn't been for Colin pulling me away, I would have burned to death. We were a pair, hollow-eyed, filthy, done-in to the bone. But he saved me . . . and I could do nothing for him. He dashed down to help recover more of the wounded men and was hit.'

He stopped, head bent once more to study his hands. 'I wish I could have brought him back for you, Miss Tarleton. He was a fine man, as good a soldier as I ever knew. Talavera was a great victory for our cause. It established Wellesley as the general who could lead the armies as Nelson led the navies. But at such cost. He was named Viscount Wellington right after that. I was invalided home before the news came to him of his new title. I wonder if he wouldn't have far rather had the supplies and animals they promised him instead.'

'And you? Is your wound healed?' Vanessa found she simply could not comment on the stark horror painted in those few words he had spoken.

He attempted a smile. 'It aches on rainy days. Better than a barometer, I daresay.'

A stir at the door brought both heads around to see Lady Juliana poised there, hands clasped before her in concern, carefully watching the two who were in such deep conversation.

'Come in, Lady Juliana. Sir Harry was just telling me about my brother. If you will both excuse me, I believe I will go off by myself for just a bit.' Normally she would never have left

Lady Juliana alone with a man. However, Sir Harry looked upon Juliana merely as his friend's young sister, and there was no danger there. She turned again to Sir Harry. 'You understand, do you not?' At his nod, she thanked him again and slipped from the room, leaving Lady Juliana in pleased conversation with Sir Harry.

Peverly was nowhere in sight as Vanessa gathered her shawl over her shoulders and slipped from the house. She walked without paying much attention to her direction. In the distance the bleating of lambs arose like an ancient chorus of discontent. The grass was long and thick as she waded through it to the south, ignoring what it might be doing to her jean half-boots. She hadn't changed after her foray in the garden, thank goodness. Before her rose the fountain, its figures spouting jets of water high into the air. Ignoring the majesty of this work of art, she chose to continue toward the lake glimpsed through the trees.

Seeing a cluster of cowslips in bloom, she gathered what she could for Lady Juliana, then went on to pick watercress from the clear stream running into the lake. At the sandy bank of the shallow lake she sank onto a bench so placed to view the scene. It was peaceful; she was totally alone. It was here that Lord Stone came across her as she dried the tears shed for her long-dead brother. Cowslips and watercress were strewn over her lap as she wiped her eyes on a corner of her shawl.

The sight of the slender figure dressed in green print cambric, her blond curls ruffled in the breeze, the gallant set of her shoulders as she tried to end her crying bout, stirred a memory buried someplace very deep. Nicholas frowned as he attempted to recall what it might be. Had he seen her before? Did she remind him of someone from the past? Nothing came to mind. Her beauty was undimmed by her spell of tears.

'I gather you spoke with Harry this morning?' He noted the damp spikes of her long lashes, the shadowed expression in her eyes. He felt as though he should offer her comfort, pull her head to rest against his chest, hold her close. He drew himself stiffly erect to keep from holding out his arms to her — welcoming arms they would be, too. She appeared very appealing with her defenses down, that womanly softness revealed so sweetly.

Vanessa jumped to her feet, scattering the cowslips and watercress over the neatly raked gravel of the bank. She didn't care for him to see her like this. 'I did. Though I expect to return now to the house. It was good to be by myself for a bit. I have made fair progress on one corner of the largest tapestry, milord.' She again thought of the odd lumps behind the birds, but her intention to tell him faded as he made a dismissive wave of his hand.

'You do not have to feel as though you must put your needle to work every hour of the day, Miss Tarleton. I am not such a hard master that I would see you lose your sight over a weaving, even if it is old.' He wanted to shake some sense into her, or was it simply a desire to touch those slim arms, that slender body? He resisted the inclination and moved away a step.

'And valuable, milord.' Something about his stiff attitude, as though he only mouthed the words, that inside he felt as though she ought to be at the table, needle in hand, led her to hastily gather the fallen cowslip and watercress, then turn toward the house. 'I shall see you at luncheon?'

At her cool words of dismissal, Nicholas curved his lips into a rueful twist. He nodded. 'I will be there.' She removed temptation from him so neatly. He wondered what might have happened if he had yielded, gathered her close in his arms. Memory of the vision in blue returned as he watched her run from him, the fluid line of her body revealed as she whisked herself off to the house.

Fleeing across the expanse of green to the house, Vanessa could sense his eyes burning into her back. How glad she was he had not seen her shedding tears, and especially that he did not know the cowslips she carried would be used to blend into an ointment, and the watercress she would turn into a night application to purify Lady Juliana's skin. She doubted he would be so charitable in that event.

A few words to Cook regarding the herbs, and Vanessa hurried up the stairs to the saloon. Sir Harry was still there, Lady Juliana shyly smiling at his attempt to entertain her. As Vanessa joined them, Peverly followed, with Mrs Hewit at his heels.

'Never mind, Peverly. I know my way here as though it were my home, you know.' She dismissed the elderly retainer with an insolent flick of her hand. Turning to face Vanessa, she noticed the high color of her cheeks, the shawl still draped about her shoulders. 'I thought you would be sewing this morning. Surely you must know Lord Stone expects his servants to give excellent service.'

Lady Juliana gasped at this pointed remark. 'Please do remember that dear Miss Tarleton is not a mere servant, Mrs Hewit. Harry knew her brother well. She is from a family of higher rank than yours.'

The last had been said in a childish fit of pique, and Vanessa could not allow such rag-manners to go unchallenged. 'But I daresay Mrs Hewit was so fortunate as to have a more prudent parent than I, Lady Juliana.' She wrapped her composure as close as her shawl as she turned to Mrs Hewit. 'I am fully aware of my place here. It was just that after hearing the account of my brother's death from Sir Harry, I felt the need for a few moments' solitude.'

'Harry . . . and Pamela! Why do you not join us for lunch?' Nicholas had come from the fields in his nankeen breeches, his top boots damp from the early-morning dew. Yet this time, he was impeccably attired otherwise, his buff waistcoat revealed as he undid the gilt buttons of his dark blue riding coat. With a start, Vanessa realized she had only noted his face before now, captivated by the expression in those dark eyes.

Sir Harry glanced unaccountably to Vanessa, who found herself nodding to him just as Mr Millbank paused at the entry to the room. Sir Harry replied, 'I'll send my groom home to let them know I'll not be returning.' He beamed at Nicholas with apparent relief.

Sauntering over to the worktable to inspect the repairs that had been accomplished this morning, Nicholas inquired in the most friendly of voices, 'How're your mother and sister these days, Harry?'

'Louisa has accepted Dunston at long last, and Mother is busy planning the nuptials. Dunston insists he wants to be wed as soon as possible, while the weather is good.'

'And well before hunting season, I suspect. They ought to do well together, both of them horse-mad as they are.'

Twirling a tassel from a drapery tie-back in her fingers, Juliana giggled. 'I enjoy a ride as much as any woman, but Louisa outdoes all of us, I am certain. Though I would hate to have my wedding set for such a convenience.' She darted an oblique glance at Sir Harry, who had joined Nicholas at the worktable.

Feeling somewhat nervous at this inspection of her morning's work, Vanessa moved protectively toward the table as well.

From her position near the door, able to observe Mr Millbank as well as the others, Mrs Hewit sweetly intoned, 'But then, one must be asked first. It would be so hateful to be presuming a wedding, then find it was all a hum.'

Glancing up to catch the fleeting look of malicious glee on the pleasant countenance Mrs Hewit usually presented, Vanessa was surprised to find it no longer twinged when she was reminded, however subtly, of her

159

recent betrothal and subsequent dismissal by Lord Chudleigh.

Nicholas looked up, surveying the suddenly quiet room to comment, 'Harry will never have to worry about those two, now that Louisa has at last made up her mind. How many weeks has he allowed your mother?'

An amused laugh was followed by Sir Harry's announcement, 'You know him better than I do. He gave her three weeks.'

Nicholas riposted, 'Once a man makes the decision to wed, there is no point in postponing the marriage. Only leads to trouble.'

Mrs Hewit sidled up to Lord Stone and placed a dainty gloved hand on his arm. 'What an interesting theory, dear Nicholas. My dear late husband was of the same feeling, I gather, for he rushed me to the altar before I could blink.'

'Poor man,' whispered Lady Juliana to Vanessa, who gave her a cautioning look in return.

Fortunately no one else heard the aside from Lady Juliana, so the group of six who entered the sunny dining room was an amiable one.

Later Vanessa reflected, as she sat quietly beside her worktable in the peace of the deserted saloon, that something would have to be done about Lady Juliana's propensity for ill-timed remarks. It would not do her one bit of good with Sir Harry. It was plain to see he was all polished manners and politeness. He also was gifted with perception, except for the matter of Lady Juliana. It wasn't ladylike to be sniping at the woman who just might become her brother's wife. At that thought, her needle was removed from the tapestry and placed carefully in the ivory needle-holder, which she tucked on the top shelf of the workbox.

Lord Stone might not desire her to wear out her eyes or give her shoulders a permanent bend, but she doubted he would approve what she planned to do as an alternative.

Cook gave her a broad smile as Vanessa slipped into the steaming kitchen. 'Everything ready?'

'Aye, that it is, miss.' A wave in the direction of a pot and the necessary ingredients sent Vanessa to work.

It took some time to carefully compound each mixture. Cook was only too happy to enter the stillroom to fetch the few missing ingredients. Vanessa thanked her with fervor as the final item was dumped into the last of the concoctions.

'Let me see,' she murmured, 'oil of almond

for smoothing her skin, elderflower and rosewater to cleanse it. The oatmeal did up nicely with the vinegar, Cook. That was a good idea to add a bit from the tear of gum benjamin. Not only does it give scent, but it acts as an astringent as well. I must remember that combination. The watercress will make a lovely lotion. She can put it on at night if she is not given to walking about. Can you not see what effect a green-tinged face might have in the middle of the night, striking terror in the heart?' She laughed softly with Cook, then added, 'She will have to wash it off before being seen in the morning.'

Vanessa didn't add that all this would have to be done as discreetly as possible to prevent Lord Stone from finding out about the scheme. Even Cook had heard about the edict and, like everyone else who adored Lady Juliana, thought it monstrous cruel to keep her from improving herself. Her efforts in Sir Harry's direction was cheered on by all the staff.

Upstairs Vanessa discovered Lady Juliana in the music room. The lotions and creams were covered with a checked cloth on a tray, concealed the best way possible. Vanessa walked up to where Lady Juliana sat, then spoke in a soft voice so only she could hear. Vanessa had learned not to be overly confident about being alone. One never knew who might be around the corner.

Beaming a curious look up at Vanessa, Lady Juliana rose from the bench, then led the way to the hall. No one was in sight — Peverly apparently taking one of his little snoozes — so the two stole up the stairs like naughty children escaping detection.

Once in Lady Juliana's room, Vanessa set to work. Tying Juliana's hair back for the moment, she applied the oatmeal concoction with tender skill to the young, plump face. Soon, only two dark blue eyes and a cherry-red mouth were visible. 'Don't speak. You will be sorry,' Vanessa cautioned.

Then, with the help of the dependable Katie, Vanessa treated Lady Juliana's hair with the special mixture of butterwort leaves and camomile flowers. Never was so much accomplished in such silence. Katie was a born conspirator, her whispers carrying without being overloud. The golden liquid bathed the hair with sunshine, bringing life and needed color to the once-drab hair.

'I believe I ought to read to you, only I cannot imagine what it ought to be. Perhaps that new book I saw by your bed, the one from Minerva Press? Just nod if you wish.' Vanessa watched as Katie rinsed the mixture from Lady Juliana's hair, leaving it slightly more golden than before, with texture that would catch light with every movement she made. While Katie toweled Lady Juliana's hair dry, Vanessa read. It was no problem to keep Lady Juliana quiet with such entertainment. Katie watched and listened with great delight. If she had not become devoted to the dear Miss Tarleton before, being included in on The Plan was sufficient to secure her regard forever.

When Lady Juliana's hair was quite dry and Vanessa decided the oatmeal compound could be washed from her skin, Katie slipped from the room to return with a basin of clean water. Also brought was a tray, carried by a footman Katie trusted, with a pot of fragrant tea.

'Now, what is this?' questioned a dubious Juliana.

'A mixture of strawberry and camomile teas. You may sip it while I apply this lotion to your skin.' Taking one of Lady Juliana's hands, Vanessa worked in the lotion, then transferred her attention to the other hand, then last of all did the sweet, plump face.

Laughing, Lady Juliana touched her face with exploring fingers. 'I feel as though I ought to slide, I am so covered with cream.'

Vanessa and Katie paused by the door, glancing at each other before looking back to where Lady Juliana perched on the edge of her beautiful crowned and draped bed.

Vanessa whispered a terse reply. 'Just finish your tea and take a nap. We must get rid of the evidence before your brother happens on us.'

With this admonition, Juliana nodded quickly, swallowed the last of the tea, then snuggled down on the bed. She scarcely felt any hunger pangs, in spite of the sparse luncheon she had allowed herself.

Spending the remainder of the afternoon diligently working at her repair on the tapestry, Vanessa wondered if the efforts on Lady Juliana would show up when it came time for dinner. In one way she hoped they would; then, thinking of Lord Stone, she decided it might be better if they didn't.

From time to time she could see Lord Stone cross the great central hall with a roll of papers in his hand, arguing in an amiable manner with his architect or conversing in serious tones with Mr Millbank. Her gaze followed him each time. It was as though she knew his step, sensed his presence without raising her eyes from her work. Of course she could not resist a peep. He was far too handsome a man for any woman to ignore, and Vanessa didn't even try.

When the sun dipped low in the sky and the flickering light from the candles offered nothing but an ache in the eyes, Vanessa put away her needle in the ivory case. She wound up the yarns neatly and placed them in the bottom of the workbox. She was pleased, even as she sighed with aching shoulders and a stiff neck, that the work looked as well it did. She could see a distinct difference in the area she had worked. Miss Linwood had made excellent suggestions regarding colors.

Vanessa's thoughts strayed to the remarks she'd overheard while at Miss Linwood's exhibit. Fixing her gaze absently on the Turkey carpet of the saloon, she rubbed the back of her neck, wondering about the gossip those men had repeated. Was Lord Stone in search of a wife? And would that wife be Mrs Hewit? The more she saw of that woman, the less Vanessa approved of the idea. Surely Lord Stone — or Nicholas, as Mrs Hewit so sweetly called him — deserved better. True, his words had wounded Vanessa. 'Rejected' was a word no woman cared to have bandied about, though 'spinster' was a designation Vanessa might well become accustomed to bearing. But the truth of that fact didn't mean Lord Stone deserved to suffer a lifetime with Pamela.

It was a pity Sir Harry wasn't there for dinner, Vanessa thought as Lady Juliana shyly joined the others in the drawing room before going in to dinner. Her skin, although still spotty, glowed from the good cleansing and her hair gleamed with gold from the lights of the many candles. The simple white dress, another of Mrs Hewit's choices remodeled by a surprisingly skilled Katie, accented her fresh appeal.

Nicholas appeared to notice nothing different about his sister. Vanessa breathed a sigh of relief as she realized the meal would pass with no trace of difficulty. He didn't seem to observe that Juliana ate far less than usual.

Outside, the wind had risen, a harbinger of another rain. Nicholas wore a set look as he consulted Mr Millbank. 'Think there will be any difficulties with the lambs tonight?'

Millbank shook his head. 'No, they are well on their way — the shepherds have the sense to get them to higher ground in this continued rain we have been plagued with lately.'

Recalling the rain that had fallen, incessant and relentless, at Blackwood Hall, Vanessa added, 'It has been a very rainy spring, I believe.'

'And shockingly windy too,' chimed in Lady Juliana. 'We need some entertainment, Nicholas. Have you given any further consideration to finding a harp for Vanessa to play?' She thoughtfully chewed a tender bite of chicken while she waited for her brother to answer.

'I believe so. I requested Millbank to send for yours, Miss Tarleton. Upon reflection, I decided that the new owner might very well decide to appropriate such a valuable instrument for himself. Your former steward might not be able to hide such a large item.'

'He did promise, you know,' Vanessa replied.

'Promises are not always kept.' His eyes seemed to remind her that her betrothal had been one of those. 'Far better to get it out of temptation's way.' He studied the needlewoman in the soft candlelight, her blonde hair glowing with seductive lights. He was going to have to get a stronger hold on his responses. He couldn't afford to be attracted to this woman. He met her gaze, wondering what her thoughts might be.

'I do most humbly thank you, milord. It is very generous of you to do this.'

Nicholas made a careless wave of his hand. 'I would do a lot to keep this puss here contented.' He seemed to take note of Lady Juliana for the first time then. 'You seem in good looks tonight.'

Lady Juliana blushed a pretty pink under her brother's teasing. Her hair was lovely after Katie had brushed and curled it, shining with health and herbal treatments.

'I am happy to have Miss Tarleton with us, Nicholas. She is exceedingly good company for me. Please say we can do things together once the weather improves. I would like to show her all the sights in the area. Surely you don't expect her to bury her nose in those musty old hangings all the time, do you?'

Surprised at this attack from Lady Juliana, Vanessa raised a staying hand, but was ignored by both brother and sister.

Lord Stone rubbed his chin, then glanced at Vanessa. 'It might be a good idea. I have been charged with neglect of you, Juliana.' His gaze lingered on Vanessa before returning to his sister. 'When the weather improves, I believe it would be quite in keeping for you two to take rides in the dogcart or to go for short walks.'

'Fine,' said Lady Juliana. 'I have all manner of ideas.'

When Nicholas moved around to assist Vanessa from her chair before the footman could reach her, he again noticed the delicate scent of bluebells about her. He drew it in, savoring the well-remembered scent as one does something very special. Looking down at the slender form, the golden curls, dainty hands, all so very feminine and appealing, he wondered what was happening to him.

8

The next weeks passed in much the same fashion. Each day Vanessa spent long hours at the tapestry repair, listening as Lady Juliana read from Scott's *The Lady of the Lake*, a charming poem with an interesting story and finely drawn characters. Vanessa appreciated the company, for it kept her entertained while she concentrated on her sewing.

Each afternoon they pussyfooted up to Lady Juliana's elegant bedroom for another treatment on her skin. The reading up there was from the Minerva Press volumes Juliana kept secreted in her room. The change in Lady Juliana was quite gradual, what with an occasional lapse. Her downfall was the muffins baked for Lord Stone. Still, she always returned to the slimming diet and tisanes Vanessa and Katie prepared for her. Her complexion improved, there were fewer spots and freckles to be seen, and her hair acquired a healthy gleam. But the improvement was not an accomplishment achieved overnight.

Today the sun had come out for once, the weather having been utterly cold, damp, and windy for the most part. Lady Juliana was restless, pacing back and forth on the Turkey carpet until Vanessa fully expected to see a path worn through it.

'I need a project, something to plan,' Juliana announced in a firm tone. 'If Nicholas is going to marry that featherhead, I must needs find a diversion, preferably one away from the house.' She paused, hands on hips. 'You see how she is? I could never settle for days and days spent in her company.'

There was a quality in Mrs Hewit that reminded Vanessa of her mother, an indolence of manner perhaps, or a way of getting others to do for her.

'Perhaps Sir Harry . . . ' Vanessa's voice faded away as she reluctantly admitted to herself that Sir Harry remained as blind as ever to the charms of his young neighbor. It was as though once he had looked at her — years ago, most likely — he never really looked again.

'And perhaps pigs will fly. I give up on him! Since I will have no other man, I may as well find something with which to occupy my time.' She stood a moment to look over the watersoaked grounds and beyond. 'The skies are clearing nicely. I think tomorrow we may be able to take the dogcart out. What do you say? Cook could pack us a picnic.'

Knowing something must be done to help her young friend, Vanessa allowed that it would be lovely.

Enthusiasm bubbled forth from Juliana. 'And I know what I shall do. I will paint all the wildflowers of Yorkshire I can find. Perhaps I may even do a book of them!'

'Oh, dear.' Vanessa envisioned days spent tramping the fields for some elusive bloom, perched on rocks to paint a delicate blossom, all the while torn by wind.

'What did you say?' Lady Juliana paused once more to send a sharp look at Vanessa.

'I said, my dear, what a perfectly splendid idea — to do a book of your very own.' Vanessa admitted it wasn't a bad idea, and it would keep Lady Juliana occupied.

Lady Juliana resumed her pacing, this time more slowly, more reflectively. 'I might even go further afield. It would take me away from Pamela, and that is a blessing to be desired. I could travel all over England, painting wildflowers. Would you join me? I will need a companion.'

Wryly Vanessa smiled back at the girl, so full of dreams and hopes. 'It depends on when you want to go. I have to finish this first.'

'Peagoose! It will take me some time to paint all the wildflowers around here. I must go up to my room to see what paints I might need. Think on it, will you?' Juliana slipped quietly from the room, leaving Vanessa in pensive silence.

As the days had passed, she had watched the odd sort of attachment between Nicholas and Pamela Hewit. He certainly wasn't very loverlike in his attitude. Rather, it seemed to her that Nicholas Leighton treated Mrs Hewit much as he did his sister or any other lady. And as far as Mrs Hewit went, it appeared to Vanessa that that lady did a great deal of the pursuing. Certainly Mrs Hewit popped up here at mealtime far more than Lord Stone was known to be at her table. Still, the lady seemed to achieve success with her wiles, practiced as they might be.

Sighing deeply, Vanessa thrust her needle into the weaving, thinking that if she continued at this pace, it wouldn't take nearly as long as she had first feared to complete the work. And then what? Could she contemplate junketing about the countryside while Lady Juliana painted wildflowers? The young woman was accomplished in the art; Vanessa had seen several of her paintings. But would Nicholas Leighton permit such an adventure? He had told Vanessa he had plans for Juliana, plans for a marriage. He was very slow in announcing them, whatever they were. Of

173

course, this allowed Juliana to lose more weight, improve her skin in the meanwhile. Lately, her dresses had begun to hang on her. It was time Lord Stone was reminded of his promise regarding the dressmaker.

Figuring she might as well approach Lord Stone now as ever, Vanessa sought him out in the nearly completed long gallery. She looked about with approval as she entered the light, airy room. Now the workmen were nearly done, the painters departed for another room, and the carpenters were doing some hammering in the old tapestry room. At the far end of the gallery she caught sight of him standing near the bust of some long-dead Roman placed on a column of red-veined marble. That red echoed the gorgeous red of the draperies hanging at the windows. Tall paintings of past members of the eminent Leighton family peered down at her as she swiftly marched through the long room.

'Lord Stone, I wonder if I might have a moment of your time?' Why did her heart have to behave in such erratic fashion every time she drew near the man? Sometimes she almost felt weak, as though her limbs might melt beneath her. She had made an effort to keep away from him, not wishing to call his wrath down upon her head again. As well, she knew in her heart that it was by far the wisest course for her. She must not become attracted to this man.

Placing aside the rolls of plans he held, Lord Stone gave her an enquiring look. 'Go on, you have my attention.'

With that rather unencouraging reply, Vanessa took a deep breath. Searching for the best way to ask for the dressmaker, she was startled when he laughed.

'Am I such a dragon that you must gather your courage to ask me for something? I'll wager it is not for yourself. What does my sister want?'

Vanessa cleared her throat, gave him a weak smile, then began. 'You may recall I mentioned Lady Juliana needed a number of things, especially some new clothes. Her present dresses simply do not fit her properly. She has just received the latest fashion journals from London — slow as they are in getting here — and I know it would please her vastly if you would tell her she might select a few new dresses.'

'Is that all you wanted? A few dresses for my sister? Seems like a reasonable request to me.'

'Well . . . we heard how difficult things are for you. I understand the crops do not look to be good in the south this year. There have been troubles here in the north as well.

Perhaps it is not best that the money be spent right now. I am aware you are a man who does not like to incur debts.'

He nodded as he studied the detail on the marquetry chest newly arrived that morning. It was an exquisite piece of workmanship, one he could now afford. For the moment. There were so many things he wished to buy for the house, and he had to carefully ration the funds, ordering piece by piece. He refused to go deeply in debt. An artist like the man who created this beautiful chest deserved to be paid, not put off again and again as he knew others often did.

Still, Juliana probably needed clothes, and she had been most forbearing with his refurbishing of the house. 'Why don't you contact the woman in York who does Mrs Hewit's clothes? She could select the fabrics you require, bring them out here, and sew them up. It shouldn't take overlong, should it? Or is there more afoot than a dress or two?'

Those dark blue eyes pierced what composure Vanessa retained when confronting him. She felt as though she was no better than a tongue-tied schoolgirl. 'Her riding dress is sadly worn. Several muslin morning dresses would not come amiss. None of her present evening dresses is fit for company, and her pelisses are a disgrace. If she is to go out painting as she wishes to do, she will need a better parasol. I would suggest one that could attach to a stand while she paints.' Vanessa thought of all the treatments Juliana had endured and murmured, 'After eliminating all those freckles, it would be a shame to risk them again.'

'And just how did you manage to do that?' His voice was a low purr, reminding Vanessa of the jungle cat she had seen at the Royal Menagerie in the Tower of London on her single visit to the attraction.

Thinking swiftly, she cautiously replied. 'Well, there hasn't been much sunshine for some time. When one is pent up in the house, one doesn't have the opportunity to freckle the skin, does one?' She slanted a hesitant smile at him, hoping she had deflected his interest in Juliana's skin.

'Hmm. I suspect you are right. If I thought for one minute you had been dabbling in those quack remedies I heard of while in London, I would wring that dainty neck of yours.' He took a step closer to her, inhaling her bluebell scent with pleasure.

'Then we can contact the dressmaker?' She sounded a wee bit breathless and hurried in her speech. To divert him from noticing the effect his closeness had upon her, she boldly proposed a shopping expedition. 'If we were in London now, we might shop at the Exeter 'Change for the little things she needs — gloves, shawls, parasols, and such items as are indispensable. Perhaps we might make an excursion to York?' The idea of traveling to the second-largest city in England brought a sparkle of enthusiasm to her eyes and a pretty rose flush to her cheeks. Her lips parted with a happy expectancy.

Nicholas ceased contemplating what it might be like to kiss those inviting lips so near to him, coldly shaken from his abstractions. 'No. There is no reason why you two cannot draw up a list of what is desired, then send it along to the dressmaker.' He was reluctant to frighten her with the stories that had reached his ears, tales of violence from the Luddites and the half-starved workers now barely subsisting on relief. York was a study in contrasts, the rising group of prosperous manufacturing families as well as the belligerent poor. He much preferred that both women remain safely at home. His own workers were living well enough, but with the Corn Laws in effect, he hated to think what it would be like if there wasn't a good harvest this year.

The light faded from her eyes as she bowed her head. 'You would not reconsider? A young girl looks forward to purchasing the little fripperies so dear to her heart with such anticipation. I fear Lady Juliana will be greatly disappointed.'

'She will have to survive, I fear,' was his wry rejoinder. As Vanessa began to turn away from him, her face an icy mask, he added, 'She is too young to go jaunting off to York, and I haven't the time to spare to attend her right now. She takes too much time from your repair as it is.'

Anger flared within her elegantly full bosom as Vanessa glanced up to meet his eyes, hers as frosty as a storm-tossed sea. In frigid tones to match her glare she replied, 'Lady Juliana has been so good as to spend hours in the saloon reading to me from a totally unexceptionable work by Scott. Far from keeping me from the needle, she has actually done the reverse. You do her ill to judge her so, milord. As to her being too young, she is of an age to marry. When she is properly dressed as befits a girl her age and position, you will make a discovery that I trust will not be unpleasant. You admitted to me some weeks ago that your little sister has grown up. She has grown up more than you realize.' Then a flash of daring came on her and she added, 'You cannot be so blind that you do not see how much she loves Sir Harry?'

'Harry?' Nicholas was thunderstruck. He shook his head. Somehow he couldn't picture Harry in the role of a brother-in-law. 'It's merely a childish case of calf love, nothing more.'

'How blind a man can be when he does not wish to see what is beneath his very nose.' Vanessa gave him another of her cool looks. 'She has stated that if she cannot have Sir Harry, she will have no one else. I believe she has made plans for that eventuality.' Prudently Vanessa omitted the form of those plans. 'If I may inquire, just who is the man you envisioned as a husband for your sister? She has mentioned no one else in my hearing.'

'He's a fine young man. I need time to prepare the thing,' Nicholas blustered. Really, this woman was getting on his nerves. He had years before he must deal with that particular subject . . . surely. Someone would come to mind . . . eventually. His eyes narrowed in sudden thought. 'You have a strange propensity for meddling in affairs that are none of your concern, Miss Tarleton. I suggest you confine your attention to the tapestry.'

Vanessa stiffened as though receiving a blow, then dipped a neat curtsy, fleeing the room before she could make a disastrous slip of the tongue. If she told that utterly insufferable man what she thought of him, he would send her off to the ends of the earth!

Storming up the stairs to her room, she rounded the corner to bump into Lady Juliana. Coming to an abrupt halt, she said somewhat breathlessly, 'You are to have a new wardrobe, Lady Juliana. Although we will not be permitted to travel to York, you may select from the swatches in the new copy of Ackermann's, and then send your order to the dressmaker in York, the same one, I suppose, who did the work before.' Vanessa took a calming breath, then gestured Lady Juliana to follow along to her room.

'How did this come about? I vow I relish the idea of new clothes, but I question whether Nicholas was willing.'

The door once closed behind them, Vanessa marched across to gaze out the window. 'I scarce have patience with that brother of yours. He said that you were too young to travel to York and that he did not have time to go with you. Mind you, he has a perfect right to say such a thing, but surely he knows your age. What think you of that!' By this moment Vanessa was fuming. She could not bear to repeat his charge of meddling. Turning to face Lady Juliana, she encountered a calm expression, almost a smile, on that young lady's face.

'No matter. We shall pore over the Ackermann's — best to do it before Pamela gets wind of the notion — and send off the order as quick as a cat can wash its ear.' Juliana placed a gentle hand on Vanessa's arm. 'I well and truly do not mind remaining at home. Although the woman followed dear Pamela's orders regarding my dresses, she was capable enough. We shall make do quite nicely. I am exceedingly pleased with the thought of new clothes. However did you manage it? I have hinted for ages.'

Vanessa sniffed. 'Apparently all you needed to do was come out and directly ask. Your brother is not a one for subtleties.'

Lady Juliana nodded, adding, 'That is true enough. He has listened to Pamela Hewit for two years and not caught on to half of what she says. Did you know Nicholas was in the Peninsula War as well as Harry? He was in Portugal when Papa and Damian were killed, and then had to come home. Though he saw only limited action, I often wonder if his hearing was impaired by the guns. If you know what I mean,' she added with a twinkle in her lovely eyes. 'There are times when I talk to him and the message appears to miss him completely.'

Not wishing to discuss her employer, aware she had already overstepped in that direction,

Vanessa simply nodded as she gathered up the most recent of the London fashion journals. The two sat down, heads together, and pored over the magazines, making notes, writing up a longer and longer list, until Vanessa threw up her hands in mock horror.

'I fear your brother will be furious if this list grows longer. I suggest we go back over and select the ones which will be most becoming.' Vanessa was alarmed. While appropriate, Juliana's choices were quite numerous. And Lord Stone would likely place the blame on Vanessa.

Juliana nodded. 'I feel positively wicked, and I find it a most deliciously pleasant sensation. The dressmaker will be surprised to see how thin I am become. And I have you to thank for this, dear Vanessa. Oh, do say you will permit me to call you by that name. And I insist you call me Juliana. You are like the sister I never had. Surely more than Pamela Hewit can ever be, even if Nicholas does marry her. He is as slow as a wet week when it comes to ladies, I fear.' Juliana bent over her list and missed the pink that crept into Vanessa's cheeks at that remark.

After a hasty scratching on the door, Katie entered, her eyes ablaze with excitement. 'If you please, milady,' nodding at Vanessa, 'would you come along with me? There's a surprise for you.'

Casting a questioning look at Juliana, Vanessa slowly rose from the bench where the two had sat while exploring the fashions from London. 'Must I?' With Katie's fervent nod, Vanessa turned to Juliana. 'Perhaps if you finish that list, and attach the swatches you prefer, we can send this off to York today.'

Juliana drew a line through one item, then declared, 'This will do. I trust the lady has the current journals, and I have noted the page for each fabric and drawing I like. I have a longing to see what this surprise is.' She winked at Katie and hurried out the door in the wake of the others.

Peverly stood before the entrance to the music room, nodding to the footman by him to open the tall oaken door as the women, led by Katie, drew near.

'Oh, my!' Vanessa rushed into the room as she saw her beautiful golden harp set close to the pianoforte. She reached up to run her hand over the graceful lines of the instrument, lightly touching the strings. 'I suspect it needs a good tuning.' She beamed at Juliana.

'Let me hand this order to Nicholas — yes, I would see his face for myself — and I will be back in a trice.'

Juliana bestowed a quiet thank-you to

Peverly and Katie for their help, then hurried from the room. The others discreetly closed Vanessa in the music room with her beloved harp while she made haste to check it over and begin to tune it. Drawing up a chair, she then tested the pedals used for changing octaves and attempted a simple melody.

Juliana returned, quietly taking her place at the pianoforte. She began a familiar tune, and Vanessa joined in the spirited rendition. Vanessa played well, her fingers slowly regaining agility with the strings. The duo performed a second piece, Vanessa's skill improving with each bar of music. The delicate rhythms floated across the room to where Nicholas stood listening in amazed silence.

At the conclusion of the music, he applauded. 'Well done. You make an excellent duet. Your talents will liven up our quiet Yorkshire evenings with a touch of elegance.'

The strings twanged as Vanessa's fingers faltered at the sound of his voice. 'Lord Stone!' All her previous anger toward the man flew away in her current charity with him. 'Oh, thank you so very much. How I have missed my music.' She stroked the beautiful instrument with a loving touch.

Nicholas stood quietly, a pensive hand rubbing his chin as he watched the golden head bent over the harp. She looked like an angel in her delicate frock of white and yellow stripes. Again that memory, elusive, haunting, rose up from the back of his mind. What was it about her that reminded him of something in the dim past? He glanced at Juliana as she silently slipped from the room.

'Is something the matter, milord?' Vanessa paused in her enjoyment to notice the abstraction that had fallen on her employer. 'Perhaps you have had a change of heart concerning the trip to York? Although your sister declares she does not mind in the least that she not be allowed to go.'

He decided he must take her into his confidence if he was to come out of this keeping her good esteem. Why it should be desirable to curry the favor of a woman in his employ didn't occur to him. He briefly explained the often-dangerous state of the countryside, ending on a placatory note. 'You see, it is not that I wish to deny her a treat, rather postpone it until she can be properly attended on the journey.'

Recalling that she had been allowed to pass through that very countryside escorted by no more than a groom and coachman, Vanessa held her tongue. Her status as a servant differed greatly from that of the only daughter of the house. 'I see. Your concern for your

186

sister does you credit. Perhaps once she acquires her new clothes she might entertain a few friends here? Sir Harry and his sister, Louisa, could be two. Surely you can think of others?'

'I could ask Mrs Hewit. I have been absent for most of the recent years, and since my return, I have found myself well nigh buried here, making improvements, refurbishing . . . ' He again rubbed at his chin, frowning at the thought that he had cut off his sister from company her own age by his concentration on the work at hand.

'Is Miss Featherston near Lady Juliana in age?'

'Gads, no! She must be over eighteen at least, if not older.' He wished he knew why the steady gaze of this young woman could disconcert him to such degree. He felt as though he was being raked over the coals.

'I see. The same age, then. Just different interests?' She could have shaken him for not remembering his young sister's age.

'But Juliana can't be that old . . . can she?' His look of confusion was amusing.

'I declare, you men are all of a kind. You pay more attention to installing that . . . that fire engine than to your little sister.' Vanessa's golden curls trembled as she tilted her head in mock dismay.

Hoping to divert what he was certain could be a scold, though why he should allow this woman to behave in such manner he was loath to explore, he inquired, 'Did you get out to see the fire engine?'

His diversion was successful. Vanessa followed his lead with surprising eagerness. 'I confess I have wanted to see it. There simply hasn't been time.'

His eyes twinkled down at her with a disconcerting fire lurking in them. 'Yes, well, I have heard you and my sister retreat to her room for an hour or so of reading each day. Mayhap if you did without that, you would have time to spare?'

Desiring the subject be changed again as quickly as possible, Vanessa nodded without comment, instead suggesting, 'Suppose I remedy it now. I should like to see your fire engine, milord. I have had a fear of fire since trapped by a blaze while away at school.'

Arrested by the haunting of dread in her eyes, he offered his arm. 'I hope you suffered no serious injury!' At the negative shake of her head, he added, 'We will enjoy another concert this evening if you are willing. Best to see the engine now.'

Urging him to the door lest he return to other, less desirable subjects, she agreed. Vanessa hoped he did not expect a professional performance this evening. While she was aware she was far better than most, he made her nervous, and that did not bode well. 'We shall do our best for you later. Let us inspect this engine to extinguish fires, if you please. That is, if you have time to show me. I realize you are a busy man, milord.'

She placed a slim, dainty hand on the smooth fabric of his coat, noting the firm muscles concealed beneath. They left the room with an unusual degree of amiability between them. As they walked down the stairs and out toward the stables, where the fire engine was housed, Vanessa felt a kindling of hope within.

She was well aware she had no call to claim his attention as her escort. She could quite easily find the dratted fire engine if left to her own devices. It did serve dual purposes, however. She got him off the subject of Juliana for the moment, and as well, removed the matter of her meddling from his mind — she hoped. Indeed, she held a delicious feeling she was getting around the man very nicely.

★   ★   ★

The size of the small group who assembled in the music room after dinner did not reassure

Vanessa. She was well aware that no matter the size of the crowd, if Lord Stone was included, she would be nervous.

Yet when her fingers plucked the strings of her golden harp in a familiar melody, the room faded away and she was once again at Blackwood Hall. How often she had played for her family. Even Aunt Agatha had remained silent during the music. Colin had been her most devoted listener, sometimes singing along with a well-known tune. How she missed him. Now her mother lived with Agatha. Colin was dead, her father as well. The family unit existed no longer.

The touch of the harp against her shoulder brought her back to the present. Her eyes sought the lean figure of Lord Stone. How very kind of him to send for her beloved instrument. Though he had his blind spot with Juliana, and must needs turn to Pamela Hewit for her money, there was an innate goodness in him. It would be impossible to thank him enough for reuniting her with her harp.

She was quite certain the warm glow in her heart was only gratitude.

9

'Eeek!' A screech loud enough to rouse the very dead sounded with great clarity from Vanessa's room.

Startled from a sound sleep, Vanessa abruptly sat up, threw the covers back, then slid from her comfortable bed. 'What is it?' Across the room a horrified Katie stood frozen, pointing at the floor.

'For heaven's sake, Katie, it is only a mouse, a very small mouse. Do not tell me you fear even such a little one?' Vanessa stood, her sheer lace-trimmed blue night-gown clutched to her in the chill of the room, laughing at the mortified Katie. 'I do believe Hercules has made me an offering in appreciation for taking him in.' Vanessa bent to pat a smug Hercules on the head. 'Good cat.'

The door, which had been ajar, was flung open, and Lord Stone dashed into the room. 'What happened? Are you all right, Miss Tarleton?' He stopped suddenly, realizing that Vanessa seemed in no harm, indeed had been laughing, and no apparent crisis was at hand. Behind him a curious Juliana peeped into the

191

room, her lace nightcap askew, wrapper untidily thrown over her shoulders.

Terribly aware of her state of undress, Vanessa shrank back against one of the bed posts, hoping the volume of blue fabric that draped from it would blend with her nightgown and shield her from Lord Stone's sharp eyes.

'There is nothing amiss,' she replied, sounding far more composed than she actually was. 'Hercules brought me an offering that Katie found exceptional.'

By now Katie had recovered her wits sufficiently to hasten to her mistress's side with an enveloping wrapper of peach satin. 'It was a mouse, milord.'

Nicholas, having caught an enticing glimpse of the slim figure partially revealed through the sheer blue silk, backed toward the door, bumping into Juliana as he did. 'I'm surprised at you, Katie. A mouse?' His eyes sparkled with appreciation at the delightful scene that met his eyes. Juliana stepped to one side, also backing out the door, a wary eye on the tiny furred object on the floor near Hercules.

'It's that sorry I am, milord, waking everyone up. I wasn't expectin' to find a dead animal at my feet when I went to open the draperies for Miss Tarleton.' Red-faced and quite obvious in her desire to sink through the floor, Katie half-hid behind her mistress.

Nicholas found his gaze caught with Vanessa's before she glanced toward the floor in embarrassment.

He couldn't hide the amusement he felt. 'Dispose of the mouse and help your mistress to dress. It is chilly in here. No fire, Katie?'

Rushing to the defense of her maid, Vanessa quickly interposed, 'I like my window open at night as long as I have a lovely down comforter to snuggle beneath, milord. Usually Katie starts a fire going after she closes the window.'

A vision of Miss Tarleton, in that sheer-blue silk snuggled in her bed, shimmered before him until he recalled he was a gentleman and ought not to be in here at this moment. 'Juliana, let us retire to our rooms. I intend to finish dressing, and I would imagine you will fall back to sleep.' He took Juliana firmly by the arm, leading her from the room, shutting the door behind them. He was thankful the servants had been occupied in other parts of the house at this hour, and no one was witness to the event.

Although Vanessa had avoided meeting his eyes after that one searing glance, she could list his attire in vivid detail. His cambric shirt was open at the neck, much like the first time she had seen him. She had noticed a bit of dark hair peeping from the opening. Had her fingers really wanted to explore, touch? Immaculate nankeen breeches met white silk stockings, both covering a muscular form that did them proud. He had been in his stocking feet, accounting for the silence of his approach. But what must he think of her in her sheer blue gown, so unlike the prim muslin worn by most women? Hers was not a practical garment in the least.

Thank heaven Juliana no longer needed the nightly herbal treatment that imparted a ghostly green tinge to her face. Nicholas would have been far less sanguine had he seen *that*!

'I might as well get dressed, Katie. I am quite awake at this point.' Vanessa could feel the heat in her cheeks slowly fading as Katie assisted her into her stays and petticoat, then her dress. The multicolored mosaic design printed on white cambric was a perfect choice for her excursion in the dogcart with Juliana today.

After Katie had arranged Vanessa's hair in a pleasing combination of soft curls at the sides and a neat coil on the crown of her head, Vanessa left her room. The hall was empty and utterly silent as she walked toward the stairs. In the breakfast room she encountered Lord Stone, intent on his morning meal. She noted the heaped-up plate before she made her own choices. The silence was uncomfortable.

'Good morning, milord.' How grateful she was that years of enduring her mother and Aunt Agatha helped her to conceal her inner feelings.

Marveling at the composure of the young woman who had been so very intruded upon earlier, Nicholas softly answered her, 'You make a good start for the day, I see.' He nodded at the equally heaped-up plate Vanessa placed on the table.

A rueful grin curved her lips. 'I do like my breakfast, I'll confess.'

Nicholas replied, 'Yet you remain slim, while Juliana blossoms forth in unwanted pounds.'

Vanessa shrugged the shoulders so neatly covered by the delicate cambric dress. 'I have always been thin. I believe some people are more disposed to weight than others. My mother also eats a hearty meal and ever remains slender. Juliana will slim down, you will see.'

He wanted to explore her abilities. What else might be concealed beneath that lovely exterior? 'I enjoyed the concert you two presented last evening. You are a very talented woman — tapestry-mending, harp-playing, and today you go painting.'

'About my harp, milord . . . I would pay for the transporting of it. It seems a very great deal for you to do for someone in your temporary employ.' She crumbled a bit of muffin on her plate as she bravely met his gaze.

'Actually it was not all that costly. It came by carrier wagon and the expense was minimal. Forget it, please. It was worth it to see Juliana so entertained. Until you came I had not realized how lonely she must be here. We have few close neighbors, I'm sorry to say. Raising sheep requires extensive land.'

'Surely there must be others within riding distance besides Mrs Hewit and Sir Harry?' Vanessa inserted the question between the last bite of her muffin and a final sip of coffee. It was pleasant eating breakfast with Lord Stone, once the initial discomfiture passed.

'I have been away too long, then too deeply absorbed in the house. Perhaps I could have Millbank investigate.'

As she watched him leave the room, following his elegant bow, she wagered Mrs Hewit would gladly offer to hostess a gathering, and she would know the people to invite, as well. That was one thought Vanessa refused to pass along.

As she left the breakfast room she observed another of the little things about the house which had disturbed her over the weeks. The chandeliers badly needed dusting. Juliana was too accustomed to having her brother handle everything to assume leadership about the house. Poor lamb had had no woman to show her what to do or how to go about it. Resolved to make a gentle hint to the young lady later, Vanessa went to the housekeeper's domain in the stillroom to compliment her on the breakfast, and perhaps find out if more help was needed to maintain the house, though it was hard to imagine with all the servants employed by the earl.

'That was an excellent breakfast, Mrs Murdoch. Not every housekeeper manages to maintain the food at such a nice temperature.'

A black look as suspicious as Vanessa had ever had directed at her came from beneath dark, thick brows. Plump hands were folded across the expanse of rusty black bombazine as Mrs Murdoch nodded politely, the white ruffle of her starched cap moving not at all. 'Thank you.'

How best to approach the matter, which was really none of Vanessa's affair? She could claim an interest in Juliana's home. Or perhaps she could offer sympathy to the housekeeper, who was getting along in years.

In reality it was her cursed curiosity that compelled Vanessa to step beyond propriety again. Yorkshire — or was it Stone's Court? — exerted a peculiar effect on her.

'Ah, I was wondering if you are short of staff?' Once asked, the question was regretted. Vanessa felt the rising anger of the other woman with acute discomfort.

The figure before her had stiffened noticeably. 'You have cause for complaint? Katie is a bit forward, miss, but I can't be getting anyone else.' The implication was that Vanessa didn't deserve that much.

'Katie is just fine, Mrs Murdoch.' Vanessa was uneasy at the look from those eyes, yet she persisted. 'This is such a large house to manage, you must get very tired indeed. Trying to cope with the dust from the renovations must drive you to distraction. I'm certain if you sought Lady Juliana's ear, she would do her utmost to see that you acquire more help. Another maid or a candle boy, perhaps?'

'I resent the implication that this house is kept in any but top condition, Miss Tarleton. His lordship has never complained.' The housekeeper made a dismissing gesture, then turned her back on Vanessa. But not before Vanessa caught the look of intense dislike that sat on that plump face.

Disturbed by the encounter, Vanessa went around the servants' area, noting the number who were occupied at the morning tasks. The stillroom maid was busy doing up the breakfast dishes, while the scullery maid worked feverishly at scrubbing pots and pans. In the kitchen Cook instructed the kitchen maid in the making of a special sauce for luncheon. Going outdoors, first crossing to the laundry rooms, Vanessa noted that this area was more neatly kept, but not up to the standard maintained by Mrs Danvers at Blackwood Hall.

Clearly things were not as they could be here, and these quarters were within the province of Mrs Murdoch. The laundry maid looked harassed, with far more to do than one person should have to manage. Only in the dairy did Vanessa see that all was as it ought to be. In one tiny room she discovered the candle boy hard at work trimming the wicks of the lamps and filling those for the main rooms with colsa oil.

A brief conversation with him revealed a puzzling thing. Normally the candle boys got to keep the candle stubs as a perquisite, selling them to the local grocer for a few shillings. Here, all stubs were handed to the housekeeper.

When Vanessa returned to the house, a

discreetly placed question to Cook got the reply that all the bones, drippings, and other fat also went to the housekeeper, instead of to the cook, as had been the custom at Blackwood Hall. A very thoughtful Vanessa slowly walked up to her room.

Moments later Juliana rapped on the door and burst in gleefully announcing, 'Nicholas has the dogcart ordered for us and it is a gorgeous day out. Are you ready to depart? I had my paints and paper sent down. Vanessa?'

'Oh, sorry. Woolgathering, I fear. All I need is my parasol.' Gathering this item from the bed, along with a sketchpad and a pencil, which she dropped into her reticule, Vanessa followed Juliana out to the stableyard, where a pretty brown pony was hitched to a dogcart.

Lord Stone rounded the corner of the stable block as the young women made to enter the cart. A groom handed Juliana up on the driver's side, while Nicholas quickly walked to Vanessa and offered his hand.

'Allow me, Miss Tarleton.' He took her hand, noting how very soft and fine-boned it was as he assisted her up to her seat. 'I hope you two will have a productive day. Juliana told me you have been nose-to-the-grindstone these past weeks. It is time you took a break.'

His hand held hers longer than she deemed

proper, yet Vanessa made no move to draw it away. It felt warm and secure and there was a tingling all the way up her arm, which was most delightful.

Smiling her pleasure down at him from her perch on the charming Prussian-blue cart trimmed in bright yellow, she nodded, finding her voice lost somewhere at the moment.

'I have had another table set up in the saloon, as the men are removing the other tapestries from the room where they hang. I want to get the painting completed and the floors redone in there. This is an ideal time.'

'That is an excellent idea, milord.' Her voice was a dulcet sound on the morning air. Reluctantly she gave a tiny tug at her hand, thinking he was no more pleased to let it go than she was to have it back.

A groom hopped up to the back of the cart before they left. She didn't turn to look again at Lord Stone as Juliana set off from the stable at a smart clip, though somehow Vanessa had the feeling they were being watched. As they turned the corner, she peeked around the brim of her bonnet, catching a glimpse of Millbank with the earl, walking toward the house.

'I have been thinking.' Lady Juliana was no novice at handling the ribbons, and turned her head to glance at Vanessa as they bowled along the neatly graveled road.

'And?' prompted Vanessa.

'Now that Louisa is to marry, well, Harry will no longer feel he must look after her. He will be free to marry as well. He may begin looking for a wife in earnest. He needs an heir, you know.'

'So I gather. That does not mean he will look far afield, Juliana.' Vanessa attempted to sound reassuring.

'If he could but see!' Juliana's vexed cry echoed the thought Vanessa had had at dinner some time go.

'Well, he will need to be shown, then, won't he?' It was all well and good to seem confident, but how did you go about making a blind man see?

'I have given up on him, you know. Completely. Totally. When I next see that man I will treat him like he has treated me all these years, a mere insignificant nothing!' Juliana nodded her head for emphasis. 'To think how I mooned over him, dreamed of him for so long. What an utter waste of time that was.'

Juliana lapsed into silence as the pony trotted along the country lane. It was a fine morning. Fallow deer grazed beneath the oaks, looking up with placid eyes at the dogcart as it went merrily past. After the abundance of rain, the grounds were deep green and lush with growth.

Juliana selected a spot some distance from the house on a rise of land after seeing a smattering of rich golden globeflowers in bloom. The pony was tied to the branch of an oak, not seeming to mind in the least being left in the care of the young groom.

For a while Vanessa was content to sketch, not the flowers, but the tranquil scene. It wasn't long before she grew slightly bored with sketching and decided to ramble about. Juliana discovered a cluster of bright red rough poppies and delightedly set to putting them on paper.

There were odd formations on the lower part of the hill, rather like barrows. Vanessa walked quickly to the foot of the rise, wondering if they could possibly be the graves of longdead Celts. Poking her foot absently at the side of one, she noted something odd. Curious, and more than a little interested, she knelt, unmindful of what Katie would say when she saw the soiled printed cambric. A nearby stick offered a tool, and Vanessa began to dig in earnest.

The sun was high overhead and she could feel drops of perspiration running down her forehead. Yet she was reluctant to give it up. Finally, just as she was about to acknowledge defeat, she caught sight of a glitter of metal. Hastily digging at the spot, she unearthed a small object that appeared to be a pin of some sort.

Scrambling up the bank, she ran toward Juliana, now on the distant side of the site, engrossed in painting a delicate branch of wood vetch. As she neared Juliana, Vanessa observed Sir Harry mounted on a fine chestnut mare, riding briskly in their direction.

'Hallo! Nicholas said I might find you out here. Painting wildflowers today? That's a welcome change from watching the rain fall, I daresay.' Sir Harry was his customary offhand self.

Juliana had been quite serious when she announced her intention to treat Sir Harry with indifference. Not bothering even to look up from her painting, she absently replied, 'Oh, hullo, Harry. Lovely out, isn't it?'

Sir Harry frowned at her, then slid from his horse, tying him to the same tree where the patient pony stood in the shade. He nodded to the groom, who smiled his assent in keeping an eye on the bit of prime blood. 'I thought to arrive in time to join you for your picnic. Your cook always does well at those.'

Waving a casual paintbrush in the direction of the cart, Juliana mumbled, 'It must be in there somewhere. I imagine the wine ought to be well-cooled, since Vanessa put it in the stream.' Instead of her usual breathless greeting, she totally ignored Sir Harry, and he looked baffled.

'I say, there isn't something amiss, is there?'

Deciding to step in before something spoiled the way Sir Harry was beginning to wake up, Vanessa held out her hand. 'See what I have found, will you? Lord Stone mentioned to me that you were interested in antiquities. Can you tell me anything about this little fellow? It looks like a dragon to me.'

Sir Harry took another look at the cool and quite slender-appearing Juliana in her pretty dress, then studied the little pin Vanessa offered to him. He picked it up, turning it this way and that before making his admittedly hesitant pronouncement. 'I do believe it is from the Late Celtic period. I have a small pin of similar workmanship, round and intricately cut. It isn't so curiously interesting as this, however. Good find, Miss Tarleton.'

Juliana sauntered over to see what was causing the discussion, and exclaimed with delight at the little dragon, as Vanessa decided to call it. 'You mean to say you have found such things as these and never told me? But how fascinating!'

Exceedingly pleased at this turnabout, Sir Harry preened slightly, then offered his arm to the impressed Juliana. 'You see,' he began, 'I discovered a peculiar object, small, bronze, and formed like a kind of mask. That was all it took to rouse interest and set me to digging on the barrows on our property.'

While setting out the more-than-ample lunch Cook had sent along with them, Vanessa smiled to herself at the absorption between Sir Harry and Juliana. She asked all manner of intelligent questions and he eagerly answered with various explanations and descriptions.

Once Vanessa had placed the picnic lunch on a checkered cloth spread out beneath one of the massive oaks, she called the two. They came with great reluctance.

'Harry has such a collection of antiquities! Can you imagine I have never heard of it? I am vastly disappointed, Harry. I should like above all things to see it.' She added coolly, with proper deference, 'If I might?' How unlike the brotherly treatment Sir Harry had received before!

Politely nodding, his estimation of Juliana rising a good many notches, he answered quickly, 'Of course, Juliana. Anytime at all. Truly, I had no idea you would be interested.' He munched on a piece of cold chicken, then commented, 'You seem quite different today, Juliana. Can't think what it is, though.'

Vanessa made an effort to study a piece of cheese as though it contained the wisdom of the ages, while Juliana flicked a casual glance at Sir Harry. 'Fancy that, would you? I don't feel any different.'

Poor Harry looked more than a little confused at the offhand treatment from someone who usually gave him her breathless attention. He frowned again, then concentrated on his lunch and the cool, delicate wine. An occasional glance at Juliana, with such a puzzled expression on his face, nearly sent Vanessa into whoops. She couldn't recall when she had been so diverted.

'Perhaps there might be something else in the barrow, Juliana. Why not get Sir Harry to assist you? After all, one does not have the advantage of an expert at hand every day, you know?' Somehow Vanessa managed to keep a straight face as Juliana accepted a hand up from Harry with an exceedingly indifferent air, albeit well-mannered, then walked at his side as he happily explained to her what might be found.

Without planning it, Juliana appeared to have found the solution to capturing Sir Harry. Now, if it could be sustained for some time, there might be a chance that Sir Harry would wake up to find himself betrothed to Juliana.

While the others dug around at the barrow, Vanessa gathered the remains of the picnic lunch together to stow away in the dogcart. The large underboot originally used to carry dogs on a shooting expedition worked admirably for painting supplies and a picnic. Vanessa leaned against the racy little two-wheeled vehicle to watch the scene below.

Sir Harry had removed his coat. Juliana stood by with her parasol shading both of them while Sir Harry used a stout stick to dig further into the barrow. As Vanessa gazed on, Sir Harry bent to pick up a small object, which Juliana exclaimed over with ladylike enthusiasm.

Just as Vanessa was trying to decide whether to join them or not, Juliana waved and then motioned for Vanessa to come down. Unfurling her own parasol against the warmth of the day, Vanessa leisurely sauntered down the hill until she came to where the two stood.

Sir Harry picked up four more tiny objects to place in Juliana's hand. 'See what we have found, Vanessa. Harry says these are jet beads.' She bent to study the beads, then handed her parasol to Vanessa. 'If you would hold this for me, I could brush off the dirt for a better look.'

Sir Harry straightened up to offer several more beads to the collection, then watched as Juliana carefully removed the dirt from each piece of jet. 'You know, I daresay we have almost enough of those beads for a necklace,' he commented. 'That is what they were originally. There may be more beads in here.' He bent to the hot work with more enthusiasm than Vanessa could have managed.

When Juliana retrieved her parasol, Vanessa sat down on the grassy bank to continue her watch. The other two were lost in the excitement of the exploration of the dig. How pleasing to see Juliana so animated — in her newly remote manner — with an interest she might share with Sir Harry. The mound of dusty black beads, varying slightly in size, grew little by little.

'I believe there now *are* sufficient to make myself a necklace!' Juliana exclaimed with delight.

Sir Harry gave her a shocked look. 'Never say you intend to wear those beads.'

'What else would I do with them?' Juliana placed the beads on the pristine white handkerchief Sir Harry spread out for her on the ground, then began to clean them more carefully.

'Why, they ought to be preserved.' He looked as though he couldn't understand anyone desiring to *use* a thing rather than just *look* at it.

'Why?' Juliana's puzzlement was sincere. 'I don't have a collection. I intend to take great care of them, you know. I just want to wear them. I haven't had many pretty things like these.' Her simple statement earned a sharp look from Vanessa as well as a perplexed glance from Sir Harry.

Thinking over the past weeks, Vanessa could not recall so much as a cameo brooch or a necklace of pearls adorning Juliana's person. Her gaze briefly met Sir Harry's above Juliana's bent head.

Juliana raised her head to see the confusion of the other two. 'Not that I mind. After all, where would I wear such things? Before Nicholas came home, Papa was too busy, and rarely here. I suspect he sold all of Mama's jewelry. Damian barely said hello to me. I guess he still considered me a nursery brat. And since Nicholas returned, he has been occupied with restoring the house and lands. Not that it wasn't exceedingly necessary, you know. Still, I would like to have something pretty.'

Caressing the largest bead with a delicate touch, she then gathered them up with a decisive air. 'I shall wear them, and no one will stop me.' Juliana sat down on the bank, her appealing blue eyes gazing first to Vanessa, then to Sir Harry, assessing each face for a reaction.

'I, for one, think it a splendid notion,' declared Vanessa. 'What better way to preserve them than to wear them around that pretty neck of yours? They couldn't ask for a softer spot, could they?' She slanted a smile at the two, who looked at each other in wary consideration. Speaking to the air in general, Vanessa added, 'I believe I shall go over to the stream. Small as it is, I can wash the dirt from my dragon.'

'Do that, Miss Tarleton,' Sir Harry replied in a vague manner quite unlike his usual decisive speech. As she slowly moved from hearing range, she heard Sir Harry say to Juliana, 'You have had a rotten time of it, haven't you? I hadn't realized.'

Looking back once or twice, Vanessa could see the others slowly trail in her path, talking quietly as they came, absorbed in a voyage of discovery. While there might be some distance to go, Sir Harry appeared to be waking up to the little beauty close to home.

Delight in the charming little dragon was heightened as Vanessa discovered the rich patina age gave to the bronze. The more she rubbed the metal, the more it gleamed. The trio chatted comfortably as they returned to the dogcart and Sir Harry's patiently waiting chestnut mare. The young groom assisted them all before they left the pleasant picnic spot. The trip home was accompanied by a great deal of conversation.

When they alighted from the dogcart, Juliana graciously extended her hand to Sir Harry. 'I am excessively pleased you came along when you did. I vow this jet necklace will be absolutely charming with my new dresses. I do hope I may see your collection before too long. It sounds fascinating.' She twirled her parasol in a delightful, flirtatious manner, then nodded an entrancing farewell. A stunned Sir Harry was left standing by the dogcart, mouth agape, while holding the handkerchief full of beads in one hand.

Vanessa could only marvel at the new Juliana who had suddenly emerged from a well-wrapped cocoon. Giving up on Sir Harry had turned out to be the best thing possible. Vanessa had caught the expression on his face as he mounted his horse, then trotted off in complete abstraction. Poor man didn't know what had hit him.

First instructing a groom to convey the painting materials to the house, Vanessa fingered the little dragon pin that had nestled safely in her hand during the ride home. She had found it on Leighton property. By rights it belonged to the earl. With reluctant feet, she sought to find Lord Stone somewhere in the house to offer her little dragon pin to him. It would have been nice to keep it as a memento of her time here, she thought wistfully.

Peverly gave her the directions to the earl's whereabouts. She slowly walked down the long corridor containing the antiquities from Rome and Greece. At the end of the passage she found Lord Stone supervising the placement of a painting in his newly completed library.

The room was done in a combination of ivory ceiling and trim with deep blue and gold paper hung on the walls. An ivory Aubusson with designs in deep blue covered most of the floor. Leather-bound volumes tooled in gold were already placed on the ivory-painted shelves. Several elegant tables sat next to comfortable-looking chairs.

'This is a warm, friendly room,' she commented while watching the workman climb down the ladder, then step away so the earl could verify the placement. It was the second time he had hung the heavy painting of the earl's grandfather, the first time being off-center. He devoutly hoped the thing was at last where it belonged.

'Fine, fine, Higgens. You may go.' Nicholas turned to face Vanessa. 'How was your day?' He placed one booted foot on the fender before the fireplace as he leaned an arm on the marble fireplace mantel. He looked elegantly casual and totally the lord of the manor.

'I believe Lady Juliana did quite well with her paintings. I made an interesting find I wish to show you.' She held out the little dragon. 'Since I found it on your land, naturally I offer it to you. Sir Harry came along just before lunch — I believe you told him where we were to be — and he was most helpful. He thinks it to be a fine piece of Late Celtic work.' She added in a polite voice, 'I imagine you would like to add it to your collection, or if you don't have such a thing, begin one?'

Nicholas accepted the trinket, still warm from her hand. The curiously shaped dragon reminded him a little of a sea horse he had seen at the shore one summer long ago. Not wishing to contradict such a charming lady, he nodded. 'A dragon, to be sure. No, I have no plans to begin a collection of antiquities. Sir Harry does it for all of us, I think. Keep it, if you wish.'

He knew full well he must turn his

attentions to Mrs Hewit now that news of the poor crop expectations had reached him. Her money would be needed to fulfill his plans for Stone's Court. The knowledge didn't cheer him. Something about the slim, attractive woman standing at his side drew him to her. She appealed to him in so many ways. Yet he had made his vow to restore his home. He could not allow himself to be deflected from his duty, as he saw it.

'Thank you, milord. I shall treasure it.' Her delighted smile enchanted him.

10

Juliana paced back and forth by the tall windows in the saloon where Vanessa worked diligently at the repair. It seemed to her that Juliana had been doing quite of bit of this sort of thing lately.

'What shall I do? The dressmaker is to come today with all the fabrics and patterns. But Sir Harry wants me to visit Eastthorpe Hall. My strong inclination is to cry off. What do you advise?' Juliana paused, hands clasped together before her. Her usually sunny face was marred by a frustrated expression. The recurring desire to adore Sir Harry warred with her new policy of indifference.

Compressing her lips against a desire to laugh, Vanessa struggled to maintain a calm facade. 'Why, go on as you have begun, my dear. Let him wait. Send a groom with a note informing him something has come up and you cannot visit. Offer the prospect of a future visit if you like.'

'I cannot believe this. All these years I have hoped, yearned. Once I decide to forget him, here he is. I declare, it is the outside of enough.' Juliana looked to where Vanessa

216

perched on her chair, suppressing a grin, then convulsed into giggles. 'It *is* rather amusing, is it not? Tell me, dear Vanessa, is there anything in your book of herbs that will ease the pain I feel when I must be near the man? Anyone who has been in love knows the distress from caring where it is not returned.'

'Alas, there are no herbs to cure love, my dear. Only time can do that — but it may not be necessary, you know. You might learn to take over the reins of the household. Who knows, it could be useful one day.' Vanessa carefully inquired, 'Have you had any success with Mrs Murdoch today? I tried to sympathize with her, but it appeared to make her angry instead.'

'Do not get carried away. Harry may be befuddled at the moment, but I cannot believe it will continue. It is simply the novelty of it all. He has looked at me and discovered *not* what he expected to find.' Glancing toward the doorway, she shook her head. 'As to Mrs Murdoch — she simply tells me not to worry and to leave everything to her. She treats me like a child. But it was ever so, you know. Never since she came has she encouraged my interest in the house. By the by, Katie told me we are out of some of the herbal remedies. She promised to get some of the ingredients in the village when she goes in later today. Could you mix them up tomorrow?'

'I do not see why not. Your brother does not suspect, does he?'

'What is it I do not suspect?' Lord Stone entered the room in long strides, pausing to look over his sister before turning toward Vanessa. 'Explain, Miss Tarleton.'

Thinking fast and furious, Vanessa tried in vain to grasp something she could repeat to him. Nothing came to mind, unfortunately.

Juliana interrupted, pleasantly inserting, 'We were discussing Mrs Murdoch, Nicholas. I have tried, as you so pointedly suggested, to take a more active part in the household affairs, and Mrs Murdoch just pats me on the head, telling me not to worry about a thing, as though I am a silly child.' She stamped a dainty slippered foot, pouting adorably as she peered up at her brother.

'Oh, is that what is going on?' Nicholas smiled fondly before turning a curious look toward Vanessa, who appeared a portrait of innocence.

'Miss Tarleton is advising me on how to manage a household. Do you know, Nicholas, she worked with their steward to supervise the entire estate. She paid tradesmen, helped keep the books, even learned about cooking! It seemed there was nothing she did not learn to turn her hand to doing. I believe I shall take the dogcart out to visit the tenants as Miss Tarleton did. She used her herbs to treat them too.'

That was quite the wrong thing to say. A dark look crossed his face. 'I believe I told you to leave your herb quacking behind you. There are enough problems today without your adding to them.'

At once becoming serious, Juliana placed a hand gently on his arm. 'Tell me what is going on . . . please? How can I begin to handle the trials of running a household if I am always kept under wraps? I know you mean for the best, but I cannot be protected forever.'

The earnestly spoken words affected him deeply. Nicholas studied his little sister, noticing how lovely she appeared in her simple white dress. Without the flounces and ruffles, she seemed slimmer and appealing. Soft golden-brown curls tumbled about her face that peered up at him so trustingly. He sighed, then spoke in simple terms he hoped she would comprehend. 'The Luddites have been at it again, smashing, destroying. As well, I have had word that the harvest looks to be a bad one. The problem extends all over the country. There has been too much rain this year. Industries may be flourishing, but with the Corn Laws in effect, the price of wheat is soaring beyond sight. With no cheap food entering the country, the poor will starve. It is not a good year for us either. I must find some means of continuing. Oh,' he reassured Juliana at seeing her alarm, 'we need not fear for our household. But my plans for improving the house are in jeopardy.'

Nodding in agreement with his statement, Vanessa quietly added, 'It is difficult for people to reconcile their lack of food with the stories they hear, much magnified I suppose, from Carlton House. If the up-coming fête the Prince Regent plans is remotely like the dinner following his appointment to the Regency, it would be better were it kept a secret. I vow, someone must lie awake at night to dream up such elaborate ways to spend money.'

'You object to spending money, Miss Tarleton? In my experience all women seem to be adept at such things.' Nicholas arched an expressive brow as he considered the calm face above the worktable.

Looking down at the needle poised above the exquisite tapestry, she studied the elegant lady whose skirt she was mending. 'It is all well and good to spend money if the need is there or if you have sufficient. It is another matter to go into debt — coping with insufficient funds, turning to the cent-per-centers as a last resort. When I was in London for my Season, I observed that a great many of the families were desperately presenting a face to the world that had little to sustain it. I believe I am better off than they, even if I have to work for my living. At least it is an honest one.' As her attractive voice ended her comments, an engaging chuckle slipped out nearly unheard.

Admiring the soft-spoken woman who had endured who-knew-what before she came here, Nicholas nodded. 'Well said. Perhaps it is a good thing you instruct my little sister in the ways of domestic management. Mrs Hewit volunteered, but something always seems to interfere.'

Juliana and Vanessa exchanged glances that spoke volumes regarding that particular woman's ability when it came to domestic management. Or were her frequent entreaties to Nicholas to assist her with her problems all a hum? Vanessa recalled one of Mr Hunt's remarks. He had said that one of the most dangerous things a single man could do was dry a widow's tears. Yet she realized Nicholas wanted desperately to restore his home to the condition it had been in years ago. He considered it his duty, and rightly so. Vanessa admired his resolution and determination. Marrying Mrs Hewit undoubtedly would be the answer, a very simple answer. He would get more land, a good deal of wealth, and a pretty wife in the bargain. It was an ideal solution. Why, then, did Vanessa have so little liking for the scheme?

'How do you feel about it, Miss Tarleton?' Lord Stone's deep voice broke in on her gloomy reflections.

'Sorry. I'm afraid I was woolgathering.' Vanessa looked in question, first at Lord Stone, then at Juliana.

'She does that a lot, Nicholas.' Juliana giggled at her friend who looked so perplexed. 'I thought only little old ladies did such things.' Her teasing was meant in a kindly way, but it cut Vanessa, reminding her that her future was likely to be just such a thing. Visions of herself in a black lace cap sitting by a window in some attic sewing endless garments flashed before her eyes.

'Juliana thinks it would be a nice idea to have a few guests over now that the music room has been restored. A bit of music and a dance, some good conversation with friends. Millbank would be there as well,' he offered, believing to entice her in that manner. He had observed how his steward made frequent efforts to be in the vicinity of the saloon, where Miss Tarleton worked at her needle.

Lowering her eyes once more as she drew out the needle from the tapestry, Vanessa nodded. 'It sounds lovely. The dressmaker can start with something suitable for the occasion so it will be a sort of come-out for Juliana as well as the room decor. Perhaps you have noticed what looks your sister is in lately?'

'Yes, I have, rather. It must be owing to the trips to paint wildflowers, all the fresh air. Though it seems you do not eat as much. You appear thinner.'

Juliana flushed under his appraising look. Her reply was made with more haste then consideration. 'Miss Tarleton has been so good as to advise me how to go on. Thanks to her, I have acquired a finer figure. I do appreciate the new dresses, Nicholas. You are the dearest of brothers. But it is not too much with conditions what they are?'

'Um . . . don't refine upon it. I can make economies elsewhere. Would you be so kind as to arrange for luncheon to be served soon?' He waited until his sister had left the room before turning back to Vanessa. 'Why is it my instincts tell me there is something afoot here? When I came in the room, you were concerned I not suspect something. What, pray tell? Does it have to do with the 'fine figure' Juliana has acquired? Has she perhaps been a recipient of your herbal potions?'

Much as she wanted to meet his eyes, Vanessa found she could not. 'Your sister merely chose to eat less and do a bit more walking, milord.' She kept silent on the improved skin and hair, hoping that a mere male would not be quite that observant.

'And what about the potions you gave to the tenants on your estate?' His voice had taken that crisp, cool tone she especially disliked. It reminded her of pickled cucumbers.

'My, you are suspicious. One would think I am a Lucretia Borgia about to pour poison into the food and drink of those about me. She only did away with those she distrusted or feared.' She glanced up at him, trying to assess his level of ire.

'Or those who got in the way of her ambitions.' Nicholas didn't know what drove him on to goad her so. After seeing her with Millbank, he wanted to strike out.

'And what ambitions could I have? I am employed here to repair tapestries. If I suggest to Lady Juliana the remedies that have proven helpful in other cases, it is to prepare her for her future life. She will not remain here forever, you know. Before too long, I have no doubt she will be a wife with her own domestics to order.'

'I said nothing about any arrangements.' His surprise could not be masked. What the devil was she getting at?

'Nevertheless, she will. Unless I am badly mistaken, it will be sooner than you think. Her new wardrobe might be in the nature of a trousseau, perhaps.'

'Are you meddling again?' His exasperation with the innocent-looking blond who haunted his nights far too often exploded. 'What have you been whispering into my sister's ears? No gentleman who might seek her hand has sought an interview with me. Besides, there is plenty of time for her to marry.' He hadn't intended to be so curt with her. But she affected him in a most peculiar manner, which he found confusing. He admired her for her courage, yet feared the way he felt toward her. At once he desired to scold her, and to kiss her. Scolding served as the safer course.

Bristling with anger, certain he had all things wrong, Vanessa replied in even tones, 'I am to keep her company by day, help her choose her gowns, teach her how to cope with domestics, and accompany her in music come the evening . . . but not meddle. Perhaps you ought to hire a companion or instructress to prepare her, milord. It is difficult to obey your directive, not knowing how to interpret it. Why do you not make up your mind, then come back to inform me how to go on?' Her words were quietly biting, with all the hauteur of the Honorable Vanessa Tarleton who'd had the ordering of Blackwood Hall for so many years.

Millbank hovered near the door. His glance darted from Miss Tarleton to Lord Stone and back again. There was a tension hanging in the air between the two. Even where he stood he could almost feel it, a tangible emotion. Surely Lord Stone considered Mrs Hewit as the object of his courting, so what existed between him and the Honorable Vanessa Tarleton? Millbank's own interest in the elegant Vanessa Tarleton — though she might be employed, there was no doubt of her air of consequence — was resigned to that of an observer. Was there mere admiration between those two? Or something deeper? Finally he decided to break the faint silence that hung suspended, both awaiting the reply to her question.

'Milord . . . the dressmaker has arrived and I believe luncheon is ready, as you requested. Miss Juliana is even now in the dining room. No doubt she is anxious to begin the fittings.' There was no hint of Millbank's curiosity.

'Thank you, Millbank,' Nicholas said, never

removing his eyes from Vanessa. Gads, the woman had breeding, to stand up to him as she did. Her life had been full of duty and continual work at tasks most young girls knew nothing about. Yet she remained fresh, unbowed. He could not help but respect her for her courage in the face of adversity. What compelled him to lash out at her as he did? Was it to see that composure break? He wasn't proud of his latest attack. Clearing his throat, he nodded. 'Point taken, Miss Tarleton. I cannot very well expect all things from you, can I?'

Her astonishment at the mildness of his reply was impossible to contain. She made no attempt to try. 'I take it I am to continue to guide Lady Juliana in her choice of clothes and deportment, should she seek my advice?' The control exerted to make that calm statement was considerable, yet she deplored histrionics.

'Yes.' His simple answer was with a sigh of defeat. How this woman could manage to vanquish him without half-trying discomfited him. They entered the dining room in wary harmony.

Juliana bubbled with excitement, scarcely able to contain her desire to be gone to her room. She managed to eat a few bites, then begged Vanessa to join her with the dressmaker.

Deciding that remaining here between Millbank, who studied her with a disconcerting gaze, and Lord Stone, who ignored her for the moment, was not a welcome idea, she agreed. 'I will be delighted to go with you. My appetite seems to have vanished.' With that, she hastily excused herself and followed Juliana from the room. The air seemed far lighter, easier in the hall.

As they hurried up the stairs, Juliana whispered, 'I do hope Nicholas did not give you a scold. I suspect he is a little confused regarding me right now.'

This bit of wisdom was met with a nod of agreement. 'Yes, indeed, my dear. I have no doubt of that!'

They spent the afternoon in the most glorious of occupations for a young girl, choosing lovely new clothes. The dressmaker had brought her assistant, because of the length of the list, she explained. The two women set out bolts of fabric as well as several pretty dresses all completed. Explaining these, the dressmaker, a Mrs Biddle, said she always had a number made up, ready for altering, as one never knew when a rush order might come.

There was a lovely waved gauze in celestial blue, quite acceptable for a young woman's evening dress, so pale was the color. It was vastly flattering to the delicate skin and newly gold-washed hair. Juliana slipped into the dress to discover she scarcely needed any alterations at all.

'I shall wear this for the party! Now, to get to the invitations.' The thrill of new clothes and a party was very evident in the sparkling eyes and radiant face that contemplated the simple gathering with an eagerness usually extended toward a London ball.

'One thing at a time,' cautioned Vanessa. 'Perhaps Millbank could handle that for you, since you have so much at hand here. I will give him your list while you begin selecting the other items you wish. That lovely dress will need immediate fitting to be ready by ... did you say tomorrow night!' She was aghast Juliana could consider so brief a time before her party.

Juliana blithely waved a slip of paper before Vanessa. 'You are a dear. These are the names. Everyone Nicholas will approve is on the list.'

As Vanessa left the room, it was to the familiar words from the dressmaker: 'Hold still, please, milady.'

She found Millbank in the library, placing books on the shelves. 'Here is the list for the little gathering Lord Stone was so kind to offer Lady Juliana as a treat. I gather it is

229

sufficient time, since there are not a great number of social doings in the country. Since she is otherwise occupied, she hoped you might oblige her.'

His bow was nicely done, she thought. He seemed a kind man. His polite smile as he scanned the short list won her approval.

'I will be more than happy. I gather you will attend? Dare I hope you will honor me with a dance? I see Lady Juliana is insisting I find some music other than our own.'

'Perhaps a fiddler or someone? You undoubtedly know who is all the crack about here. In answer to your question, I will be happy to dance with you, Mr Millbank.' She dipped a polite curtsy, then left to return to Juliana, nearly bumping into Lord Stone as she rounded the corner to the hall.

Nicholas watched Miss Tarleton make her way up the stairs, a thoughtful look on his face. He had heard the remark about dancing with Millbank. It made no difference to him, yet he wondered what it might be like to touch her, perhaps hold her for that most daring of dances, the waltz.

Vanessa was breathless when she reached her room. If there was to be a party, even a small affair, she must look over her modest array of dresses. Though no one would pay much attention to her, she desired to look her best.

Katie bustled in, Hercules padding after her. She took one look at the plain green jaconet muslin held up for inspection and said with horror, 'Never say you intend to wear that to the party, miss! Never! Right, Hercules?'

His gold eye winked in agreement, it seemed, while Katie removed the offending dress to plow through the limited contents of the wardrobe. 'Here, this is the one.'

A concoction of pale blue gauze over white satin shimmered at Vanessa. 'I do not wish to draw attention to myself, Katie. This is Lady Juliana's evening.' Vanessa thought of Mrs Hewit. 'Still, I would not wish to bring Lord Stone's reproach upon my head.' She caught a smile of comprehension on Katie's face that revealed the maid's thoughts far too clearly.

'You'll look a real treat in that, you surely will. Mayhap that Mrs Biddle person will have a flower or two to tuck in your hair?'

'Katie, I forbid you to even think of such an extravagance. I simply cannot afford to spend one farthing on trimmings for myself. This will do nicely with that cashmere shawl I saved out. I was more vain than I thought, to do such a thing.' She gave Katie a stern look, then dissolved in laughter at the antics of

Hercules as the cat batted at the fringe of the white cashmere shawl. 'I do believe Hercules has set a seal of approval on it.'

Vanessa was feminine enough to wonder what Lord Stone would say to her appearing in such a dress. It was quite unexceptional in color and fabric, and the neckline didn't plunge all that low. Perhaps the white satin clung to her figure too closely? It might not be the sort of dress a needlewoman employed in the house ought to wear, but it was the prettiest she had, and she desired to look her best.

After Katie left the room, Vanessa delayed joining Juliana, going instead to stand by her window to gaze out on the great court. She had tried so very hard to pretend to herself that all those sensations she experienced, the feelings she knew when Lord Stone neared her, were simply imagination, nothing more. Now she wondered how much longer she could deny her true response to him.

Tomorrow she would be compelled to watch him partner the dainty Mrs Hewit throughout the evening. Could she retain an unaffected calm? She hadn't wanted to face her inner feelings; she still didn't. Perhaps if she ignored them, they would disappear. It was for the best that Lord Stone marry Mrs Hewit, she reminded herself. There was nothing to say he felt it merely a marriage of convenience. Though his sense of duty was strong, with Mrs Hewit's beauty, it probably would not be all that *much* a duty.

Which thought so depressed her that she abandoned the window to return to Juliana, where she could watch the pinning and final decisions. Once done, the dressmaker and her assistant, with several footmen to carry bolts and parcels, retired to the sewing room in the upper regions of the house to commence the work.

The following hours were spent in continual bustle as Juliana asserted herself in a new and delightful manner. She directed Mrs Murdoch to see to it that the music room was polished to a fine state. Peverly fussed at the footmen more than ever. By late afternoon of the next day, Vanessa was pleased at the improvement wrought in the house. While it had been neat before, it now gleamed as it should.

The nervousness Vanessa felt about her dress, fearing an adverse reaction, was for naught. Juliana completely stole the day. It seemed she blossomed all at once. The loss of weight, the new dress, her charming looks all combined to endow her with the radiant glow that entranced the three who watched her as she made her entrance to the dining room.

'Very nice, little sister. It seems as though you have grown up overnight. I must say, I approve your appearance. If Miss Tarleton contributed to the change, I must applaud her help.' Nicholas bowed to Vanessa, an ironic gleam lurking in his eyes. If he noticed the pretty rose Katie had tucked into her hair arrangement, or the charming fall of her gown, he certainly didn't reveal it by an eyelash.

Vanessa nodded with serene grace, seeking to remain in the background during the meal and later when the guests began to arrive. It would not do for the needlewoman to assert herself in any way. She decided she would behave with utmost propriety this evening.

The bemused state last observed on Sir Harry's face as he rode off to Eastthorpe Hall was still there, perhaps a bit less distinct. He joined Lord Stone and Mrs Hewit as they swept toward the redecorated music room, towing a cool Lady Juliana at his side. His sister, Louisa, and her fiancé, Dunston Blaine, wore polite smiles when introduced to Vanessa. They were rigid figures, seeming ill-at-ease in evening dress. Louisa bore the same air as her brother, only a feminine version. She firmly linked her arm with Dunston's, then sailed along behind the others. Vanessa hid a smile at the parade they formed.

Pamela Hewit was gushing over the freshly decorated room with her usual enthusiasm when Vanessa slipped inside the door, Millbank at her side. The golden gown of delicate satin brocade Pamela wore reflected the candlelight quite charmingly. She was in first looks, and she knew it.

At a nod from Lord Stone, the musical trio set in the corner commenced to play a delightful country dance, the first of several. Nicholas extended his hand to Pamela while Vanessa clenched her teeth and smiled politely at something Millbank said.

A laughing Juliana swirled out to the floor with Sir Harry, flirting in a most amazing manner with him. 'Of course I know my steps. Miss Tarleton has been in London and is quite up to snuff about all sorts of things.'

The casual brushing off of what had been a most grueling time until Juliana finally mastered the new steps was almost too much for Vanessa. Only the sight of Louisa and Dunston cutting the stiffest of figures saved her from disgracing herself. Undoubtedly they were superbly at home on horseback, outshining all there. But not in the dance.

'I am pleased to see they have not succumbed to the latest craze from London, the waltz. I understand it is to be seen in Devonshire House; but then, such outrage is not a surprise from that quarter.' Mr Millbank gave Vanessa an intent look with a hint of hauteur about it.

Vanessa slanted a startled gaze at Mr Millbank. She hadn't thought him to be so stuffy. Not that she didn't hold reservations about the dance that caused such talk. Yet when offered a chance to learn the scandalous steps, she had accepted with an eagerness her Aunt Agatha would have denounced with fervor — had she known.

'While it certainly is different from an Irish jig, I cannot feel it is so very bad. True, it is not done at court as yet, but I think it will not be long before it is taken by society to its heart. The steps are very simple. Come, I will demonstrate.' She motioned to one end of the room where there was sufficient space with no one around.

Mr Millbank gazed at her with undisguised dismay. 'Oh, never could I do such a thing.' As he spoke the words, the latest country dance ended and his voice sounded clearly in the sudden lull.

Curiosity brought the irrepressible Juliana to their side. 'Never could do what?'

Not wanting to embarrass Mr Millbank, Vanessa was inclined to dismiss the subject. She found the waltz too daring anyway. It would not give credit to her determination to behave with propriety. She said nothing.

Not so Mr Millbank. His heroine had come crashing down with quite a thud. 'Miss Tarleton endeavors to teach me the waltz.' The horror in his voice was too much for Lady Juliana. She had the misfortune to laugh.

From behind them, Mrs Hewit darted a calculating look, first at Lord Stone, then at Vanessa. 'Why not teach the dance to all of us? Perhaps if we see it performed, we may find it quite diverting.' She noted the tightening of the muscles on Nicholas's face, the coolness of his eyes, and smiled.

Taking a deep breath, Vanessa calmly nodded at the trio of musicians, who were up to the mark regarding the latest music. In spite of her desire to remain in the background, it seemed she was destined to put her foot out. She extended her hand to Mr Millbank, who seemed reluctant to accept it. Further embarrassed, Vanessa glanced to Juliana for help. However, it was Lord Stone who took her hand in his, nodding for her to commence.

'It is really quite simple: one, two, three . . . one, two, three . . . an easy series of steps.' She lifted her satin skirt so her feet could be seen as they moved through the steps.

No man could fail to appreciate the pretty turn of ankle displayed. A flash of vexation crossed Mrs Hewit's face, gone before Vanessa might see it. Vanessa swallowed with care before placing her other hand on the earl's shoulder. 'Now you lead thus, milord.' The shock of his hand so intimately on her back was quelled with only the greatest of fortitude. She glanced up to find his eyes studying her face, and she sensed a warmth stealing over her that must reveal itself in some shade of pink. They moved away from the others in the basic steps, neatly performed. Vanessa ventured an approving smile. 'You do well, milord.'

She was amazed when Lord Stone deftly spun her around in a very good turn about the room in perfect time to the threequarter beat of the music. It felt as though she skimmed across the sky on a cloud.

Lady Juliana grinned at Sir Harry, then dared him to attempt the dance as well. He was game, and another couple, albeit rather clumsy, joined Vanessa and Lord Stone in performing the dance. Louisa looked as though she might like to try the dance, but knew the limitations of her partner too well to do so. Pamela looked fit to kill, as Juliana was wont to say.

The closeness of Lord Stone, Vanessa's

hand clasped lightly in his, the warmth of his other hand on her back, felt so clearly through the delicate fabric of her dress, nearly made her dizzy. The relief at the conclusion of the dangerous dance was mingled with a deep sense of loss. She made her curtsy, then backed away, trying to hide her confusion from the others. The touch of his hand was imprinted on her back in searing heat. Never had she imagined such sensations.

'Disgraceful!' Chagrin mingled with jealousy. Pamela Hewit dared not ignore that gracefully swirling figure as a potential rival.

'It is nothing of the kind.' Juliana laughed, though with girlish charm, at Pamela. 'I think it prodigiously delightful. What think you, Nicholas?'

Rubbing his chin in a gesture revealing his nettled mood, Nicholas said, 'I had the advantage of seeing the dance performed while in Portugal. It has been popular in Europe for some time, you know. Miss Tarleton is as graceful a dancer as I have observed.'

Determined to remove attention from Vanessa, Mrs Hewit signaled the musicians to play, sweeping Nicholas off in a country dance with Louisa and Dunston along. Juliana followed with Sir Harry, leaving Vanessa with the disapproving Mr Millbank.

There was little to be said, so she simply enjoyed the music, ignoring the sight of Nicholas paying court to the figure in gold satin.

Vanessa was far too well-bred to allow her gaze to follow him as he moved about the room. Yet she knew precisely where he was every moment of the evening. She wondered if hearts actually crumbled to little pieces when wounded.

Later, after the pleasant supper and bidding the guests good night, she listened to Juliana proclaim it the most agreeable of evenings. The two women walked up the stairs to their rooms, Juliana quite tired and pleased with the party. She danced down the hall to her room on happy feet after leaving Vanessa at her door. Nicholas and Millbank were still downstairs in the library, enjoying a last glass of port before bed.

In the quiet of her room, as Vanessa removed the pins from her hair, allowing the flower to fall ignored to the floor, she acknowledged the bitterest of truths. Lord Stone would undoubtedly ask Mrs Hewit to be his wife. The marriage so neatly solved his problems, and in view of his behavior this evening, did not appear to be all that objectionable to him. He had positively doted on the widow tonight!

And Vanessa? She had made an utter cabbagehead of herself, dancing the waltz. But it had been wonderful, and delicious . . . and she wished she might do it once more.

11

The Celtic dragon winked back at her from the mirror as Vanessa stroked its tail, pleased with the way it looked at the neck of her green jaconet gown. The polished bronze felt like cool satin to her touch. Who had worn this so many years ago? What had happened to cut short her life? For a moment she visualized the violent clash of Saxon against Celt. A second check in the girandole mirror that hung in the saloon reminded her she ought to be working at the tapestry, not admiring her discovery and dreaming.

Settling on the chair where she spent so many hours, she considered the previous night as she threaded her needle. She began to skillfully weave the color in and out of the tapestry, being careful not to catch in the lining.

She shook her head in dismay at her actions of the previous evening. How had she allowed herself to be urged into the position of demonstrating the waltz? Mrs Hewit had declared herself scandalized. Though Lord Stone had defended Vanessa — mildly, to be sure — he'd spent the remaining evening with

Mrs Hewit, never once, as far as Vanessa knew, glancing in her direction.

Well, what did she expect? Her foolish heart could never think Lord Stone might look at a needlewoman when he felt it his duty to marry for money. And, she reminded herself, she would never be a party to anything less than marriage.

Smoothing the heavy fabric of the tapestry, she observed how the yarns were so closely intertwined, in and out across the breadth of the weaving. Red turned to blue to green much like the days of her life changed subtly as time flowed by, a never-ending thread. Her hand encountered another of the strange lumps. Just as she was about to explore it, Juliana danced into the room, her face wreathed in a smile.

'It was a frightfully marvelous party, was it not? I declare, I am excessively pleased with our little evening. I wanted to tell you how much I appreciate all your help.' She giggled, making a face at Vanessa. 'You sit so prim and proper today after dancing the waltz last night. I vow, when Pamela said she found it disgraceful I simply had to join in the dance. Harry surprised me. I never dreamed he would be such a good sport. Maybe there is hope for the man after all.'

'It would appear you are correct, the way

he behaved last evening.' Vanessa suppressed a smile at the lavish speech Juliana favored. What a dear young woman.

'She was in good looks, was she not?' Juliana tossed out her remark, watching Vanessa's reaction with shrewd eyes.

'Mrs Hewit?' An imp took hold of Vanessa's tongue and she replied, 'She was like a full-blown rose — a yellow one, to be sure. You did not exaggerate when you said she wears naught but yellow. However, since she looks charming in that shade, who could fault her for it?' The woman was past her prime, but Vanessa could not bring herself to be catty in her remarks. If Lord Stone had fixed his interest in Pamela, that was the end of it.

'I thought Harry prodigiously handsome.' Juliana held out her arms, waltzing down the room to a tune she hummed in a pleasing soprano.

Murmuring a noncommittal reply, Vanessa let her thoughts turn to Lord Stone. Distinguished, handsome, well-set — how best to describe the man? His elegance of last night had not been that of a country squire, but of a man of polish. The sparkle, as rich as any sapphire, that had lurked in his eyes was such that she wished she might see it more often. What heaven to be held in his arms, if only for the length of a waltz. Annoyed at the direction of her thoughts, she resolutely applied herself to Juliana and her problems. 'What do you plan to do today?'

'I have a fitting, then I am free. I believe Harry said something about coming over to check with Nicholas regarding a problem with the sheep or some such thing. I shall be very indifferent.' She turned to waltz down the room again, her humming louder this time.

Smiling to herself, Vanessa bent her head over the tapestry to resume her work. The central tapestry was nearly completed. Long hours of diligent weaving accomplished a good deal of work. Soon this one could be transferred and the second begun.

Juliana peered over her shoulder. 'That is certainly an elegant hanging, is it not? Grandpapa was so proud of them all. I suspect they are quite valuable. I am pleased Nicholas decided to honor his promise to him and have them repaired. It certainly was not a project my father or Damian would have considered undertaking.' Her fingers traced the figure of a hunter with his catch of wild boar, the jewel tones of his doublet and hose bright and bold.

'I quite agree with you regarding the tapestries. The depth and richness of color appear undimmed by the years, in spite of the neglect. The gradations of color continually amaze me. See how subtle the change is done, yet the outline remains crisp and the detail sharp? The story of the hunt with all the information of what life must have been like for them is there if you but search for it. At Blackwood Hall our tapestries were of the seasons. I dearly loved them. I wonder who will care for them now?' she mused softly.

'Have you ever thought of weaving one yourself?'

'Like Penelope at her loom? Not really. Though now you mention it, such a venture would be exciting. I should like to attempt a bed hanging, I believe. Perhaps someday I may have the time to try such a thing, although it would be an expensive undertaking, I fear.' Vanessa sighed, then turned her attention to the needle in her hand, the lumps she had intended to explore earlier completely forgotten.

'What did they use for dye?' Juliana continued to examine the section Vanessa was working.

'This blue is either indigo or woad, the yellow from weld, which resembles mignonette. I imagine the red is from madder. The other colors are most likely mixtures. They used bark, leaves, berries, and moss, even insects, I understand. I am thankful I can buy my thread. Miss Linwood told me she has hers all dyed for her.'

'It's a bit like your herbs, I think — all the natural ingredients used.' Juliana lost interest and wandered away from the worktable to gaze longingly out a window. 'I wonder when I will be able to take the dogcart out again. I shall want you to come along.' Her look was as pleading as her voice was coaxing.

'Let me finish this central hanging. While the footmen shift it about to transfer the second one, I will come with you. Tell me, do you plan to paint, or search for more jet beads?' Vanessa held her needle poised in midair, glancing up to Juliana, wondering if she hoped Sir Harry might join in the outing.

Juliana moved restlessly to the next window to stare up at the cloudy sky. 'I shall paint. As far as the beads are concerned, Harry promised to have them strung for me. There are enough to make a pretty necklace.' She paused, then continued. 'I told you I mean to be indifferent to Harry, and I meant what I said. No more languishing looks!' She ruined her dramatic speech by peeping at Vanessa like a naughty child expecting to be reprimanded.

Vanessa merely laughed at her, shaking her head in rueful amusement.

Suddenly Juliana stiffened. 'Here comes Pamela's carriage. Surely I must be needed for a fitting . . . or something. Excuse me.' She hastily slipped from the room, leaving Vanessa trapped at the table.

The lute-toned voice drifted in from the central hall, where Peverly greeted Mrs Hewit with frosty hauteur. Vanessa approved his disdain in this instance, though she never would have admitted it to anyone. When Pamela Hewit failed to materialize, Vanessa concluded she was to be left in peace. Obviously the widow, garbed, no doubt, in daffodil or sunflower yellow, sought Lord Stone. The thought failed to bring any comfort.

As Millbank left for an errand in York early that morning, Vanessa felt safe from his reproachful gaze. The house was strangely quiet with Juliana secreted in her room with her dressmaker, the carpenters working elsewhere for the present. No echoes of dropping lumber reached her ears today. She picked up the tune Juliana had hummed earlier to amuse herself with a rendition that, if it wasn't perfect, gave her spirits a lift.

A rustle of silk at the door brought Vanessa's head up just as Mrs Hewit entered the room. The daffodil dress — Vanessa had guessed aright — was slightly mussed and her usually perfectly ordered hair was disarranged. In point of fact, some of the young ladies who dallied with young bucks during a ball looked much the same. The smug expression on her face didn't sit particularly well with Vanessa, who chided herself for a suspicious turn of mind, when Lord Stone entered the room from the same direction.

Vanessa knew her eyes must have widened at the sight of him. His hair was tousled, to be sure, but not in the perfect arrangement his valet created, nor in the absent-minded disorder Nicholas tended to make when deep in thought. His cravat, earlier a pattern card of perfection, looked as though it had been scrunched badly by . . . Her mind skittered to a halt, refusing to consider what her eyes noted.

Yet she had promised herself to be realistic. It seemed Nicholas — Lord Stone, that is — would not find marriage to Mrs Hewit the least bit of a hardship. Vanessa discreetly lowered her eyes to the tapestry once more, resolving to retain a measure of cool composure in the light of their obvious dalliance. Her cheeks warmed in response to their apparent lack of conduct. Still, she couldn't deny there was an ache in her heart at the thought of Lord Stone in the arms of Mrs Hewit.

'I vow, Nicholas,' Mrs Hewit cooed, 'this room could be so wonderful. I see drapery hangings of rich gold and dark red with a carpet to match. Have the painters redo those insipid chairs, paint them a white to match the walls, then cover the seats with a tapestry in gold and red as well. It would be monstrously elegant.' Her dainty hand reached up to straighten his cravat, thereby making a greater hash of the thing. Bestowing a limpid smile into his eyes, she turned to face Vanessa. 'Do you not agree with me, Miss Tarleton? Gold and red would be vastly appealing in this room.' Her expression dared Vanessa to disagree.

A devil seized hold of Vanessa, who raised her twinkling eyes to meet the sardonic gaze of Lord Stone. 'Why, no. I cannot see gold and red in here at all.' She knew full well the two colors would become the chestnut-haired Mrs Hewit very much. 'There is such a wealth of sun in here, I believe an elegant cerulean blue with delicate gold would be better, at least to my mind. And the wood of the chairs left as is. I have always admired satinwood. Perhaps Juliana could create worked seat covers done with bellflowers or bluebells to carry out the blue theme.' She paused for effect, then added mischievously, 'On the other hand, winged lions might be nice. They would go well with those caryatids on the fireplace. Perhaps carved paw feet on the tables as well? And quite definitely a shell-shaped couch with alligator legs, to be right up to snuff, don't you know.'

'If you wait for Juliana to work seat covers for these chairs, they will sit in their present state forever,' said Lord Stone. He walked to the window to look across the parkland. It seemed to Vanessa his shoulders shook ever so slightly. He cleared his throat, then turned to face the women.

The sight of him with that tousled hair and the devilish blaze in those dark eyes riveted Vanessa's attention and she couldn't help staring at him, despite her resolve to remain cool.

'I wonder . . . deep red and gold versus cerulean blue and delicate gold. I shall have to ponder on it. Thank you both for your suggestions.' He awarded them a wicked smile.

Pamela stamped het foot in vexation. 'Horrid man! Knowing you, I shall find a totally different color scheme in here when the drapery is installed, such as pale green with ecru. You ought not have to bother with all this, Nicholas dear,' she coaxed. 'A wife could take this burden from your shoulders so easily.'

His grin widened. 'And work the seat covers for me as well, true?'

Pamela blanched, knowing her talent with the needle to be her poorest skill. She shrugged eloquent shoulders, the deep neckline of the daffodil gown revealing a vast expanse of creamy shoulders, and more — or less, depending on one's preference — to appreciative eyes. 'If you desire worked seat covers, get someone like the Duchess of York, who plies her needle without ceasing, so I understand.'

Vanessa covered her quivering mouth with her hand. Somehow, she doubted if Mrs Hewit had planned this scene to go quite this way.

'However, I do believe one of those charming Greek-style sofas would be lovely in here. A nice red and gold satin stripe, I daresay.' Pamela gave Vanessa a defiant look, daring her to contradict her.

'Oh, I agree with you about the couch in the Greek style,' said Vanessa in the most dulcet of voices. 'In fact, I believe two would be even better. Those curved arms are so graceful, and I so enjoy tucking a bolster at my side while I do my needlework. I find it so pleasantly relaxing, don't you, Mrs Hewit?' Not waiting for a reply, she continued, 'But as to color and fabric, I should think ivory silk with a faint stripe of blue would be eminently more suitable for this room . . . as I see it.' Mrs Hewit didn't have a monopoly on limpid looks. Vanessa couldn't resist batting her eyelashes in the direction of the nobleman who now lounged against the marble fireplace mantel with the ease of a conquering hero.

'Ladies, please. What other improvements come to mind for this room? Hmm? I'm sure your fertile mind can dredge up something, Pamela dear.' The look Lord Stone cast in her direction was anything but loverlike.

Sending a puzzled glance first at Mrs Hewit, then at the earl, Vanessa considered his words and tone of voice. It sounded as though he didn't like the woman in the least! This ought not have cheered her — but it did.

Impervious to his tone, Pamela began again. 'A clever folding card table and a pair of those consoles in the last copy of Ackermann's Repository would be fitting.' Her enthusiasm growing, she added, 'And a pair of torchères to set by a lovely sideboard as well. This could be a magnificent room, Nicholas!'

He moved away from the fireplace to again look out at his parkland, his hands clenched behind his back as he considered her words. 'You make it all sound so simple.'

'Of course it is. All you must needs do is place the order.' Life was easy for Mrs Hewit. With her money, all she had to do was follow her own advice: if you want it, buy it. Now she wanted Nicholas and she had the funds to tempt him.

'Aye, and pay for it as well,' he muttered softly. If Pamela Hewit noticed that last remark, she made no reaction to it. Vanessa wondered at the bitterness in his voice.

'Do come outside a bit,' Pamela said to the earl. 'A walk in the garden will be just the thing. I fear you have been teased about this room long enough. We are keeping Miss Tarleton from her work . . . and I know how you feel about that, dear Nicholas.' She extended her hand in a graceful, imperious gesture.

Nicholas glanced to where Vanessa bent her head over the tapestry, seemingly unconcerned about the other two people in the room. He didn't know what he had tried to prove by his actions here, but the consequences would have to be mulled over later. 'That seems an excellent idea, Pamela.' He walked to where she stood waiting, a smug look flashing briefly across her face as she glanced at Vanessa. Before leaving, he paused to add a final comment. 'I shall see you later, Miss Tarleton. Pity Millbank found it

254

necessary to travel to York today. You might have managed to persuade him to attempt the waltz.'

At that last remark, given so slyly, Vanessa raised her head to stare at the departing couple. Perhaps they deserved each other. He knew perfectly well that Millbank would as lief jump off a bridge as learn that wretched dance.

The following days brought the construction work in the tapestry room to a finish. All that remained was for the painters to blend the precise color Lord Stone desired, and the room could be completed. He envisioned forest-green walls below the ivory-and-gold ceiling.

Vanessa was surprised when he sought her out to question her about the color to go with the tapestries.

'I thought to flatter the tapestries best with a shade of green.' He considered something at length, then turned from the window, where he seemed fond of regarding his parkland. 'Have you seen my mother's room?'

The needle jabbed her finger as she started with his sudden question. She dropped the long needle to press the wounded finger to her lips, then shook her head. 'No, milord. The only rooms I have seen, other than Juliana's and my bedrooms, are those you

255

showed me that first day.'

They both remained silent as their thoughts returned to the day Vanessa had arrived at the house to mistake Nicholas for Millbank. Nicholas placed his hands behind him, cleared his throat, and replied, 'Well . . . I would like you to see her room. The tapestries in there are blended nicely with the paint and furnishings. Perhaps you will know what I mean when you view them.'

She rose from her chair to walk toward where he stood. 'Very well, milord. Are you certain it is *my* opinion you should be seeking?' It wasn't precisely the question she ought to ask, but she found she simply had to.

'Probably not. Yet I find I like your taste . . . in most things. No lion heads or paw feet, mind you.'

'I thought we were discussing paint color.'

'I meant to talk to you about that conversation long before this. Paw feet and lion heads, indeed! Not to mention a shell couch with alligator feet! Whatever were you thinking of, dear girl? You know I don't think along those lines.'

Vanessa fought to control the tremors that threatened her at his touch when he guided her from the room and up the stairs. Her response was light. 'Well, I thought they *did* go with the caryatids on the fireplace.'

'I see I shall never be allowed to forget your first day.' They walked along the hall in silence. He motioned to a door, where he stopped, then opened it to usher her inside. 'Here we are. Tell me what you think.'

'What a lovely room. The colors are truly gorgeous. I quite see what you mean about blending.' She turned to face him. 'I like the idea, picking up the central color of the tapestries to use on the walls. The ceiling is another matter.' She angled her head around to inspect the picture in the center of the square ceiling. 'Whatever is that painting supposed to represent?'

He was drawn closer to her, desiring to again know the fragrance that reminded him so much of his dear mother, that delicate scent of bluebells. 'Umm, I believe it is supposed to be Diana and Jupiter, the goddess of the moon coming to the god of the sky and storms. It implies a rather tumultuous bedroom scene, does it not?' His comment was highly improper; he could see the flaming of her cheeks as she strove for control.

Her voice was high, thin with strain as she looked away from him, anywhere but at Nicholas. 'This needlework is very fine. Is it Indian?' An unsteady hand reached out to lightly touch the delicate flowers and elegant birds embroidered on the hangings.

Nicholas experienced a twinge of conscience. He knew it was wrong to have her here. He ought to stay away from her. He should never have brought her up here alone with him. But he could not deny he wanted her more than any woman ever before. 'Vanessa?'

She had drifted from his side to stand by the window. She stood quietly gazing up at the beautiful embroidered bed hangings and the tapestries on the wall. It was the room of a woman who had wished to surround herself with needlework of the highest quality. 'They are perfectly preserved. How fortunate she was to have lived in such a room.'

'Vanessa, look at me.'

'No.'

Nicholas moved in front of her, grasping her shoulders in tense hands. She stood waiting. Her gaze slowly, reluctantly met his.

Her eyes were wary, her lips moved as though to say something further, but nothing came forth. As his face neared hers, those hauntingly beautiful sea-blue eyes fluttered shut, her face like carved marble in stillness. The scent of bluebells engulfed him.

The touch of his lips, their warmth unwanted yet cherished, overwhelmed her. A soaring joy floated through her as his strong hands clasped her so tenderly to him. He must care for her to hold her, kiss her like this. She yielded to his seductive touch — for the moment, she assured herself. She had dreamed of this, longed for it. Such incredible bliss to be in his arms, to be his. Could she really dare to claim such happiness?

Then reality intruded.

She tore her lips from his, placing her head against his cravat, ignoring his urgent whisper. This was how Mrs Hewit no doubt crumpled his attire. The thought chilled her blood. 'Please . . . milord. This cannot be.'

'Dare not say you cared naught for that kiss. I refuse to believe it.' His voice was hoarse, arms tightening their hold as though to deny her words with his strength.

'What has that to say to anything? I should not have come up here with you, you know that.' Her voice was low, agonized. 'I am not a maid to be trifled with as you please. But for my father's gaming debts I would be now preparing to wed a baron, a respected woman. I will not be party to a clandestine affair. Let me go. I want none of this.' The lie trembled on her lips as she awaited his reaction to her words, her body quiescent, hurting deeply.

She sensed the sharply indrawn breath as

his hands released her, falling to his sides. 'I apologize.' He turned from her toward the window, listening to her steps as she crossed to leave the room.

At the door she paused, looking back to where he still stood staring out the window.

'This places me in a nearly untenable position, milord. You must know I need this work unless I go to live with my aunt.' Her voice grew bitter. 'There is precious little a woman can do when rejected by her fiancé and family as well. It will go hard for me if I beg to return. May I plead that we forget what has occured between us in this room? I will strive to keep my distance, and there will be no repeat of this kiss.'

Nicholas braced himself to turn, wondering what he would see in those eyes the color of the fathomless sea. Never in his life had he been so torn between what he conceived to be his duty and what he as a man wanted for his own sake. Her grace, charm, and bewitching appeal could not be his. Duty to his heritage demanded an heiress. He knew that. But for one aching moment in time he had captured all he desired in his arms. He admired her more than any woman since his mother had died years ago. She exhibited the same spirit, sense of taste, and good humor.

Her eyes were guarded, figure tensed. 'Well?'

'So be it. I shall endeavor to be the gentleman at all times when near you. Forgive the lapse, my dear.'

Sagging with relief, she nodded, then fled down the hall and stairs as though the very hounds of hell were behind her. For some reason she couldn't understand, she felt a crushing disappointment. Had she momentarily believed he might abandon his duty for her?

Breathlessly she entered the saloon, where Juliana paced before the windows.

'Where have you been? I have the dogcart ready to go out. Cook packed a picnic for us if you care for a bite to eat. If I intend to collect paintings of all the wildflowers in Yorkshire, I ought to get busy, don't you think?' At the dazed reaction from Vanessa, Juliana walked to her side, touching her lightly on the arm. 'Vanessa? Are you all right?'

'What? Oh, I am fine, quite fine, I daresay. Let me get my bonnet and parasol if we are to go out.' She moved reluctantly to return to the upper level of the house.

'Katie gave me your things to save you a trip upstairs. They are on the table by the door.' Juliana gestured to the items so close to

261

where Vanessa stood.

Vanessa dropped her gaze to see her bonnet, the cottage straw trimmed with canary silk ribbons, and her parasol placed where she must have nearly touched them when she entered the room. 'Thank you, dear Juliana. How thoughtful you are. Shall we go now?' Vanessa picked up her things, absent-mindedly crammed the bonnet on her head, and marched out the door.

Following slowly behind her, Juliana wondered what had upset Vanessa to bring her to this abstracted state. Far too polite to question her friend, she joined her in the dogcart and the two women jogged off down the graveled path.

The day was productive for Juliana, who produced three exquisite little watercolors. Vanessa contented herself with hunting for herbs, shutting from her mind the events of the morning as best she could. Upon their return to the house hours later, she left Juliana at the entry to the stable area.

'I will go to the stillroom to tend to those mixtures I promised you yesterday. These herbs I gathered will be a welcome addition to what Katie brought from the village.' With a casual wave, Vanessa set off toward the kitchen court of the house.

Everyone was bustling around the kitchen.

Cook scolded the scullery maid as the stillroom maid washed up the luncheon dishes. Apparently company had sat down to lunch during their absence. Vanessa wended her way through the activity, saying little, but nodding in her pleasant manner.

In the stillroom she located the purchases made by Katie and set to work. Off to one side she heard voices, arguing. Without intending to, she listened, growing intrigued as she heard more. Her hands stilled at their task of blending herbs as her dismay grew.

There were only the two voices, Mrs Murdoch's and a man's, obviously a tradesman. At home Vanessa had dealt with tradesmen, paying their bills when Danvers and Mrs Danvers were otherwise occupied. Now it seemed Mrs Murdoch had worked out an arrangement with this shopkeeper to cheat the earl out of money! It was an ingenious scheme. The bill was to be padded, with the amounts charged greater than warranted, with the difference between actual and listed cost to be split, Mrs Murdoch naturally getting the greater sum.

Thinking furiously, Vanessa realized she couldn't go to Lord Stone with this tale. He had in the past accused her of meddling, and she had no proof of the scheme to defraud. It would be the word of a temporary employee against a trusted retainer hired through the recommendation of the lady Lord Stone intended to marry.

The herbal mixtures completed, Vanessa gathered them up with as much haste as possible, wishing to be far gone from this spot when Mrs Murdoch returned. Just as she went out the door, Mrs Murdoch pushed open the one on the far side.

Vanessa hurried up the stairs to her room, not pausing when she heard her name called. No matter who wished to speak with her, she was deaf until she secreted the remedies away in her dressing room. Had Mrs Murdoch observed Vanessa as she whipped around the corner of the door? What would happen now? What a quandary to be in — to know of wrongdoing but be unable to speak up!

She would find a way to do something to correct the situation. She must. It needed a bit of time and care, but she would see to it the thief was apprehended. Somehow.

12

''Tis something mighty strange, I tell you,' muttered Katie as she rather vigorously brushed Vanessa's hair. 'Her highness is acting more peculiar-like than ever. Come all over queer at times, she does, peering over her shoulder like she thinks a devil be at her heels.' Katie gave a shrewd look at the face in the mirror. 'I'll wager her past sins are catching up wi' her.'

'Mrs Murdoch is not herself these past weeks?' Since overhearing the housekeeper in the act of arranging an illegal transaction, Vanessa had been extremely careful to keep out of her way, while still trying to note what went on belowstairs. Lately the desserts served at dinner had been either curdled or burned, with breakfast dishes deteriorating as well. Since these were both the province of the housekeeper, could anxiety be the root of these culinary disasters?

'Not herself? Not much, I'd say! Fergot to check the linen yesterday! And told Cook to mind the roast, as though Cook didn't do it every day of the year! Acting mighty fearful, she is.' Katie gave a satisfied pat to the arrangement of braids and curls, then carefully placed atop this the dainty bit of muslin and lace that passed for a cap before standing aside to allow Vanessa to rise from the chair by the dressing table.

'I expect she will bear watching, but ought not you to inform Lady Juliana of this?' Vanessa tried to cling to a last vestige of propriety regarding her interest in Stone's Court. She had no business in trying to help. Ought she not simply to turn the matter over to Lord Stone instead of attempting to solve the mystery herself? Doubtless he would say she was meddling. Again.

'Me, milady? Never say so! It ain't my place to be speakin' to her. Asides, she be so intent on Featherston, I doubt the cautioning would do much good.' Then, in a confiding manner, Katie added, 'There's much talk belowstairs about it. Most figure 'twill not be long before Lady Juliana leaves here to be at Eastthorpe Hall. They are wagerin' about the month and day of it.' She nodded her head in pleasure at the thought of a wedding.

Uncomfortably aware she should not be discussing the housekeeper or the family affairs with her maid like this, Vanessa walked toward the door. Still, Katie knew more of what went on than anyone else, with her sharp eyes and quick mind. Coming to a decision that was of a certainty slightly improper, but for the best regarding Lord Stone and his interests (she told herself), she turned to face Katie. 'If you note anything else, please inform me, Katie. It is possible I could pass the knowledge along to Lord Stone.'

She shut the door on the knowing gleam in Katie's eyes. Sometimes that girl saw *too* much.

The hall was silent and empty, the maids and footmen busy in other parts of the great house. Vanessa reflected on the past two weeks since she had first discovered the nefarious ways of Mrs Murdoch. While the housekeeper appeared rattled, undoubtedly wondering how much Vanessa knew about her underhanded schemes, she hadn't approached Vanessa in any way. Instead, the household suffered with the burnt offerings and neglects of the apparently distracted woman. Perhaps if Vanessa adopted a bit of Katie's knowing airs, Mrs Murdoch would tip her hand? The vision of herself skulking about the halls, listening in to stillroom conversations, and sneaking a look at the household accounts brought a grimace of distaste to her face. Was she so past redemption in her interest for Lord Stone that she would stoop to anything? Then she realized that if it meant improving life in any manner for him, she would attempt it.

As she entered the saloon, Vanessa's heart lightened momentarily as she saw how much work she had accomplished on the tapestries. The second tapestry had now replaced the central, larger one, and was well under way.

To be honest, she knew periods of despair now, wondering what would become of her when she must leave this house. Her regard for Lord Stone confronted her at every turn as she went about her work, moved about the house she had come to love. How silly she was to even contemplate romantic notions about him. While he was cordial to Vanessa, he continued to press his attentions toward Mrs Hewit.

Needle in hand, prepared to attack a patch of flowers and greenery that was sadly worn, Vanessa considered the odd attitude of Mrs Hewit in regard to Juliana. At first, Vanessa had thought Pamela Hewit guilty of jealousy toward the girl. As time progressed it became evident Pamela hoped to ensure a devoted slave in Juliana, one who could remove the tedious burdens of the household from her shoulders once she snared the title of countess. All those sweetly worded requests for help, the misguided assistance at choosing dresses. Or was it misguided? If Juliana never

268

married, Pamela Hewit could have a spinster to take the burdens from her shoulders for years to come! Given those awful dresses and the encouragement to eat sweets, chances were that Juliana would have remained unwed instead of being on the verge of marriage with Sir Harry. Having smarted under the hand of Aunt Agatha, Vanessa recognized the little signs Juliana ignored, or perhaps didn't see.

At this point Juliana entered the room with a flourish, as though conjured up by Vanessa's thoughts. 'It is an utterly miserable day, is it not?' she sang out in the gayest of voices. 'I vow the fog is hanging over the hills in a most sinister manner, as though setting the stage for a tragedy.' Her laughter bubbled out as she stalked across the room like a villain preparing to attack. Her giggles brought a smile to the worried countenance above the worktable.

'I believe you are right,' said Vanessa. 'I do not know if the rain or the fog is more annoying. Perhaps tomorrow will be better.' Returning to her earlier thoughts, she enquired, 'Is Mrs Hewit to dine with us this evening?'

Juliana sobered instantly. 'I very much doubt she will wish to venture out in such weather. It almost makes me glad for the fog.

Oh, I cannot bear to think of dear Nicholas married to such a woman. I had begun to entertain thoughts in another direction.' She peeped at Vanessa to gauge her reaction to the too-casual words tossed out in seeming innocence.

'I beg of you, no nonsense, please. I am persuaded his marriage to such an admirable lady will solve all his problems, financial and otherwise. She is quite lovely,' Vanessa sighed, thinking with great lack of charity of the lamentably flat bosom displayed in the elegant, though slightly unfashionable gowns worn by the widow.

'Lovely she may be, but never kind. Did you observe how she continually demands — in the nicest possible way, mind you — that I fetch her a shawl or perform some other service for her, as though I were her personal servant? I vow, if it were not for Nicholas I would tell her to either do for herself or call her maid. I am out of patience with her, you may be certain!' Then she ceased her pacing about to break into a cherubic smile. 'However, things do progress with Harry. If this beastly weather ever breaks, you must go with me on another painting expedition. Harry mentioned there is a particularly fine patch of bloody crane's-bill not far from Eastthorpe Hall that ought to bloom before too long. Also, he knows where I may find a large plant of the deadly nightshade.' She assumed her villain pose once more and giggled again as she added, 'It's as well Mrs Murdoch does not venture into the woods or you might find it in your soup one day.' Catching Vanessa's look of alarm, she added, 'Oh, I have seen how she glares at you. Whatever did you do to put her back up?' Juliana perched on the edge of the worktable, studying Vanessa with frank curiosity.

'I suspect she resented that expression of sympathy I made some time ago — you know, when I asked if she needed more help. Poor woman undoubtedly needs spectacles and is too vain to wear them, or else she would see the dust about here. I do not know what possessed me to step beyond the line in that fashion. It is not my usual thing, I assure you.' Vanessa hesitated to mention the scene in the stillroom, when she had overheard the bargain struck by Mrs Murdoch. A check of the estate books *might* prove wrongdoing. Surely the woman would attempt nothing as drastic as Vanessa's demise, would she? Just to be on the safe side, Vanessa resolved to eat nothing not first tasted by others.

'You are all that is proper, dear Vanessa. I doubt you ever get an *im*proper thought in your head.' Juliana suppressed a grin at the rising hint of pink in Vanessa's cheeks. 'Well, I, for one, am going to see what is offered for luncheon today. I live in hope it is better than yesterday's presentation. That was truly horrendous!' She slid off the table and strolled toward the doorway, then paused to look back to where Vanessa sat at her needlework. 'Do you know, I tried to consult with Murdoch on menus, as you suggested, and she acted as though I was trying to take over her job! Fubsy-faced old woman. Pamela Hewit is welcome to her. I intend to be gone from here before too many months pass by.' With a flounce of her skirts, Juliana turned, leaving the room as suddenly as she had entered.

The afternoon passed quietly, Juliana reading out loud while Vanessa continued at her work in the fog-induced gloom with the aid of two branches of candles.

After Juliana left for her room, claiming a dry throat, Vanessa slipped from the saloon to find her way to the estate office. Mr Milibank was out on business, she knew. Peeking into the books was extremely distasteful to her, but if she was to discover any proof of Mrs Murdoch's cheating, this was one spot she might find it. She made a number of notes regarding transactions from the housekeeper's domain, then carefully left the office, first checking to see if anyone was about, while wondering just how she might have a look at the housekeeper's account books. Had anyone told her she would ever resort to this manner of skulduggery, she would have said he was daft in the head.

'Miss Tarleton! Have you lost your way?'

Startled, betraying the guilt felt at snooping into the estate books, though she had learned nothing she had not already suspected — that it was doing well enough — she felt the warmth stealing into her cheeks. 'Lord Stone! No, I, . . . er, was looking for Mr Millbank.' The reply was not exactly an untruth. She *had* taken care to see him . . . depart.

The gloom that had settled over the surrounding hills appeared to have entered the house, judging from the expression on Lord Stone's face. 'He's too busy for dalliance, though I must say I believe you two to be an ill-matched pair.'

Since Vanessa had reached the identical conclusion some time ago, she could scarcely argue with the earl. 'Ah, it regards some purchasing needs.' She stole a look at the watch pinned to her bosom, then fluttered a hand. 'I must dress for dinner, milord. I will see you then.' With barely disguised relief, she rushed off, clutching her slip of paper hidden in the folds of her skirt.

Nicholas stared after her precipitate flight and wondered what she was hiding.

It was a dismal dinner. Nicholas wore a rather grim expression. Vanessa wondered whether it was because of the absence of Mrs Hewit or the ill-prepared meal before him. Juliana chattered on, freeing Vanessa from the task of attempting conversation. She was relieved when she could safely escape to her room from the depressing company in the drawing room. Even her harp hadn't drawn her tonight.

She fussed at Katie as she dressed for bed. 'I have not seen my little dragon pin today, Katie. Know you where it is? I looked earlier, but cannot for the life of me recall where I put it.' She watched Katie in the mirror while that redoubtable miss brushed Vanessa's long golden tresses.

'Nay, milady. I've not seen it for several days. Sleep on it. Perhaps it will come to you in the night.' Katie took the question in good humor, knowing Vanessa to be the best of ladies, never demanding or accusing.

'Maybe. Come, Hercules, up on the bed. I never knew what an excellent foot-warmer you would become when I took you in.' She stroked the soft white fur, smiling as his green eye gave her a pleased wink.

'What you need is a good man to keep you warm at night. If you be thinking it cool now, what will you do come next winter?' Katie paused by the wardrobe in the act of checking a dress.

'I may be gone by then, Katie, and have no need for a masculine foot-warmer.' Vanessa bent her head, the sudden image of Nicholas Leighton arrayed in a night-shirt too overwhelming to contemplate.

'We'll see, milady. We'll see.' Taking her candle with her, Katie left the room, plunging it in darkness.

Vanessa suffered an uneasy sleep.

Sometime during the night she awoke with a start, as she was wont to do when something was pestering her mind. She sat up, recalling precisely where the dragon pin was to be found. Lighting her bedside candle, she made her way to the maghogany highboy, where her fingers searched the top drawer, then found the little pin. She had tucked it in with the linen cap she wore the day before, completely forgetting it until her dreams prompted her memory.

Holding it carefully in her hand, rubbing at the patina with a fond finger, she glanced to where Hercules sat on the windowsill watching the courtyard below. The cat turned his face toward her, blinking those peculiar eyes in a canny way.

'What is it, Hercules? Do you fancy you see something out in the night?' Still clutching her dragon, Vanessa walked to the window, her bare feet wincing at the cold wood along the wall. A draft from the slightly open window caused the candle to sputter and go out, leaving Vanessa in total darkness.

The fog had lifted, with tatters of clouds sweeping across the sky. The moon, now half-full, cast strange shadows before the house, floating wisps. It looked much like a running figure, which was nonsense, of course. Yet it seemed as though someone was there, moving in an erratic path away from the house. A cloud cut it from sight, plunging the courtyard into an unfathomable gray.

Vanessa continued to watch, puzzled at what she thought she saw, while knowing it must be her imagination, then turned her glance toward the entry. She drew in her breath sharply as she placed the dragon on the windowsill while leaning forward to see better. Was that a rosy glow from two of the windows? It was highly unlikely anyone would be in that part of the house now. The library, where Nicholas often sat until the wee hours of the night, was far removed.

Pausing only to grab up her robe from the

foot of her bed, she groped her way from her room, impelled by an unreasonable fear. The candles in the hall were burning very low, near the guttering point. She tore down the stairs and rounded the corner at a panic. That untold dread urged her to hurry, in total disregard of her bare feet and possible dangers. At the door to the green room, now standing tightly closed, she paused. If she had guessed correctly, this ought to be the room. She opened the door, then gasped.

Holland cloths torn from the furniture blazed in the center of the room, chairs heaped up catching fire even as she watched. She tore her hands from where it had touched her mouth in horror and ran for the bell pull. It would be useless to scream for help, for the servants slept far from this part of the house.

Not waiting for the arrival of whoever might answer her summons, she ran to the pyre of furniture, pulling at the chairs, tugging at the holland cloths. A small rug near the door caught her eye in the light of the fire. She whipped it at the fire, a frenzied figure silhouetted against the rapidly rising flames.

'Good God!' Peverly's voice reached Vanessa through her frantic efforts. The stunned butler froze at the door.

'Ring the alarm! We need all the help we can get!'

Moments later she was startled by the sound of a bell clanging with eerie vigor as she continued her battle against the fire. It was spreading, creeping along the fabric of the holland cloth, licking at the writing desk Vanessa strove to push away from the blaze.

When Nicholas joined her, his shirt hastily pulled over hurriedly donned breeches, he ordered, 'Get out of here, Vanessa! You could be burned to death.'

'Never! Help me pull this writing desk away so the fire can't damage it further.' As they shifted the delicate desk away from the flames, footmen hurried into the room to assist.

Outside, the fire engine was pulled up to the front door, with the well-drilled men, seven on each side, rushing into action. The flexible leather hose snaked around the corner of the door, then down the hall, pulled by a team of fierce-eyed men intent on getting the water to the fire.

Side by side Vanessa and Nicholas fought the blaze, carrying exquisite pieces of furniture, selected in order of value, to a place close to the door, where others could remove them. The men sought to repel the creeping flames that coiled out, writhing, snapping at the wood in its path. Water came, but the stream was pitifully small in such a large room. Vanessa rubbed her cheek in frustration as she watched the footmen tear down the newly hung draperies, flames curling up the green silk, while the room filled with thick, suffocating smoke and the terrible smell of burning wood and fabric. The men bundled up the draperies, now ruined beyond any hope of repair, to extinguish the fire.

Buckets of water were also brought from the pump, nearly thirty men now involved, gaining in the fight on the blaze. In the hall Juliana joined the maids in continually sweeping the water out the hall door.

Mr Millbank paused by the door as he carried another burden from the house, valuables, papers, jewels — just in case. He hurried on his way, intent on saving as much as possible, his nightcap — forgotten in hasty dressing — tipped at a comical angle on his head.

Nicholas wiped his brow with his arm. The advance of the fire was stemmed; it only remained for embers to be stamped out, the debris to be removed. He studied the soot-streaked face of the woman at his side. 'I think we have it under control. Come, we will let the men finish putting out the embers. You must be exhausted.' He gently drew her from the ruined room.

She glanced down at herself, dismayed to see her good robe covered with charred holes, splotches of soot everywhere, her nightgown meeting a similar fate where exposed. Her hands were bruised, small burns now beginning to hurt where they had been ignored in the heat of danger.

Nicholas fared no better. The branches of candles lit by Peverly to show the way revealed soot-stained breeches above bare feet, a shirt so spattered with burns it scarcely held together.

'Aren't we a pair, though?' Her amusement also made clear her shaken state, for her voice trembled badly. Her extreme pallor alarmed Nicholas.

'Vanessa, dear girl, how did you get into this?' He wrapped an arm about her, guiding her away from the debris of the fire toward the drawing room. Seeing Peverly, he ordered, 'Tell Mrs Murdoch to see to it the men get refreshments of some sort . . . ale and cheese with bread. 'Tis hard work, this firefighting.'

'I have not seen her. Perhaps she is a sound sleeper. I'll rouse her myself, if need be, milord.' His bow was, as ever, correct, and he disappeared as Vanessa sagged down on the floor of the drawing room near the fireplace, refusing to sit in the chair Nicholas pushed toward her. She felt utterly filthy.

She asked the dreaded question. 'What — or who — do you suppose started the fire? Of a certainty, it did not start itself. A person had to light the holland covers, place the chairs atop the pyre.'

Nicholas poured out a glass of brandy for each of them, then sank to the floor beside Vanessa, taking the poker with which she nudged the fitful fire from a trembling hand, replacing it with her glass.

Vanessa stared at the deep amber brandy in the glass, then downed the fiery liquid in one swallow, shuddering at its impact on her poor stomach. To Nicholas she appeared about to collapse. He removed the glass from her unresisting fingers, setting it aside with his.

'Here, allow me to help you.' He slid an arm around her shoulders, drawing her against him. He had been so wary of this woman. It wasn't that he didn't trust her, rather that he didn't trust the way he felt about her.

Plucking at a hole burned in her robe, Vanessa looked up to Nicholas, her eyes a storm-tossed blue. 'Sorry-looking spectacle I am. I ought to get to my room to change. You need your burns attended to as well.' Her voice trailed into a whisper as she continued to meet his eyes, trying to see what emotions lay in their midnight depths.

It was irresistible. They drew together slowly, both aware of details — the smell of smoke in her hair, his soot-streaked cheek. The kiss was at first tentative, a hesitant touching of lips. Then Nicholas found he could no longer hold back the desire that had been growing within him these past months. He crushed Vanessa to him, molding her body against him, caressing the beautifully modeled curves as though he had every right to do so. His lips sought hers in a kiss as fiery as the conflagration just left behind.

Could she be dreaming? Was this heady sensation singing through her body true? His mouth persuaded her response. Fatigue slipped momentarily from her as she yielded, trembling with awakening passion. Vanessa permitted her hands to slide up the tattered cambric shirt to clutch at his broad shoulders. His skin was warm, his body rock solid. Oh, it was real, all right. She wasn't asleep in the least! Sanity wrenched her from his arms. She stared up at him, eyes wide and wondering.

Nicholas slowly dropped one hand from where it had caressed a slim shoulder. In a voice that was deep, husky with emotion, he rasped out, 'Why the devil did you have to be poor?'

Stung as though he had slapped her across the face, Vanessa pulled away from him, wrapping her arms about her in an ageold gesture of defense. 'I fear I had little to say about it. I am as much the victim of circumstances beyond my control as you.' Bitterness seeped into her eyes as she stared at him. Her anguish tinging the words with her pain, she lashed out at him. 'I sought an honorable way to solve my dilemma. At least' — she bit off her words sharply — 'I am not selling myself or a title.' Her eyes flashed with scorn, defying him to deny the truth.

Nicholas gave her an anguished look. Her charge cut deeply into his conscience-stricken soul. If she only knew how tortured he was. Lord knew he'd tried to find a different solution. What else could he do? Could love withstand hardships? He recalled how it had been for his mother, for Vanessa too, like as not. Could he offer Vanessa a life of straitened circumstances? He failed to recall that she would know that regardless of what he did.

'Vanessa . . . '

She cast him a desolate look, silent yet not condemning, and pointedly turned again to the fireplace, shivering as though ill with an ague.

A sound, a stirring at the door, and Juliana wearily entered the room, dropping down on the floor close to Nicholas. 'The water has been cleared out of the room and the hall. I told the maids to go to bed — we can do the remainder in the morning. How strange Mrs Murdoch never joined us. Cook saw to food and ale for the men.' She leaned against Nicholas and he put a gentle arm about her, drawing her against him while he studied Vanessa, wondering what might be in her mind.

Vanessa bestirred herself to add, ''Tis a blessing the tapestries were from the room. What a shame if they had been destroyed as well as all else.'

'They meant a great deal to my grandfather, to me as well.' Nicholas tried to catch Vanessa's gaze, to assess her feelings. She had every right to accuse him of stepping beyond propriety. He found himself thwarted when she refused to so much as glance his direction. 'You have done a fine job of restoration. I am thankful they were spared.'

Ready to drop with fatigue, Vanessa pushed herself to rise, then looked to the door when Peverly entered, obviously agitated.

'Milord, Mrs Murdoch — she is not to be found anywhere!' He wrung his hands in an extraordinary display of anxiety.

Vanessa straightened, suddenly recalling the furtive shadow seen from her window before she discovered the fire. 'I daresay you will find she has departed the house, Peverly.'

Pulling Juliana up with him, Nicholas frowned at Vanessa. 'How can you be so sure?'

With a movement betraying her extreme weariness, the altercation with Nicholas, and the pain of her injuries, Vanessa replied, 'I suspect a check of the household account books will reveal all you need to know. I believe your housekeeper was indulging in some underhanded dealings, milord. If you do not mind, I will leave the explanations until morning. I doubt I can manage any at the moment.' Her voice faltered, fading into the silence of the room.

Then, with a rare show of sensibility, Vanessa swayed on her feet and fainted dead away.

13

There was a presence in her room. She could sense it. Vanessa opened her eyes. Juliana bent over her, critically studying her. Vanessa, still fuzzy from sleep and pain, tried to sit up. There were bandages over her hands. 'What happened?'

'You recall the fire?' At a slow nod from Vanessa, Juliana continued, 'Later you swooned in a most dramatic way. Fortunately Nicholas caught you before you chanced to hit the side of the table near the fireplace. He carried you up here, only leaving your room so Katie could put you to bed. Never have I seen Nicholas look like that. Frantic, he was. Katie dressed the burns on your feet and hands before allowing him to return.'

Bending closer to the bed, Juliana continued in a whispery voice, 'Nicholas refused to permit anyone else to watch over you. He spent the entire night at your bedside to make certain you were all right. I convinced him to get some sleep this morning. He looked positively worn to the bone. He allowed Katie to put some ointment on his hands and feet, but nothing more. He was very worried for you.'

Vanessa used her elbows to push herself up in the bed a little more. She needed time to think. 'Might I have a cup of tea, perhaps? I assure you I shall be quite fine. Is . . . er, Lord Stone asleep now?'

Nodding thoughtfully, Juliana replied, 'As far as I know. I'll send down for tea. You must be perishing for a cup. Toast too.' She bustled away from the bed, leaving Vanessa in blessed peace.

Moving up further in the bed, she drew the covers aside to inspect the soles of her feet. There were nasty burns on both, generously slathered with the ointment she kept with her store of medicines. Katie had done well. Given a day or so of rest, her feet ought to be back to near normal.

'Just where do you think you are going?'

Startled, Vanessa swiveled around to see Nicholas standing in the open door, hands on hips, an awesome frown marring his forehead. She hastily slid her feet beneath the down comforter and pulled the bedcovers as high as she could. It was ridiculous to feel exposed when she wore a nightgown of white cambric that came nearly to her chin and with sleeves that extended a little beyond her wrists. But she did.

'Nowhere! I was simply inspecting my burns. Juliana said you carried me up to my bed last night. Thank you.' She dropped her eyes to study the bandages on her hands. 'It must have been difficult for you with your own burns needing attention.' She peeked up to find him at her bedside.

'How are you this morning? That was a damn fool thing of you to do. Why didn't you leave the room when I told you to last night?'

'It could be much worse, considering. I stayed because I wanted to help you, and you needed me. You had better sit down. Your feet must be giving you pain. Mine are.'

When he eased himself down at the foot of her bed, she gave him a severe look. 'That wasn't quite the place I had in mind.' Her expression softened as she inquired, 'Your hands — are they very bad?'

'About like yours, blisters mostly, some scratches. Katie put ointment on them. Felt surprisingly good. I suppose it is something you concocted?'

In spite of her discomfort, she had to smile at his expression of wry acknowledgement. 'It is. Herbal, you know.' She picked at the covering of the comforter with the tip of a nervous finger that poked from the end of her bandage. 'It was most kind of you to sit with me all night. I suspect it was unnecessary, as I undoubtedly slept well. It was fatigue, the smoke, and excitement that did me in, I would imagine.'

Vanessa gave him a considering look. Even tired and disheveled, he outshone every man she could recall. 'Should you be in my room . . . now that I'm awake? Perhaps I ought to call Katie or Juliana.' Her blue eyes held the merest hint of a twinkle in them. 'To observe the proprieties,' she added, relishing the rueful twist of his mouth.

He shifted as though uncomfortable, then met her eyes with a troubled look. 'Not only must I give you my thanks for the help you gave me, I must beg your pardon for what happened afterward.'

Vanessa decided the kiss was best forgotten. 'Did something happen I ought to remember? I confess the evening is somewhat of a blur. I do seem to recall entering the drawing room and your giving me some brandy to drink. Beyond that . . . ' It annoyed her to see the look of relief that flashed across his face before being carefully replaced by one of polite concern.

Nicholas studied the innocent face. Did she really not remember what had happened, that fiery kiss that had rocked him to his very core? A man didn't challenge a lady about such a thing, and perhaps it was better she not recall it. He knew he couldn't forget, no matter what. He looked to the soft slippers on his feet as though they might have a clue to what he ought to say to her.

The tension broke when Juliana breezed into the room carrying a long slim account book tucked under one arm. Katie followed behind her, bearing a large tray that held three cups and plates as well as fingers of toast and a fat pot of steaming tea.

'Just wait until you hear what Millbank and I discovered! You were right, Vanessa. When we carefully compared the housekeeper's cash book with the estate accounts ledger. Millbank found Mrs Murdoch had been cheating Nicholas from the time she arrived! She made some very clever entries. Can you imagine? And to think Pamela Hewit recommended her so highly.' Juliana cast a sly glance at her brother to see how he accepted this criticism of the woman he pursued. 'Millbank sent a note to the local magistrate, but he doubts we shall see more of her. Did Nicholas tell you he believes she started the fire in an insane attempt to destroy us as well as the evidence? The woman was clearly not in her right mind. He suspects she has taken her loot and headed out of the country!'

Juliana was quite obviously excited at the dramatic events that had crashed into the quiet of her life. She placed the cash book on the table, then proceeded to pour out tea for Vanessa, Nicholas, and herself. Before discreetly leaving them alone, Katie first checked the bandages on Vanessa's hands, then her feet. The maid totally ignored the protestations from Vanessa regarding the latter.

Pink-cheeked at the thought that Nicholas would see far too much of foot and ankle, Vanessa tried to rise above such things. 'I expect you have the right of it. We can only give thanks that her evil did no more harm.'

'If you hadn't raised the alarm, the entire house could have gone. By the by, how did you happen to be awake?' Nicholas had walked to the window, and stood staring out, his face impossible to read. He absently sipped from the tea while awaiting her reply.

'I misplaced my dragon pin, and during the night I recalled where I had put it. While I was up, I noticed Hercules sitting on the windowsill, watching the courtyard. I couldn't see anything other than ghostly shadows, which now I suspect was Mrs Murdoch fleeing after starting the fire. I chanced to look at the front of the house and observed a rosy glow in the windows. The rest you must know.'

There was still little expression on his face, other than the faintly grim one he had worn since entering the room. Vanessa watched as he returned to stand by her bed, cup in hand.

'Very gallant of you. We owe you a debt that is nigh impossible to repay, my dear. Tell me, why didn't you simply raise the alarm and let the others fight the fire?'

'That is what Pamela would have done,' Juliana softly inserted from her chair near the window.

Noting his look of irritation at the aspersion cast at his future wife, Vanessa took a sip of restoring tea, then replied, 'It did not occur to me. Quite foolish, I suppose. I told Peverly to raise the alarm, then began what was necessary. It seemed the practical thing to do. The sooner the fire was attacked, the sooner it could be put out.'

Vanessa leaned back on her pillow after finishing a satisfactory cup of tea and several fingers of toast. Wanting nothing more than to be left in peace to soothe the wounds to her spirit, she feigned a sigh of fatigue. It brought an instant response.

'You must get your rest. Forgive us for disturbing you after all you have done for us.' Nicholas set his cup on the tray with a loud click, then walked closer to her bedside, wincing at the discomfort from a blister on his foot.

Vanessa narrowed her eyes in speculation.

Did Nicholas accept her fakery, or did he see through her ruse to rid the room of his presence? 'Thank you for your consideration, milord. I am most conscious of your concern.' With that, she allowed her eyes to drift shut as though tired.

The rustle of Juliana's gown fading into the distance, followed by total silence, convinced Vanessa she was alone. She opened her eyes, then attempted to push herself to a sitting position once more.

'I suspected you were doing it a bit too brown. Why not just tell us to get out if you wanted peace?'

'Get out. See, it does no good. You are still here.' She was breathless at his closeness. It brought back the memory of last night's kiss far too vividly.

'I'll go, but not before I give you my thanks once more. It was very courageous of you, and I shall find some manner of showing you my gratitude.' He held out his hand, then dropped it to his side with a sigh of frustration as he again observed her bandaged hands.

Vanessa turned her face toward the window. 'Please, it is enough to receive your thanks. I want nothing else.' Except your love, which is an impossibility! she admitted morosely. She admired his dedication to what he believed he must do, while she wished with all her heart he wasn't so committed to duty.

The door closed and she was left in silence. She had wished him gone so that she might know peace . . . and now there was no tranquillity for her. How contrary the heart is. A lone tear slid from the corner of one eye, causing her to blink quite hard, then close her eyes with the hope of a nap.

She must have been more exhausted than she suspected, for she slept some time. A light tapping at her door roused her from her slumbers. She called permission to enter. Katie bustled into the bedroom with another tray. This one carried a bowl of broth and fresh bread. 'Compliments of Cook, milady. Everyone belowstairs is anxious for you to be well again and on your feet. As soon as you finish, I expect Lady Juliana will be up to keep you company.' She paused. 'That is, if you be wantin' company?'

Vanessa met those shrewd eyes with unswerving calm. 'I quite like the idea, Katie. It would get exceedingly dull in here by myself.'

Nodding happily to herself, Katie left the room. It wasn't long before Juliana bounced in with the cash book under her arm and a sheaf of papers in her hand.

'You will never imagine what I am about! I have decided I will take command of the household! Is that not daring? I do hope everything doesn't tumble down about our ears before Nicholas can get a new housekeeper. He sent off a request to an agency in York first thing this morning. Now, I desire your help. I scanned the entries, and I had no idea what manner of things a housekeeper must needs order. Fancy this, cotton reels and pin papers, carpet thread by the pound, and wadding by the sheet! Here she ordered fifty-four yards of calico at a time! I expect that was for new dresses for the maids. I have no notion of how she used this China silk or scarlet braid. How do I go on?' Juliana plumped herself on the bedside chair, an air of expectancy about her as she waited for the reply.

'I doubt if Lord Stone will be long in getting a new housekeeper. Instead of plunging into this, just see to the day-to-day care of the house. Linens in the morning, that sort of thing. I shall dress and come down to help you.' When Juliana put out a restraining hand, Vanessa brushed it aside. 'I am determined to go downstairs. There is nothing wrong with me other than a slight burn or two.'

She felt much better when seated in the

saloon by her worktable. 'I can assist you much better from here.' Juliana seemed too grateful to argue.

Lord Stone was displeased to see Vanessa had quit the bedroom so soon, but she wasn't too concerned about his reaction at this point. She spent the remainder of the day guiding Juliana into the intricacies of managing the household. With her customary enthusiasm, Juliana made the task a distinct joy. She bubbled and bounced in and out of the saloon following yet another foray into the housekeeper's stores after checking the cash book entries. There was a great deal to be learned.

Vanessa knew a faint pang of regret as a footman carried her back to her room at Juliana's insistence when it was time to retire. What a pity she hadn't been able to enjoy the journey in Lord Stone's arms.

The following morning Vanessa felt so much better she resolved to go down the stairs before any fuss might be raised. Consequently she entered the breakfast room at her usual early hour, her feet gingerly negotiating the distance.

'I might have known you wouldn't keep to your bed,' Nicholas scolded, his expression a study of exasperated disapproval.

'I am not ill, milord. Why remain in bed on

what promises to be a most glorious day?' The look on his face might have been comic at another time. Today it simply annoyed Vanessa. 'I fare well, I assure you. How does the work progress on the aftermath of the fire? I noticed the charred part of the floor has been removed. It will be like starting anew on the room.'

Nicholas paused a moment in reflection, then replied, 'I can only be grateful the tapestries had not been rehung in there.' His gaze swept the room before coming to rest on Vanessa. 'Millbank has ordered new draperies, and the carpenters, as you noticed, have begun their work. If all goes well, the painters can return before too long. What do you do today?'

'I expect Juliana will want to go out.'

'See that you don't overdo. Sit quietly,' he ordered, 'for there is no need to have a needle in your hand.' He flung down his napkin beside a partially eaten meal, leaving the room in what Vanessa suspected was a high dudgeon of some sort.

When Juliana joined Vanessa in the saloon, she was bubbling with happiness. 'We shall take the dogcart this morning, and I shall paint those flowers Harry told me about. I sent a groom to Eastthorpe Hall to tell Harry I desire his assistance today. You will be fine

297

as ninepence in the cart, will you not?' Juliana's concern for Vanessa's well-being briefly nudged aside her delighted contemplations of Sir Harry.

Vanessa smiled, amused at the capriciousness of the young woman's attention span. Juliana's desire to oversee the household was short-lived. Her intentions were of the best, and Sir Harry happened to come first at the moment. Vanessa had managed to suggest a few pressing tasks to Peverly, assuring him Lady Juliana would want them to be done. The maids set to work in the hallway, scrubbing and polishing under Peverly's eagle eye. Footmen tended the chandeliers. Already the house was attaining the sparkle it always should have had. Vanessa was pleased if she could assist in this small way, though she made certain Juliana believed the orders stemmed from herself. Turning her attention to the day ahead, she hastened to settle Juliana's doubts.

'Of course, I shall have no problem. I don't know why everyone makes such a fuss over a little thing like a couple of blisters and a scratch or two. I notice your brother is up and about today.'

'Oh, well, he is a man.' And that said it all. It was pointless to argue on that score.

If truth were known, Vanessa had enjoyed

the bit of fussing yesterday. She had had little enough of it while growing up. With a mother who succumbed to every ailment imaginable, then demanded the attentions of the entire household, Vanessa had far greater experience in nursing than being nursed.

When Nicholas heard they were to leave, he insisted he be allowed to carry Vanessa from the house, gently placing her in the dogcart with further admonitions to take care. From a point down the drive, she turned to wave farewell, only to be disappointed that Lord Stone had returned to the interior of the house. Memory of his strong arms about her, his face wearing a determined expression she simply could not fathom, stayed in her mind.

The sky was as blue as ever she could recall. A song thrush sang from a hedge by the road, hidden from view. In the distance a chiffchaff added his vibrant melody. The pony trotted along the grassy lane, the ruts thankfully not as pronounced as in the road from York. The two girls considered it a very fine prospect indeed. Vanessa gaily twirled her parasol a time or two, taking care not to dislodge the spyglass in her lap. While Juliana painted, Vanessa intended to study the local bird life. It should prove to be an unexceptionable diversion.

They passed meadowland and pastures of clover and vetch until they saw Sir Harry coming to meet them on his chestnut mare.

'Beautiful morning, is it not, Harry?' Juliana waved in girlish enthusiasm that Vanessa had not the heart to depress.

'Happy to join two such lovely ladies. Ready to have a go at your painting?' Sir Harry reserved all his attention for the attractive Juliana. Vanessa hid a smile at his slight air of bewilderment, as though he were uncertain how all this magic had come about, turning Juliana from an awkward duckling into a lovely swan.

The day progressed at a leisurely pace, Sir Harry assisting Juliana at every turn. Vanessa could only be amused at his eagerness to attend the young lady he had known since nursery days — and ignored most of that time. As for herself, she found that her feet tolerated a bit of walking with no great difficulty. When bothered, she simply found a grassy spot and sat down. After urging the groom to remain with Sir Harry and Juliana, ostensibly to have the cart close by to hold paraphernalia, she slowly made her way along a gradual rise, making note of wildflowers worth mentioning to Juliana.

Rough poppies of deep red with black-pepper centers sprang up along the track, interspersed with pert blue tufts of sheep's-bit. Off to one side she espied tall stalks of elecampane, the large golden heads reminding her of bright, fringed suns.

A ring ouzel scolded her — for coming too close to its nest, she guessed. Wheatears and stonechats along with redstarts and goldcrests darted about overhead. She was charmed by the sight. A wee hedge sparrow, its cinnamon color blending in with the twigs of the hedge, peeked at her more boldly than his fellows. Vanessa sank down on a nearby stone to rest her feet. 'What do you say, my friend? A fine day to be alive, is it not?' From the crest of the rise, Vanessa could see across a long, narrow valley. Down the center of it a trail wound alongside a stream, with clumps of weeping willows trailing branches in the meandering water. A peaceful scene of great beauty, she thought placidly.

Then two figures on horseback approached from the south, a man and a woman. Vanessa watched, idly at first, then with interest, as they neared. The woman was dressed in a gay yellow habit, the man in deep blue coat, nankeen breeches, and shining boots. Unless she missed her guess, it had to be Lord Stone with Mrs Hewit.

Without conscious thought that she was doing something she abhorred, Vanessa raised the spyglass to her eye, bringing it to focus on the couple in the shade of the largest of willow clumps. They stood very close, Lord Stone having assisted Mrs Hewit from the back of her chestnut mare. Mrs Hewit raised her face to the earl's, her hand clinging to his coat.

Had ever a pain so sharp thrust through her breast? Vanessa wondered. The sight of that dark head bent in unmistakable intent over the figure in bright yellow drove all else from her mind. Nicholas was kissing Pamela Hewit, and it wasn't the briefest of kisses either. Lowering the spyglass to her lap with hands that trembled noticeably, Vanessa turned to look at the little hedge sparrow once more. He seemed curious about the large bird so close to his perch. Vanessa stared at him. 'Can I bear it, dear sparrow? I know it *must* be the wisest thing for him to do, but oh, how it hurts me to see it so plainly.'

She had no notion how long she sat on the stone near the top of the rise. She could feel a gentle breeze against her face, feel the warmth of the sun where her parasol and bonnet failed to shade her. It didn't grow cold, as it should have, as in the novels she read. No disaster befell the two in the valley. Birds continued to warble in the scrub and low trees as though nothing of import occurred this day. She watched, her heart numb with a frozen kind of grief, as Nicholas helped Mrs Hewit back on her horse and they cantered off to the south once again. The sun moved on until Vanessa heard Juliana and Sir Harry calling her. Summoning her courage, she faced them as the cart jolted its way up the path.

'At last you join me. Did you see the elecampane and sheep's bit along the path? If the weather holds, you will have quite a number of additions to your collection. May I see what you have accomplished thus far?' Vanessa was determined to present a normal façade, though she longed to retreat in silence.

Though it was not a simple matter to feign delight, Juliana's watercolors drew Vanessa from her unhappiness as she viewed the paintings. 'How lovely, my dear. Truly you have a wondrous talent.'

Sir Harry bestowed a fond look on Juliana's face peeping up from her bonnet. 'She does, doesn't she? Never knew she had it in her. Devilishly clever of her, don't you think?'

Juliana joined Vanessa in gentle laughter. Vanessa was assisted by a gallant Sir Harry into the cart for the journey home. If she seemed a trifle subdued and spoke but seldom while they bumped along the track toward the main path, her companions counted it as fatigue. And truly, it was a rough ride at first, so one could be forgiven for not talking.

Rather than part from them at the boundary of his property, Sir Harry elected to ride the entire distance to Stone's Court. His decision brought rich roses to Juliana's cheeks, though her offhand treatment of Sir Harry seemed to confuse the poor man no end. He did all he could think of to please her. But Juliana had discovered the power of a woman admired. She intended to catch the man she'd adored all these years, so she demurely put him off.

As they reached the front entrance, Peverly opened the door. The sight of two horses being led toward the stables prepared Vanessa for the appearance of Mrs Hewit and Lord Stone at the entry. Rather than flee to her room, she nodded graciously to Pamela and motioned Juliana ahead of her up the steps. Vanessa ignored the odd look from Lord Stone.

He studied her pale face and his voice seemed concerned as he spoke. 'How are your feet this afternoon? You did not attempt to do much walking, did you?'

'I am quite well, milord. I believe I may

return to my needlework tomorrow. I am certain you will want to have the tapestries completed by the time the room has been restored.' Stiff with dignity, she entered the house, wondering how soon she could escape.

The group gathered in the central hall, a degree of ill-ease settling on various of the members. Juliana cast a guarded glance at her brother, then spoke. 'Why don't we all go into the drawing room for tea?' She recalled the lack of a housekeeper and tossed Vanessa a perturbed look.

'Tea! By Jove, just the ticket.' Sir Harry stepped close to Juliana to escort her, while Mrs Hewit moved near Lord Stone. Nicholas turned to Vanessa. 'Do you feel up to tea? Or should I carry you to your room again?'

Vanessa could see the narrowing of eyes, the calculating expression that crept over Mrs Hewit's face, and she shook her head as she untied her bonnet strings. 'I am fine, milord. Please go on without me. I shall persuade Mr Millbank to join our little group. I shan't be a minute.' She dipped a fine curtsy, then hurried down the hall.

Perhaps it might be best if she pretended an interest in Millbank. Heaven knew the man was dull as ditch water and prosed on like a Methodist, but he would divert attention from herself. She found him in the library.

'Would you care to join us for tea, Mr Millbank? Sir Harry escorted Lady Juliana and me home from our outing. When we arrived, we found Mrs Hewit with Lord Stone at the front entry. Lady Juliana has called for tea — there is someone in the kitchen who can be relied upon to prepare it properly, is there not?' She sensed he enjoyed the confidence placed in his judgment.

'Peverly and Cook get along quite well, you know. I believe that until a new housekeeper arrives, things will not be too difficult here.'

'I assured Lady Juliana I will do all I can to ease things for her. Though of course I have my own work, you know.' She extended her hand to him, drawing him into the hall and toward the drawing room with her as she spoke. When they entered, it was to a pleasantly burning fire, enough to keep a chill from the room, and animated conversation. For a moment, while pausing on the threshold, Vanessa felt the veriest outsider. Then Juliana caught sight of her.

'Come join us.' Juliana gave a gay wave of her hand. 'You must be careful of your feet, you know.'

Mrs Hewit studied the pair who entered the room, seeming to relax as she saw the polite care Millbank gave Vanessa. Vanessa knew it was mistaken for a greater interest than actually existed.

The chestnut-haired beauty smoothed the bright yellow of her habit with a coy manner. 'I vow I am utterly desolated to see how you and Nicholas suffered as a result of that viper, Mrs Murdoch. Who could have believed she would do such a thing?'

Vanessa thought much, but said nothing.

Not so Juliana. 'Did Nicholas tell you of her manner of cheating? The woman was a thief, making infamous deals with merchants from the village. Feathered her nest from the day she came here, I daresay! Then to attempt to destroy our home!'

It was not to be expected that Mrs Hewit would accept this thrust without a parry of her own. 'How terrible! I placed such trust in her, too. It seems I need a hand stronger and wiser than mine to guide my affairs. I am so pleased Nicholas has offered . . . ' Here she paused with dramatic effect. Juliana and Vanessa scarcely moved a muscle, straining to hear the next words that would fall from the pouting lips. ' . . . to give me the assistance I require.'

The words themselves were not too bad, Vanessa mused. It was the air of complacency with which they were uttered that stabbed at the heart.

Nicholas moved from where he had positioned himself by the fireplace to stand behind Pamela's chair, as though to add power to her statement, placing his hand on her shoulder. She slowly reached up to stroke his hand in a seemingly absentminded gesture, the kind one does with a husband . . . or lover.

If it was not a declaration, it was near enough. Vanessa could no more remain in this room or consume a polite cup of tea than fly. Yet she dared not run to her room now. It would reveal too much to the eagle-eyed woman preening herself beneath Nicholas's regard.

So Vanessa remained, drinking two cups of hot tea, welcoming the scalding liquid with reckless disregard for her tender tongue.

Juliana must have sensed the strained atmosphere in the room, for she chattered on about her findings of the day, allowing Sir Harry to assist her with the display of her paintings, smiling at him with such charm and grace that he nearly tripped over his own boots.

It was the most depressing tea Vanessa could recall. Mrs Hewit had established her claim on Nicholas Stone with an ease that belied how long and hard she had worked to reel in her catch.

At last Vanessa felt free to excuse herself. She hurried down the hall, pausing at the door of the saloon to stare thoughtfully at the tapestries spread out on the work-table. As of now, she felt as though she had aged ten years in the past four months. How much more heartache must she endure before she left Stone's Court forever?

14

'Good morning, milord. I trust you are feeling better this morning?' Vanessa entered the breakfast room with her fortitude firmly tucked in place. She simply would not permit herself to dream over the impossible.

Lord Stone nodded while buttering a muffin. 'Well enough. My sister is indifferent in her attentions regarding the house at this point, although I am certain she tries her best. The sooner we replace Mrs Murdoch, the better. We have had a communication from the agency regarding a new house-keeper. Milbank will go to York to interview the applicants immediately.' He gave Vanessa a quizzing look, one touched with a hint of archness. 'You can survive without his company, Miss Tarleton?'

She quelled a desire to cry a denial of interest in Millbank. Instead, she smiled calmly, which took more effort than she expected, and replied, 'I imagine anything is possible, milord.'

He sipped at his coffee, then said, 'If that were only true. The bills mount each day for the repairs to the damage caused by the fire.

Dashed costly thing.' He shook his head in gloomy reflection.

Her usual reticence set aside, she leaned forward in concern. 'You really have little alternative as regards your solution, do you? That is, if you desire to fulfill your promise to yourself and your grandfather. Juliana has spoken of your admirable motives in the restoration of the house.' She was certain he could never imagine how she felt in her heart, or how terribly difficult it was for her to encourage him to wed another. It wasn't a nobility of purpose on her part. It was simply that she loved him. If Nicholas felt honor-bound to pursue this path, she would not hinder him.

Nicholas didn't pretend to misunderstand her intent. He met her gaze, his eyes revealing how torn he was in regard to his solution. He could continue apace with his program of refurbishing or abandon it to a sort of holding action. Glancing down at his plate, then back up to her once more, he nodded. 'I fear you are right. A man cannot always follow his heart.' Then, as though he had said more than he intended, he rose from the table, hastily excusing himself.

Vanessa was left to mull over the brief conversation in silence. It seemed that while Nicholas accepted his fate regarding Mrs

Hewit, he did not welcome it. If he could not follow his heart as regards Mrs Hewit, it stood to reason his affections lay elsewhere. That absurd bit of reasoning lit her eyes with hopeful speculation, until she decided it was a rather fruitless pursuit.

A disturbance in the central hall drew her from the now-unwanted breakfast. She strolled out the door of the breakfast room, then along toward the hall. She was rewarded with a glimpse of Sir Harry walking behind Peverly in the direction of the library. Above, Juliana peered over the banister, straining to see what was going on.

Running up the stairs to greet her, Vanessa chided, 'Keeping an eye on the guests, Juliana?' It was hard not to laugh at the outraged expression on the young woman's face.

'That was Sir Harry who entered the house just now. I happened to be looking out my window when he rode up. I thought he was coming to call on me. Instead I saw Peverly show him down the hall toward the library to see Nicholas. It makes me out of reason cross. Unless . . . ' Irritation gave way to a dawning look of joy. 'Do you suppose he intends to ask for my hand? I wonder if Nicholas will be surprised.'

'Somehow I doubt such a thing, my dear. Sir Harry has been living in your pocket some weeks now.' The two young women began to walk down the stairs, Vanessa intent on reaching the saloon, Juliana desiring to be nearby in case her presence was requested.

'Yes, he has, hasn't he?' A complacent smile settled on Juliana's appealing little mouth. She peeped up at Vanessa, then burst into a fit of laughter. 'Am I past all redemption, dear Vanessa?'

'Hardly, my dear. You shall do well, never fear.'

It was then that Vanessa noticed the becoming gown Juliana wore. Unlike her customary morning attire, usually quite plain, it was deliciously charming. Blue sprigged muslin with dear little bows scattered around the hem and neckline was just the thing to set off her fair skin and newly washed hair. The morning sun that beamed into the saloon they had entered during their quiet conversation brought hints of gold to the light brown. Never had Vanessa been so pleased with her efforts as this morning.

'I owe you so much.' Juliana clasped Vanessa's hand in fervent gratitude. 'If you had not come to stay with us, I would not know this happiness today.'

'Wait until he speaks to you before you crow.'

Juliana shook her head. 'He will. I know it.'

Threading yarn of the richest blue through her needle, Vanessa began to work an area on the gown of one the stately court ladies in the tapestry. 'I pray you are right.' At least some good would come from Vanessa's stay at Stone's Court.

Before long Peverly paused at the open doorway, nodding to Juliana in a friendly manner. 'Sir Harry wishes to speak with you in the drawing room, Lady Juliana.'

Her triumphant glance amused Vanessa. She watched the younger woman sail out of the saloon, ribbons fluttering, the scent of primroses drifting after her. How she envied Juliana, on her way to receive the address of the man she loved. Vanessa bent her head over her work, concentrating on weaving her needle in and out of the tapestry.

'I trust you approve?'

Startled, Vanessa looked up to see the mocking countenance of Lord Stone. She hadn't heard him enter. Of course, she had been deep in thought. 'I assume you mean Lady Juliana and Sir Harry? But of course I approve. You do not?' She held her needle poised above the tapestry while she awaited his answer. It was unthinkable he might have denied Juliana her heart's desire, but one never knew.

'I must confess I am surprised. I knew he had been riding out with you both on the excursions to paint, and he danced only with her that evening of her party. But to ask her to wed? Why now? Is she so altered?'

Vanessa chose her words with care. 'Perhaps he has come to see her with new eyes. She has been growing up all these years in proximity with him, I know, but the scales of familiarity do occasionally fall from one's eyes to reveal the changes wrought by time.'

'Plus a little help from a friend, I think. At least in this case. I have been rather blind about my sister. Yesterday I took a thoughtful look at her during dinner. Her change is not simply owing to the passage of time, my dear. She is far slimmer, her skin is clear, and her hair has charming highlights. I believe you helped her with those dratted herbs of yours. Am I not correct?'

'Would that be so terrible, if it were true?' She held her breath as she awaited his reply.

'No, I suppose not. I've been rather a bear about that, haven't I?'

His sudden capitulation on the subject brought an astonished, 'Will wonders never cease!' from Vanessa. A wry smile touched her mouth.

'Do you now choose to hold it over me? I am about to get my sister off to the very best of fellows, a good friend and neighbor. And I suspect it is much your doing, my dear.' He pulled up a chair to the worktable, then continued with his speech. 'I have much to thank you for, I know.'

She met his gaze with a shyness not like her normal manner. My dear. He'd used the term twice. What meaning could it have for her? Those dark eyes, so eloquent, seemed to reveal a yearning to match her own. She shook her head as though to deny the reality of what she saw. His hand reached out to cover hers, a tender touching. she glanced at it, then met his gaze once more.

'You are quite welcome, milord. I am always glad to be of service to my employer.'

'What? You know there is far more closeness than that between us.' His anger was almost tangible.

'That must not be, milord.' Her calm voice amazed her. His unexpected approach must be deflected — for his own good if nothing else. There could never be more between them. If they were to marry, she knew he would come to hate her for denying him the means to continue with the improvement to his property. Although she desired him, she could never bear his hatred.

316

'Speak plainly.'

'I helped your sister because I felt sorry for the dear girl. The assistance I gave you during the fire was such that anyone of heart might have done, you know. You must make nothing more of these incidents, milord.'

He rose to pace before the long expanse of windows. 'I believe you mean what you say . . . as far as that goes. I must respect your words, but I cannot like them.'

Vanessa glanced up to see Juliana and Sir Harry arrive at the door. She made to rise, thinking she ought to leave the room. Nicholas frowned at her, waving her to her chair once more.

The two who entered smiled self-consciously before Juliana sought Sir Harry's nod of reassurance. Her gaze remained fastened upon him as he began to speak.

'She will have me, Nicholas! I am the luckiest of fellows. I am determined we shall wed soon, for I dare not allow this darling girl time to change her mind.' His warm, possessive look as his own large hand was placed over the little hand tucked through the crook of his arm was enough to bring tears of joy to Vanessa's eyes.

On the heels of this announcement, Mrs Hewit was ushered into the room by Peverly. She was swiftly apprised of the betrothal. 'I vow I wish you both happy.' If there was a dissatisfied gleam in her eyes or her smile lacked sincerity, none but Vanessa caught it.

Juliana sent her a jubiliant look. 'Thank you. Harry wishes to marry as soon as possible.'

'Aye. We'll have the banns read this Sunday.'

'Then you must have a betrothal party! Oh, Nicholas, permit me to help you with this joyful task!' Pamela darted a sharp look at Vanessa. She seemed content to find her rival submissively plying her needle in the tapestry, and turned again to plead her cause.

'Of course, of course. My dear little sister and the best of friends. What better arrangement could one wish? When Millbank returns with the new housekeeper, you may confer with her, Pamela.' He glared at Vanessa, who returned his taunting look with a bland one of her own, concealing the death of any hopes she might have nurtured with admirable composure.

The others strolled from the room, Nicholas calling to Peverly for champagne to be brought to the drawing room to toast the engaged couple. He looked back at Vanessa from the hall.

'Do join us, Miss Tarleton.'

With a stubborn tilt of her chin, Vanessa

shook her head. As much as she loved Juliana, it was far preferable to stay away from Pamela Hewit. 'No, I thank you most kindly, milord.'

Nicholas glared at her again, taking note of that defiant chin, then gave an exasperated shrug and followed the others.

Vanessa watched them disappear from view, their voices floating back, echoing in the marble confines of the central hall before fading away. So much for his protestations of gratitude. She attacked the tapestry with renewed vigor, glad that the second tapestry was nearing completion. The third contained the least of the damage, it being away from the western sunlight. A few more weeks and she could leave here. The months had sped past so quickly, she could scarce believe it had turned from spring to summer since she arrived.

Her head rose abruptly as a sound from the hall caught her ear. Lord Stone entered, carrying a glass of bubbling liquid.

'You may wish to toast the happy couple.'

'You might have sent Peverly, you know.' Her chiding was halfhearted.

'I wished to remind you that you chose your path.' His voice was cool, proper, yet held reproach.

'No' — she shook her head sadly — 'that was chosen long before.' She accepted the glass and sipped the champagne.

'I would dissuade you of that nonsense.'

'Would that it were such, milord.' Defiantly she drained the glass and handed it to him. 'Mrs Hewit will not like your absence, I believe. You had best return to the woman who can realize your dreams.'

It was more than she had intended to say and it angered Lord Stone, mainly because it was so accurate an assessment. 'So be it.'

The effervescent comfort of the champagne seeped through her body as she contemplated his final words. He wouldn't seek her out again.

Millbank didn't return until late the following day, bringing a pleasant, neat-looking woman of middle years with him. Her plain dress of black bombazine was offset by a crisp white apron and white cap when Vanessa encountered her in the breakfast room the next morning. Katie had praised the new housekeeper with a lack of her usual sharpness when she came up to wake Vanessa that morning. Apparently Mrs Barkham won support without half-trying.

'Good day, Miss Tarleton. Would you care for a berry muffin?' She set forth a basket of steaming muffins that smelled deliciously tempting. Vanessa accepted one with pleasure, then applied herself to a light breakfast.

'You have come to a joyful household, Mrs Barkham. I hope you will not feel too pressed with all the preparations for the upcoming wedding.' Vanessa smiled at the woman, who looked as though nothing was beyond her capabilities.

'I daresay I shall come about well enough,' Mrs Barkham replied crisply. 'You are mending tapestries in the large saloon, Mr Millbank said. That is an exacting task. I expect you are a fair hand at your job. May I call on you if need be?'

The request was unexpected and Vanessa revealed her puzzlement.

'Lady Juliana has her head in the clouds. Mr Millbank is a fine man, but not, I think, aware of some details. Cook informed me you have done much of assistance here before I arrived. If I may?' she repeated.

'But of course,' said Vanessa, flattered to be consulted. Then she recalled her place. 'However, I believe Mrs Hewit will be here to work on the betrothal party. Lady Juliana may find herself quite amenable to applying herself to *that* task.' She smiled with an understanding shared by Mrs Barkham.

'Aye, that she may.' Nothing more was said about consulting Mrs Hewit, but Vanessa was certain the staff had already filled Mrs Barkham in on the family details. It never ceased to amaze Vanessa how so much information could be passed along in so brief a time, as though the servants possessed some manner of abbreviated communication.

Determined to remain in the background during the preparations for the betrothal party, Vanessa worked at the tapestry with renewed vigor. The second one was completed and shifted about so the third and final one could take its place. She studied it, absently rubbing her finger over one of the odd trapunto humps while assessing the work to be done.

'Are you avoiding me, dear Vanessa?' Juliana bustled into the room, searching out her friend where she was half-hidden by the mound of tapestry.

'Never! I *am* trying to do my work, however. I suspect you are too much occupied with your plans to be knowing what else goes on about here.' She sent an amused look at the miffed younger woman, hoping to allay any suspicions. 'You have Pamela Hewit to assist you with your party.'

'Fiddle! That woman has the most atrocious taste I ever saw. Can you fancy she wishes me to have an *orange* dress with *puce* ribbons for the affair? Me . . . in a ghastly orange? Now, I ask you!' Indignant at the vast number of frightful notions promoted by

322

Pamela, Juliana had nearly reached the point of tears. 'And Nicholas! That ninny agrees to everything Pamela suggests, as though he didn't give a farthing how the party turns out.'

Vanessa wondered if he did care one whit. He had been absent from the house as much as possible, claiming visits to tenants, consultations with Sir Harry, even a trip to York for something or other. It was as though he fought admitting the inevitable. There had been no declaration of an engagement between Nicholas and Pamela . . . yet.

Pamela had intimated that Nicholas would wait to ask her to wed until after he fired off his younger sister. While the waiting was agony, Vanessa knew she welcomed any postponement of that announcement.

'I believe men feel differently about parties than we do. Be patient with him, my dear. This is a difficult time for him, trying to meet the additional costs of repair. He is admirable in not wishing to store up debts, but that means he must find a way to finance the work.'

Abashed for a moment, Juliana nodded. 'I know. I will try to get along with Pamela, truly I will. He intends to wed her someday, although how he can stand that jingle-brained, bird-witted goosecap is beyond me.'

She threw up her hands in dismay. 'I must have your help in choosing a dress. Since she insists on orange, I cannot allow her to be present when the dressmaker comes. Please, Vanessa . . . I loathe orange!'

Shaking her head in amusement, Vanessa carefully placed her needle in its case, then rose from her chair at the worktable. 'I'll come.'

Arm in arm, they tiptoed up the stairs quietly lest Pamela discover Juliana escaping her keen-eyed gaze.

A blue so pale it was almost white was agreed upon as the most happy choice. Matching slippers, the pearl necklace that was a betrothal gift from Sir Harry, and the elegant fan given her by her brother were decided as all that was needed to complete the outfit. Vanessa slipped away to her room for a moment, returning with a scarf of silver gauze.

'I never had a chance to wear this. It was bought for my wedding. Please do me the honor of wearing it.'

Emotions overcame Juliana and a few tears slipped down her cheeks. 'A pleasure, I promise you.' She tenderly placed the scarf across her bed, then enveloped Vanessa in a warm hug.

With the important decision of what Juliana was to wear out of the way, Vanessa returned to her needlework. Mr Millbank found her there, bent over a hunting dog that was shredded into a haze of color.

'The party is approaching. You will go?'

She nodded, reluctant to admit she much preferred to hide in her room away from the sight of Pamela Hewit in the arms of the man Vanessa loved.

'May I claim the first dance? It will not be a waltz, so I am safe.' His wry smile pleased Vanessa; the man could jest about his own stuffiness.

'I would be honored, Mr Millbank.'

'Would you be lost to all propriety if you called me Robert?' There was a boyish charm about him today that Vanessa found appealing. If she couldn't have Nicholas, Mr Millbank — Robert — would be good company.

'Perhaps between us it might be possible. I wouldn't want to cause a breakdown among the staff.' She compressed her lips to stifle a giggle. 'I cannot imagine what Peverly's first name is, nor Mrs Barkham's, and I have no notion what Cook's entire name might be. This could lead to chaos, you know.' They shared comfortable laughter before Vanessa held out her hand. 'I shall save you my first dance and as many of the others as you wish . . . Robert.'

'And do you save one for me?' The cold gaze from Nicholas's eyes could have frozen enough ice for the entire betrothal party.

Their laughter died. Millbank hastily excused himself from the room, though Lord Stone and Vanessa barely noticed his departure. 'If you desire a dance, milord, of course I shall save one for you. After all, you are my employer — it would not do to antagonize you. Robert will understand, I am certain.'

'Robert, is it? He isn't right for you.' Nicholas completely forgot that not so very long ago he had planned to place these two together.

'I don't see that it is any of your affair.' Dignified anger sparkled in her eyes, her back rigid with the effort to control her trembling body.

He ran a frustrated hand through carefully arranged hair, making a mess his valet would shudder to see. 'No, you are right. It is none of my affair. Miss Tarleton . . . Vanessa . . . ' He looked at her, the agony of his love, the hopelessness of his dream so clear for a moment — before a shutter dropped and he assumed a bland mask. He turned, leaving the room at a brisk walk.

Vanessa sat, stunned at what she witnessed. He really did care for her. Though no words were exchanged, she knew it in her bones. Her previous suspicions had been confirmed by that unguarded look. She ran a hand over the tapestry as though trying to hold on to reality in its touch. As long as he also held to his goal, there was nothing to be done. Sighing with the knowledge of how fate can get so muddled, Vanessa turned again to her needle.

★ ★ ★

Mrs Barkham turned out to be the most tactful of women. It seemed she had considerable experience in social assemblages, and she quietly assumed command of Juliana's betrothal party. The servants bustled about their jobs. Every room, even the saloon where Vanessa sat with the tapestries, was made to shine.

The evening of the great event, Juliana alternated between tears and laughter, even after an enforced nap during the afternoon. Katie proffered her a cup of herb tea while Vanessa inspected her toilette, from the white flowers in her hair to the blue slippers on her feet.

'Lovely! Quite, quite lovely, dear Juliana. But you had best be calm. Think that only two more Sundays are required for the remaining banns to be read. Your Harry is impatient to be wed.'

Juliana drank her camomile tea, promising to try for serenity or at least something close to it. Yet her eyes sparkled with joy as she shyly joined her brother at the entrance to the newly remodeled long gallery. The beautiful room admirably suited the purpose of the betrothal party.

Nicholas gave Juliana the kind of warm smile Vanessa hadn't seen from him in some time. 'Well, well. My little sister has come of age, I believe. I am impressed . . . and pleased. Harry is a lucky devil.'

Flicking her eyes from Nicholas to where Vanessa stood quietly in the shadows, Juliana replied in clear accents, 'If it weren't for Vanessa, I wouldn't look like this and Harry would still think of me as a part of the furniture. The best thing you ever did for me was to bring her here. I'm glad Grandfather's tapestries needed repair.'

Watching in admiring silence from her recess, Vanessa decided Nicholas was a sight to stop the heart of the most world-weary of women. His black velvet jacket embraced those broad shoulders so marvelously well, and the black knee breeches were molded to handsome legs above black silk hose and black shoes. Only the sharp white satin of the waistcoat, cut with elegant discretion, worn over the nicely tied cravat, kept him from looking like a pirate.

Her own gown of sea-green silk was cut rather deep in the bosom and swirled about her figure in a clinging manner perhaps not fitting for a mere needlewoman. However, she could not afford to purchase a new gown, and this was another one the romantic Betsy had tucked into her trunk. She wore no jewelry and insisted her hair be dressed in the most simple of styles.

Juliana impetuously caught Vanessa's hand, drawing her forth from her shadowed retreat. 'Nicholas, see how regal and elegant Vanessa is this evening? She looks like a princess.'

Before Nicholas could reply to his sister's praise, Sir Harry entered the room, closely followed by Mrs Hewit and Harry's sister, Louisa, with her Dunston. Recently married by special license, she was now a Blaine, Dunston having no more patience to wait than Sir Harry.

Sir Harry had eyes only for Juliana and whispered compliments to rather rosy ears. The evening began on this happy note and proceeded to get better. Though Vanessa resolutely looked the other way when she saw Nicholas was to dance with Mrs Hewit, she knew where the couple was every minute of the evening.

It was helpful, that sensory acuity. When Robert Millbank left her side to find a glass of lemonade, Vanessa was able to drift with seeming aimlessness away from where she knew Nicholas was headed. It enabled her to dance with several of the local gentry whom Nicholas had suggested Juliana invite. Eventually she unwittingly let her guard slip and he caught up with her.

'You have been avoiding me all evening.'

Rather than deny the truth, Vanessa, in a spirit of resignation, replied, 'So I have.'

'It won't wash, you know.' His voice was low, intimate, sending shivers down her spine.

'And what will this accomplish? A dance, milord? Nothing more?' She strove desperately for serenity.

'A waltz, if you must know. I especially requested it, and gave Juliana permission to dance it with Harry. You will partner me.'

'I suppose I dare not say no.' She extended a hand that trembled ever so slightly as she made her prosaic observation, then performed a deep curtsy.

'Indeed not. I wouldn't allow it.' The warmth of his murmured threat sent a tremor of apprehension through her.

'This is madness, milord. You know you

must place your attentions elsewhere.' Her whisper was fierce; no one must overhear their conversation.

'I wish you would call me Nicholas just this once.'

She shook her head, then glanced to where Mrs Hewit sat, her thin bosom swelled with indignation. It gave Vanessa curious pleaure to whisper, 'Nicholas . . .'

She wondered if Nicholas had told the musicians to select the longest piece of music they knew, for the waltz seemed to go on and on. She whirled around the room in his arms, at first alone except for Harry and Juliana; then gradually the floor filled with a few more couples. The waltz was still very new, yet it was amazing how word had spread, eagerness for something different teasing others to try. Mrs Hewit sat in tight-lipped silence while Mr Millbank stood behind her chair, a look of patient resignation on his face.

'You shouldn't hold me quite this close, milord.' Her words were breathless, her inner joy not quite concealed.

'Nicholas. For the duration of this dance, I shall be Nicholas to you.'

'Nicholas . . . please.'

'I know. You said madness. I am a man possessed, unable to do a thing about it.' He executed a number of skillful turns that left her even more breathless than she had been before. She longed to place her cheek against the fine velvet of his well-cut jacket, to again feel the warmth of his body. Instead, she pulled away from him, her eyes flashing a warning as he tried to draw her close once again.

At last the dance concluded. As she curtsied, she looked steadily up into his face, her concern quite clear. He bowed elegantly, then walked away as though they had not been in passionate confrontation during the entire dance.

Somehow Vanessa managed to move through the remainder of the evening, accepting a country dance with Mr Millbank before excusing herself from the festivities. As she slipped from the room, she looked back to see Nicholas bent over the hand of Mrs Hewit, then leading her into the next set.

15

With the strains of music filling the house with delightful sound, Vanessa felt little like going to her room. Yet she could not bear to watch Nicholas pay his attentions to the woman he must wed. Somehow, she felt her noble resolve might falter if she tarried any longer. The urge to fight for what she desired had surfaced all too often of late for comfort. Certain no one was watching her, she edged her way to the door, then swiftly walked from the long gallery. Once free of the room, she slowed, in no hurry to go to her bed.

Swinging her reticule with one hand, she idly strolled into the saloon, now softly lit with two branches of candles. They provided sufficient light to allow her a muted view of where the third section of tapestry billowed across the worktable.

Such beautiful things they were. She smoothed a gentle hand over the weaving. Even in this dim light the colors glowed with remarkable life, like rare gems. The areas where she'd woven in new threads could scarcely be detected. She had done well. Meticulous care, attention to detail — these were the attributes required in addition to the knowledge of weaving and yarns best suited for the work.

Soon this piece would be ready to join the others, draping across the walls, adorning them like tapestry jewels. She raised her head to stare into the shadows. Wasn't that what Nicholas's grandfather had called these works of art? His jewels on the wall? She shrugged slim, weary shoulders and walked away from the table to stare out into the night.

There were few clouds in the sky tonight, the nearly full moon blessing the countryside with its benevolent light. The guests would have no difficulty in returning home after the party. The countryside had been quiet of late as well. No danger should lurk from robbers, or the Luddites Lord Stone feared, along the way.

She ran her fingers along the smooth wood framing the window with restless motions, then turned to go to her room. She was being foolish and overly sensitive. There was no place in her life now for stolen kisses, enticing words. Lord Stone simply could not afford to love her — much less marry her. Though if she had been a gambler she would have staked a great deal on the wager that he did. Love her, that is. He wouldn't have sat with her all night following the fire if he considered her a mere servant, would he? Nor would he defy the regard of his nearly betrothed by performing the waltz with Vanessa, telling her he was a man possessed. Possessed of what? A family promise? Or perhaps he wished he had made no promise, no resolution to restore this ancestral pile of stones to its former glory. She swung her reticule around in the air, wondering what he had thought as they swirled about the floor. It had excited her far more than the sedate dancing she had performed with her ex-fiancé, Lord Chudleigh.

Odd, she could scarcely recall his image. How much had happened since that fateful day when the news came that her father had been killed. She hoped her mother was well. Even though there was little affection between them, they were still related. But she was determined *not* to join Aunt Agatha and her mother when she left here. There *must* be something available for her to do. She would ask for references from Lord Stone. Perhaps he cared enough to see her to another position.

The vibrant melody of the music greeted her as she left the saloon to stroll thoughtfully up the stairs. She passed a footman standing rigidly at attention in the central hall, his powdered hair a white patch in the dim light.

She held out her skirts, swaying to the lilt of the country air with each step she took to the upper floor.

Vanessa really didn't wish to return to her room, nor did she welcome the hours that would drag by before she could manage sleep. But she had chosen her path. Odd, that was what Nicholas had said to her earlier. As though she had any choice in the matter. Unless she happened to be a widow, a woman had little to say about her life: schooled by nanny and governess, wedded by order of her father, and controlled — until one or the other's death — by her husband. Vanessa wondered what it was like to be as free as a widow . . . like Mrs Hewit. Society was not kind to spinsters, but widows were something else again. The way some women talked, the chief advantage in marriage was that it might lead to a rich widowhood. But then, those women hadn't met a man like Nicholas Leighton. Pamela Hewit had.

In Vanessa's room Katie was turning down the covers of the bed, Vanessa's nightgown neatly spread out near the foot, where Hercules eyed it as a possible blanket.

'Back up here so early, milady? Aye, I thought you'd be staying until the last guest left the house, I did.' Katie gave a final pat to the bed, then turned to study her lady.

Vanessa dropped her reticule on the dressing table, then removed the pins from her hair with a languid hand, allowing the spun gold to cascade down her back.

''Tis not my place tonight, Katie. Tonight they honor Lady Juliana and Sir Harry — and I am not family, you see.' Suddenly overwhelmed by a feeling of being cut off from family and friends, she dropped the last of the pins, then walked to the window to peer out at a carriage and the first of the guests to leave the house. Louisa and Dunstan were departing for their home. Such a well-matched pair with their mutual interests.

'Never mind me, Katie. I am blue-deviled tonight for some reason.'

Katie planted her fists on her hips, cocking her pert head to one side as she studied Vanessa. 'Aye, it should be you at his lordship's side, not that widder in yellow. She has no high birth, naught but her poor dead husband's money to recommend her. She'll lead him a merry dance.'

'Katie,' said Vanessa with little spirit.

'Poor dearie. You should be cosseted and loved to distraction. I doubt you've had your share in this life so far. Seems 'tis the common people who marry purely for love and nothing else.' She turned to plump up

337

the pillows once more, then added, 'I'll see to a nice hot posset to help you sleep. Don't worry, Katie will tend to you.'

Vanessa watched the door swing silently shut behind the departing maid. How shocked her mother would be if she knew of Katie's familiarity. Vanessa found it comforting, giving her a sense that someone cared about her. At the window, she could observe more carriages leaving. Apparently country parties did not last all night, as London affairs did. She noted a flash of yellow from the open door as Nicholas and Juliana, with Sir Harry at her side, waved farewell to the celebrants. Mrs Hewit had assumed a place with the family, as undoubtedly would be her right before too long. Vanessa pulled the draperies across the window to shut out the moon as well as her thoughts of wives and widows.

Two more Sundays for the remaining banns to be read, and Juliana could be married in the village church, as was her desire. By that time, if Vanessa kept her needle busy, she could leave when Juliana moved from the house to join her new husband. Vanessa prowled restlessly about the room, considering how to ask for the reference from Lord Stone.

A hasty knock at her door was the only

warning she had before Juliana burst into the room. 'Was it not utterly divine?' The younger woman whirled about the room in a dreamy dance, her arms gracefully extended, face rapturous. 'Dear Vanessa, once again I owe you much. I can never begin to repay you. Harry liked my dress excessively. *He* does not like orange either.' She giggled like an impish child, adding, 'Pamela was not best pleased to see me in blue tonight. It made her gold look bold and brassy.'

Vanessa made a dismissing gesture. 'You have charming taste. Once you are at Eastthorpe Hall, you will have full rein to demonstrate your good judgment. I believe you mentioned Sir Harry has an excellent housekeeper. You will get along rather well there, I fancy.'

'You will come to visit me, won't you?' Juliana paused in her perambulations around the room to give Vanessa an anxious look. 'I know I must not depend upon you, but I vow it would be nice to have you to turn to if things get a bit . . . well, sticky. Harry's mother will live in the dower house and Louisa is not far away. Not that I believe they will interfere. Louisa cannot see further than their horses, and his mother seems fairly pleasant. I hope. Did you notice her?' Juliana chewed at her lip in anxious silence.

Vanessa admitted she had failed to observe the lady. She ignored the request to visit. Juliana would know soon enough that her departure would coincide with Vanessa's.

'No matter. She was the tall, thin woman with the excess of purple plumes in her hair.' Juliana plumped herself down as though to spend the rest of the night discussing her prospective mother-in-law.

'I did see her, come to think of it. She certainly didn't appear to be a dragon. Cheer up, my dear. To-morrow will remind you how good your life will be.'

'Almost anything would be better than staying here to wait on Pamela. You'll stand up to her, though, won't you?'

'I won't be here by the time she arrives to take up residence. I expect I shall be far away come the day your brother takes his bride.' Vanessa knew her voice sounded dull and flat. There was no possible way she could display any enthusiasm in that coming marriage.

Juliana smoothed the soft leather of her long white gloves over her hands with thoughtful fingers. 'I hoped once Nicholas got to know you he would see how well you would suit as his bride. I caught a glimpse of his face tonight as you waltzed about the room with him. He is not indifferent to you.'

'No, I do not believe he is. But that has

nothing to do with marriage, my little innocent. Mrs Hewit has the money necessary to complete the alterations and improvements to the property. Most marriages, at least those of the *ton*, are based on economics, not love.' She recalled Katie's words. 'It seems there are times we can neither love where we wish, nor help loving where we would not. I admit I wonder how a marriage can survive without any real affection on either side. I have always thought of love as a tender plant to be kept alive by great delicacy of care. A lack of love would see any marriage wither into a business arrangement.' Her own evaluation of marriage had altered considerably over the past months. Vanessa seated herself on the edge of the bed, proceeding to caress Hercules into a blissful snooze.

'I know the portion Nicholas settled on me is a fair one, in spite of his straitened circumstances. But Harry loves me, I know he does.' Juliana seemed to seek reassurance in spite of Sir Harry's devoted attentions.

'The portion is a matter of honor. Sir Harry is utterly besotted with you.' This thought led back to Nicholas and Pamela Hewit. The conversation with Juliana was becoming more painful by the moment. Vanessa was grateful when Katie quietly entered the room bearing a small tray with a cup of steaming liquid on it.

Katie took one look at Lady Juliana and shook her head. 'You may sleep till noon, but if I know milady, she will be up with the birds. Off with you now. Annie is waitin' for you and half-asleep on her feet.' Katie placed the cup of posset on the small table by the bed, then helped Vanessa from her dress, fussing all the while. 'A real treat you were tonight, milady. If one don't see what's in front of his eyes, he deserves to suffer.'

Pausing by the door on her way to her own room, Juliana stared at Katie. 'You have the right of it, but whom do you mean?'

Hastily interrupting, Vanessa shook her head: 'Pay no attention to Katie. She thinks I should encourage Mr Millbank. We can talk on the morrow.'

After the door closed on a confused Juliana, Katie crossed to hang up the dress in the wardrobe, muttering under her breath, 'Never heard such a whisker in all my born days. Mr Millbank, indeed.'

'Katie,' cautioned Vanessa, 'I'll have no more on the subject tonight, please.'

Once alone, tucked up in bed and sipping the posset, Vanessa considered the conversation with Juliana. If it hadn't been for the tapestries, she might be far from here, never have met Lord Stone, and be heart-whole. Yet she had enjoyed her work, found the tapestries beautiful and historically interesting. She placed the half-empty cup on the table, determinedly shutting her eyes in hopes of sleep.

It was sometime during the middle of the night that she woke, sitting bolt upright in her bed. Something had niggled at her memory, enough to wake her from her unsettled slumber. What had preyed on her mind before she slept? Ah, yes. The tapestries.

Hercules stirred, then walked across to find out what bothered his mistress. Slipping her hand through the cat's fur, scratching behind his ear where it was best liked, Vanessa considered the notion that had flashed in her mind. Was it possible? Could there be anything to this crazy notion?

Well, there was only one way to ascertain the truth of it. She dragged the covers back, Hercules protesting rather loudly as he was dislodged from his comfortable position.

'Sorry, old boy. I am on a trip of investigation. Stay here if you like.' She put on her slippers, then pulled her watered-silk robe over the pretty matching blue nightgown.

The hall was eerily silent. All were asleep but a silly goosecap with a bee in her bonnet that would not permit her to enjoy her slumber. Hercules paused in the doorway, then trotted behind Vanessa down the stairs and into the saloon. The cat sat by the door, gold and green eyes glittering as they watched her light the candles.

Vanessa studied the tapestry on the table, then took out her sharpest scissors and approached it. One nervous finger stroked the weaving, rubbing the carefully woven threads, done so many years ago. Should she? She glanced at the cat as though he might help her. Hercules merely sat, narrowing those peculiar eyes as he tilted his head to one side in expectation.

She nodded decisively. 'I will do it! I can always repair it from the back side. No one would know.' She rolled the tapestry over to expose the lining, then ran a sensitive finger along until she came to one of the strange lumps she had reckoned to be trapunto. She turned, then brought a branch of candles to the table, placing it where she now worked. Taking a deep breath while saying a prayer, she picked up her scissors and slashed through the backing.

There it was! Just as she must have dreamed it! She set down the scissors and with trembling fingers gathered the jewel into her hand to hold it up before the light of the candles. 'How beautiful!' The large ruby

344

glittered, light dancing through it in exquisite patterns.

She set the jewel aside on a small table, then turned once more to the tapestry. She must be trembling from head to foot. Could it be possible there might be more? She found another lump. And slashed!

Light from the candles picked out an emerald of rare purity and size. This went to join the ruby. A feverish gleam lit her eyes as she picked up the scissors once again. Another lump was behind a falcon, she recalled. She searched until she found the regal bird, then flipped the tapestry over again. Slash!

A sapphire as deep blue as Lord Stone's eyes gleamed up from its nest in the weaving. How long had these jewels been secreted here? Surely, had Lord Stone's father known, they would have been sold to permit more gambling. That must have been why Nicholas' grandfather ordered him to care for the tapestries. Clever man.

She replaced her scissors on the table, gathering the ruby and emerald up with the sapphire, jewels that had hung on the wall. She didn't know the mystery of it, but here was a means for Nicholas to have everything he desired — whatever it be.

There must be more jewels here! She

couldn't wait until morning to tell Nicholas. He must be here to see for himself the wealth that had been hidden away. Vanessa tore from the saloon, with Hercules dashing madly after her, up the stairs and down the hall to where she paused before the chambers she knew belonged to Nicholas.

Should she knock? She most assuredly didn't want to wake anyone else just yet. This was special. She selfishly wanted to share it with Nicholas, not daring even to think what changes it might bring. With greater stealth than she knew she possessed, she depressed the elegant lever handle of his door, then slipped inside, carefully closing it behind her, although not before Hercules managed to squeeze past.

The room was dark, only the glowing coals in the fire-place of help to show her where the great canopied bed stood. She slowly crossed the room, reaching the side of his bed without stumbling once. He was breathing quietly, asleep on his side.

'Lord Stone! Nicholas! Wake up!' She shook his shoulder, shocked to discover bare skin. Her hand rose to cover her mouth a moment before she searched for his candle. They needed light. With resoluteness surpassing any previous intent, she put the disturbing, entrancing warmth of his body from her mind.

'What is it? Vanessa? Is something amiss?' He pushed his hair off his forehead with a slow, puzzled motion, then sat up, reaching for his dressing gown with one hand while sliding from the covers. Vanessa crossed to the fireplace, using an ember to light a candle.

'I have something I must show you.' Her voice was unsteady, but there was no panic or fright in it, rather rising excitement. She discreetly kept her back to him, talking over her shoulder.

'It could not wait until morning?' He was out of bed now, his robe tied about him. He went swiftly to her side, staring at her as though she were an apparition. There appeared to be no dire emergency, yet he tensed, awaiting the news she found so imperative that he have it right now.

'It is not bad news, but good!' She was conscious of the three stones in her hand, and what they, and possibly others still concealed, could mean for both of them . . . perhaps.

'Let it wait a moment,' he commanded gently. He placed a hand on her shoulder, drawing her closer to him. He studied the charming face, her golden hair tumbled in such unusual abandon down her back. Those luminous sea-blue eyes were warm and inviting. Where was the proper miss now? 'There is something I *must* tell you. A decision I reached tonight. I was coming to speak with you, but your maid informed me you were asleep, not to be disturbed. I fully intended to disturb you first thing in the morning. I must speak now.' The other hand reached up to tenderly smooth a curl from her brow, then settled on her other shoulder.

He stared down at her, absorbing her rare beauty. He had wondered more nights than he could begin to count just how she might appear in that robe. Delicate lace peeped out from the deep opening left by the hastily tied wrap. The view was enticing.

Nicholas found his hands caressing her arms, relishing the feel of that warm body beneath the watered silk. Her hair tumbled about her, its threads catching the candle-light, reflecting pure gold. He studied the cascade of gold a moment; then a dawning smile of recognition crept over his face. Reaching up to weave his fingers through strands of silken hair, he mused aloud, 'Now I recall — you are the princess. When Juliana was a little girl I gave her a book of fairy tales. She loved the princess the best, and begged me to find her and marry her. I knew you reminded me of someone.'

Vanessa gazed at him with such trust in her eyes. No matter how badly he desired her, he wouldn't destroy that. But he needed something. And she was here. His arms slid about her, urging her closer. He could see her skin through the gossamer silk of her gown, bringing him an ache he couldn't hope to assuage honorably . . . at least not tonight.

Vanessa's heart beat very fast, like a captured bird who fears being consumed by its predator. The momentous news could wait a bit longer, she decided; the jewels had been hidden a long time. She took a step closer to him.

'I fully intended to ask Pamela to be my wife tonight.' He felt Vanessa stiffen, but refused to let her draw away. 'I said I intended. I found I could not do it. The words refused to form on my lips, the ones I knew I ought to utter so I might continue the work I have begun here.' He glanced about the room as though reminding himself of all that remained unfinished.

'I tried to make love to her. I took her out riding, kissed her.' At the strange expression on Vanessa's face, he nodded. 'I must be honest with you, and I want you to know everything.' He saw her silent, wary nod, and continued, 'Her kiss was like water compared with the heady champagne of yours.'

Nicholas bent his head to touch Vanessa lightly on the lips. She found herself swaying toward him. The hard, muscular body she had admired from a distance was pressed against hers with devastating reactions. She felt herself melting, turning into a warm pool of the most delicious sensations.

With a great effort, Nicholas drew away from the temptation of her lips, the soft, warm body tantalizingly scented with bluebells. 'I found I could not even feel affection for her. Nothing. Polite regard seems a terrible basis for marriage.' Nicholas reflected it hadn't seemed so terrible until he fell in love with Vanessa; then everything had changed.

His hands communicated the urgency he felt, pressing ever so slightly into her arms as he studied her eyes. They seemed so trusting, so honest and open. Would she be willing to accept the difficulties and straitened conditions he offered?

'If you will only . . . I know it will be difficult at first . . . and it will take more than a year or two . . . but if you love me . . . we could do it, I know we could. Oh, my dearest little love, I need and want you so much.' Nearly incoherent with wanting to convey the depth of his desire, Nicholas took a deep breath, noting the sparkle of mirth in her eyes, promising himself she would pay for that later, and forged on. 'What I am trying to do, my little improper — you do realize it is shocking to find you in my arms, in my rooms, in the middle of the night, do you not? — my most improper little love: I desire to marry you. The sooner, the better.'

'You are sure ... The money you need ... Her assets must be very tempting.' Vanessa had a desire to know his true love before he discovered the jewels.

'I do believe you might call me Nicholas now. Seeing how things stand.' He placed another tender kiss on her lips, and somehow they both lost track of time and where they were. At last Nicholas demanded in deep tones, husky with emotions, 'Marry me.'

'If you are certain that is what you desire, I will, for I confess I love you most dreadfully.' Her eyes were shining with love and unshed tears of happiness.

It took the determined efforts of Hercules rubbing against their legs to bring them back to the present world. Nicholas cleared his throat and glared at the cat. 'What is that dratted animal doing in my room?'

'He followed me downstairs ... then upstairs again. He was with me when I found them. Oh, my dearest, I have been meddling once again. Come see what I have, Nicholas, see!'

His eyes focused on the dainty fist extended to him as it slowly unfurled. There lay three large jewels, red, blue, and green, sparkling up at him with the brilliance of expertly cut first-rank gems.

His jaw dropped; then he burst out, 'Great heavens, where did you come by those? They look incredibly real!'

Vanessa tugged at his arm with her other hand while offering him the jewels. 'They are yours, Nicholas! Come with me to see what I uncovered.'

He picked up the jewels one by one, shaking his head in utter amazement. Then his eyes sought hers. 'Incredible!'

She didn't need to pull at his hand very hard. Nicholas was all curiosity. This was a mind-shattering turn of events. He ran with her, hand in hand, flying down the stairs with bare feet and flapping robes.

In the saloon they skittered to a halt by the worktable, the branch of candles still burning with cheerful though barely sufficient light. On the table, the tapestry was in a tumbled heap, the slashes in the lining gaping like dark wounds. Vanessa cocked her head, her eyes dancing with excitement. 'Shall I cut, or do you wish the honors?'

'You, by all means.' His gaze devoured the luscious figure generously displayed as she bent to unfold more of the tapestry. She searched, then eagerly reached for her scissors. In moments a large diamond came to view. As Nicholas stood in stunned silence, trying to absorb what this find would mean to him, Vanessa continued.

'Another diamond, milord!' She handed him another stone of slightly smaller size with a flourish, then turned back to the table, first brushing a wisp of hair from her face. 'There are many such lumps in these tapestries. I meant to speak to you about them, but I feared you might feel it silly . . . or meddling of me.'

'Ah, yes, I suspect I have a great many accusations to live down.' His rueful grimace was totally missed by his busily searching love.

Nicholas brought a second branch of candles. After at least forty-five minutes of exploring, Vanessa paused to stare at the collection of sparkling jewels of every color and size — some magnificently enormous — piled on the table.

Picking up a large sapphire from the glittering pile, Nicholas said, 'This explains a great deal.' At her questioning look, he continued, 'I believe Grandfather feared, and rightly so, that my father would run through all our wealth. I often wondered why the old man stressed that I care for the tapestries. He even willed them to me, as they were not entailed.'

Vanessa thought of her father's reckless ways, and added, 'I know well how gaming can destroy a fortune. How terrible if these jewels had been taken to pay those debts of honor.' Scorn threaded through her voice for those gaming debts that took precedence over all else.

'My poor darling, how you have suffered for that.'

She placed a finger gently over his mouth. 'Hush. We both have known what it is to cope with the results of an obsession for gaming. It is behind us now. With the legacy from the tapestries, you can proceed with rebuilding the estate. It will be the gem of Yorkshire.' Her eyes sparkled with delight at her intentional pun.

He chuckled. 'We shall do it together.' He drew her close to him, cradling her in his arm.

'It means you won't have to choose. You can have everything you want. Oh, Nicholas, I am so utterly happy you wanted me the most.'

'Not half as pleased as I, my darling.'

Vanessa found herself enfolded in strong arms, far too contented to object to the impropriety of it all as Nicholas again sought her lips.

With that, the candles were allowed to

gutter out. Beyond the windows could be seen the pink of an approaching dawn. Hercules sat in puzzled quiet until, seemingly disgusted with the lack of attention from his mistress, he left the room to the two entwined in each other's arms, and retreated to the soft bed on the upper floor.

We do hope that you have enjoyed reading this large print book.

Did you know that all of our titles are available for purchase?

We publish a wide range of high quality large print books including:
Romances, Mysteries, Classics
General Fiction
Non Fiction and Westerns

Special interest titles available in large print are:
The Little Oxford Dictionary
Music Book
Song Book
Hymn Book
Service Book

Also available from us courtesy of Oxford University Press:
Young Readers' Dictionary
(large print edition)
Young Readers' Thesaurus
(large print edition)

For further information or a free brochure, please contact us at:
Ulverscroft Large Print Books Ltd.,
The Green, Bradgate Road, Anstey,
Leicester, LE7 7FU, England.
Tel: (00 44) **0116 236 4325**
Fax: (00 44) **0116 234 0205**

Other titles published by
The House of Ulverscroft:

A PERILOUS ENGAGEMENT

Emily Hendrickson

After the untimely death of his reckless cousin Ivor, Jordan Robards inherits a barony — and the wealth, property, and responsibility that go with the title. Upon moving onto his new estate, Jordan encounters the things his cousin left behind — including a bereft fiancée. Lady Ariel is definitely the most diverting thing in the neighbourhood. But far from diverting is the suspicion that Ivor's death may not have been an accident — and that Jordan himself could be the next Baron of Harcourt to meet with foul play . . .

GENTLEMEN IN QUESTION

Melinda Hammond

In the closing months of 1792, the terror of the French Revolution forces Camille, the young Comte du Vivière, to flee his homeland and seek refuge with his relatives in England. For Madeleine, the arrival of her handsome French cousin marks a change in her so far uneventful existence, and soon she finds herself caught up in a dangerous web of intrigue that also entangles Camille. But is he victim or villain?

A DISSEMBLER

Fenella-Jane Miller

When Marianne Devenish arrives in Great Bentley she expects to find her great-uncle in residence but instead meets the Earl of Wister, Theodolphus Rickham, pretending to be Sir Theodore Devenish. She is compelled to move in with Lord and Lady Grierson at Frating Hall. But what is their mysterious connection to the local smugglers? As Theo's dissembling leads to heartbreak, Marianne's tattered reputation forces her to flee. Ostracized by society, she seeks refuge at a small estate in Hertfordshire, but her life turns into a nightmare. Can Theo rescue Marianne before she is lost to him forever?

THE OTHER MISS FROBISHER

Ann Barker

Elfrida Frobisher leaves her country backwater and her suitor to chaperon Prudence, her eighteen-year-old niece, in London. Unfortunately, Prudence has apparently developed an attachment for an unsuitable man, which she fosters behind her aunt's back. Attempting to foil her niece's schemes and prevent a scandal, Elfrida only succeeds in finding herself involved with the eligible Rufus Tyler in a scandal of her own! Fleeing London seems the only solution — but Prudence has another plan . . . Elfrida yearns for her quiet rural existence, but it takes a mad dash in pursuit of her niece before she realises where her heart truly lies.